EQUITES

THE LIGHTRIDER JOURNALS, VOL. II

ERIC NIERSTEDT

iUniverse

EQUITES
THE LIGHTRIDER JOURNALS, VOL. II

iUniverse books may be ordered through booksellers or by contacting:

iUniverse
1663 Liberty Drive
Bloomington, IN 47403
www.iuniverse.com
1-800-Authors (1-800-288-4677)

ISBN: 978-1-4917-5588-4 (sc)
ISBN: 978-1-4917-5590-7 (hc)
ISBN: 978-1-4917-5589-1 (e)

Printed in the United States of America.

iUniverse rev. date: 01/05/2015

Author Photo by Christina De Marco

Cover Art By Derrick Fish

The Elemental Knights (and the Architects)

Lightrider – Joseph Hashimoto, Knight of Light (Ralin)
Nightstalker – Bat, Knight of Shadow (Rastla)
Wavecrasher – Cat, Knight of Water (Ruta)
Groundquake – Dog, Knight of Earth (Chirron)
Firesprite – Gila Monster, Knight of Fire (Darya)
Windrider – Falcon, Knight of Air (Aeris)
Forester – Squirrel, Knight of Forest (Demtia)
Thunderer – Ram, Knight of Thunder (Zueia)
Forger – Tarantula, Knight of Metal (Hephia)
Sandshifter – Wolf, Knight of Desert (Nabu)

Here are the writings of the Lightrider, once a mortal man named Joseph Hashimoto, chosen by the Architects, makers of the universe itself, to hold the power of light and lead the half-animal Elemental Knights in their quest to uphold the balance between good and evil.

But his quest was not an easy one. Taken at the moment of his death and thrown into a struggle with increasingly gray moral solutions and a fractured team, Joe felt torn between his duty and his longing for home. Worse still, his powers had a dangerous edge, a rage that could send him into fits of unbridled fury. It was one of these rages that nearly drove Joe from the knights, even as they faced their greatest enemy, the Chaos Demons. Born from nothing, the demons sought to unleash a great power to return the world to its formless beginnings. But with the help of Nightstalker, Knight of Shadow, Joe faced his own demons and rejoined his brothers and sisters in time to defeat this enemy and accept the new life he had been given.

But that was only the first part of the story …

PROLOGUE

He opened the door to the room, where once again the light from the window blazed forth, the colors shining through like fire through stained glass. He took a minute to admire them and then walked past them, to where the book sat on the little desk, its pages open and ready. He sat there, drew out the pen, and readied himself. All he needed was the right moment to continue. And for a man like Joseph Hasimoto, once the Lightrider and now the caretaker of the Obelisk, the right place was buried in a sea of options. After all, he had lived through events spanning centuries, perhaps even millennia. And for every moment, he expected the twinge of memory to either flicker briefly like a dying candle or to cut him like a sudden knife.

He looked down at the book—his journal, his life. He had begun the book nearly a month ago (as least, as he reckoned), to lay bare his long life and judge for himself if it had been worth all the sacrifice it had required. Thus far, he had only written down a part of it—the ending of his first life and the beginning of his second one. He had written down all the details— his death; his rebirth as the Lightrider; the formation of the Elemental Knights and their doctrine of spiritual balance; and their first great battle against the enemies of all forces good and evil, the Chaos Demons. And when it was done, he had laid the pen down and looked at the life he had written. And he had deemed it worthy.

But that was not all.

There was how he had chosen the long, lonely life in this place, forever bound to uphold the great lynchpin, until the time finally came for it to fall and bring all of existence down with it. Compared to those choices, the knighthood had been as simple as choosing red and green lights for Christmas. The Knights had given him a family, a group of brothers and sisters all in the same boat with him. That boat may have been tied far from the shore of humanity, but he had always been able to swim to it for a time. But where had the choices after that led him?

He was the only one of his kind, a being of great power, capable of channeling all the powers of the Obelisk to form great wonders and miracles. But all he knew now were the books and the magic and the laws that this place contained. He could not remember the last time he had felt the touch of another human hand. Nor could he recall the smell of fresh air or the sounds of the busy city.

That, he knew, was why he had begun the journal, not only to think upon the past but to remember those things again, to cast a light on those dimming memories. That was why he had given the book its name; for he was still the Lightrider, if only in name (his replacement had not taken that from him). The journal would be used not only to brighten the memories of long ago but to illuminate his own soul and allow the reasons for his choices to shine again as well.

Joe nodded and then dipped the pen in the ink and began to write. His thoughts moved to a city he had not been to in years and a bar that had been the catalyst of his greatest and most painful adventure.

BOOK ONE

AN OUTBREAK
OF MADNESS

I

THE MIDNIGHT RAMBLER WAS a bar that had been named after a Rolling Stones song and had spent every moment since trying to live up to its reputation. Entering the place, the customers got the familiar scents of beer, the sweat of men and women getting a pick-me-up after a hard day's work, and cigarettes, and the bathrooms, greeted them with the smell of piss and vomit that comes from having one pick-me-up too many. The walls were covered in pockmarks, holes, and cracks, which had been mostly covered with sports banners, pictures, and a few flat screen TVs bolted into the wall. The hardwood floors had more than a few stains from the aforementioned pick-me-up residue, but otherwise, were generally clean. Besides, no one ever came into a bar to comment on the floor.

And that was just fine with Emilio, who stood behind the bar pouring a customer a fresh drink. He'd owned the Rambler for the last ten years, and ever since he'd bought the empty pub in the Lower East Side, he'd run it as he saw fit. Everyone else had seen the wear and tear of the old building and thought it an easy victim for the wrecking ball. But Emilio had looked at it and seen a place whose damages, with some work, into signs of character. It had been a long-standing trait of his to see the potential in something others had given up on. He had been smart enough to set himself up in an area with a lot of hardworking people who wanted a hard drink after a hard day. And as time went on, he'd been able to attract a more interesting clientele, people who allowed him to keep the Rambler going with ease.

Still, there were always plenty of regular customers to help out. He finished pouring the drink for the dark-haired woman in front of him. She took it with an exaggerated reach, nearly bringing her bosom down onto the bar as she picked it up. Emilio watched as she straightened, stretching her body back, giving him a good view. He smiled then and stroked his goatee as the woman smiled back. She sat there, took a sip, and then said, "Not many men would leave the gray in like that."

"It makes me look distinguished," Emilio replied.

"Hmm. Can't say I disagree," the woman said.

Emilio nodded, but before he could respond, he heard a voice call out for drinks.

"Another time," he said as he turned toward the voice.

Normally, he would've waited until he'd gotten a name before taking another order, but for the last several nights, things had had to be different. And Emilio knew the longer he kept waiting for things to change back, the longer he'd be watching things inch closer and closer to disaster and the greater the chance was that everything he knew could be taken away. He could only hope that the little he'd been able to do would be enough to stop—

"'Bout time," the customer snapped as Emilio put those thoughts out of his head and focused on his job.

"What'll it be?" he asked, reaching below for a glass.

"Heineken. With a chaser."

"Okay, can you be a little more specifi—" Emilio began, but as he looked up and saw this man, he understood. Nodding he said, "That'll take a moment. Be right back."

The man gave an impatient nod as Emilio left the bar and headed for the door that led into the storeroom. Flipping on the light, he walked through, ignoring the boxes of alcohol and bags of chips, until he came to a worn-looking section of the wall. Reaching out, he tapped it three times, and as he finished, the section pulled back and to the side, revealing an empty space with a refrigerator inside. Emilio pulled it open and surveyed a single shelf, filled with Tupperware containers that glinted red in the dim light. He took a moment to find what he was looking for and then reached in and removed a container labeled A-B +. He then reached into his pocket and drew out a small glass bottle. Popping its lid, he opened the Tupperware and dipped the bottle into the red liquid inside. He waited a few seconds and then pulled it out. He checked the bottle, making sure it was as full as possible; capped both it and the Tupperware, returned the container to the fridge, shut it; and then, after stepping back, tapped the wall again. The section slid back into place.

As Emilio turned and started to walk back to the bar, he took care to wipe the excess blood from the bottle with a rag. He could tell that his friend upstairs was someone who didn't enjoy his current surroundings, and could be dangerous drunk and at full strength. Emilio had more than a few customers like that, on both sides of the mortal/immortal scale, and so he took whatever precautions he could. He was just grateful he could always tell who the troublemakers were.

Vampires always knew their own.

II

"Thought you'd never get back," the vampire snarled as Emilio returned to the bar.

"Sorry. Wanted to get you something fresh," Emilio replied as he grabbed a glass and drew a Heineken from the tap. He took a quick glance around to make sure no one was looking and then drew out the small bottle. He poured its contents into the beer, gave it a quick swirl, and then handed it to the vampire, who took it eagerly.

Emilio watched the vampire slurp his vile cocktail with a mix of disgust and envy. It had been close to two hundred years since he had tasted real human blood. He'd been a solider for Spain during the Spanish-American War, turned by a vampire after surviving one of the last battles in Puerto Rico. He still remembered crawling through the battlefield after midnight, near death and praying the enemy wouldn't find him. But someone had. A man, dressed in the garb of the Spanish Army had found him, saying he was a medic and would bring Emilio to camp. Emilio had taken the hand offered, focusing on that instead of the glowing red eyes of his supposed rescuer. He could never remember clearly what happened next. There had had been a flash of movement; a moment of tremendous pain; weakness; a cold, sweet taste filling his mouth; and then blackness.

He'd awoken some time later, his "rescuer" vanished but his body free of pain. He had gotten to his feet, hoping to find his camp and tell his superiors about the thing that had attacked him. But he was lost and was nowhere close to camp when the sun began to rise. And as the first rays of the sun hit his body, he had started to smoke and burn. Racked with pain, he ran to a nearby cave and dove inside, hiding from the light. Inside the cool darkness, he watched in amazement as the wounds on his body healed in seconds. He had stayed in the cave until nightfall, and upon exiting it, saw one of the American soldiers looking around for enemy survivors. Seeing his enemy and remembering the horrors of the battle, Emilio had flown into a rage and attacked the man. He'd beaten the man brutally, breaking bones and beating flesh until he saw the blood dripping down. It had been that moment when his fangs had come out for the first time, and with his eyes glowing red, he'd fed on the solider, draining him until there was nothing left. But when the body slumped to the ground and the last taste of blood left his mouth, he'd felt something change in the air. Turning, he saw his "rescuer" again, who applauded the body of the solider. It was then that monster had told him what he was—vampire.

The creature had offered a chance to feed on the blood of the living together. But Emilio had refused. The vampire had laughed, saying that, sooner or later, the thirst would take hold. But the vampire had been wrong. Emilio had survived the centuries, living first in Puerto Rico, surviving on the blood of animals as he learned the ways of the vampires, as well as the other truths about his kind (garlic didn't work, silver and stakes did, and crosses, holy water, and the like only worked on evil vampires). And as time had passed and his hatreds faded, he'd come to America to make a life for himself. He had been here long enough to lose his accent and perfectly blend in—at night anyway.

But there were times, like now, as he watched this vampire greedily chug his blood-laced beer that Emilio wished he could do more. As a vampire, he had the freedom to live as he chose—take whatever blood he wanted and interact with the humans as he saw fit. Uninterested in the predatory nature of many vampires, Emilio had chosen to mix and live among them as best he could.

But when he'd come to America, he had learned that things were truly different inside the United States. The country was divided, with several territories that were each ruled by a different lord and each one dedicated to keeping the vampire race secret from mortals. All of them worked under the command of the Eldeus, an ancient group of vampires believed by many to have been the first of their kind. It was they who judged who entered America and, afterward, the task the newcomers must do. It was understood each vampire had to contribute to his or her society in exchange for being able to keep his or her individual lifestyle. For Emilio, who had been judged worthy, since he avoided contact with most of his kind and was considered neutral, his responsibility was to offer the local vampires a place where they could go and be served their sustenance in secret. Luckily, vampires drank most liquids with ease, and Emilio was able to steal his blood from various hospitals. He never drank of it, but after living on rat and pig blood for so long, he still on occasion found himself with a longing he could not shake.

But Emilio's minor cravings were nothing compared to his current problem. The sated vampire now looked around the bar, most likely for a human he could kidnap and make into a "feedbag," as these types of vampires called human familiars.

A server of the living and the undead could not play favorites, so Emilio ignored that disturbing practice and mused on the problem. Three weeks ago, a vampire lord had come to him with a task. But the one task had stretched on for weeks, and as the lord had put more and more of his plan into motion, Emilio had realized two things—that it was a plan destined to fail and that its failure could spell disaster for both him and all other vampires.

"Thinking hard again?"

Emilio started at the voice and then slowly turned toward the source. Seeing it, he quickly bowed and asked, "What can I do for you, Lord Jason?"

"Quite a bit," Jason replied, grinning at Emilio with his sharp teeth bared. He was a tall man, who appeared barely over twenty-three, despite his centuries. His black hair was short and spiked, and he wore jeans and a black T-shirt to show off the powerful frame of his body. His face was narrow, and with his sharp, penetrating eyes, he would've seemed like a hawk, if not for his sharklike smile.

"Has…has something happened with the plan?" Emilio asked, keeping his voice low. "Do you need to…to move it?"

"Oh no no. The package is fine where it is." Jason said, his grin seeming to grow as he spoke. "What I need you to do is simply prepare yourself."

"Why? For what?"

"I have changed my plans. We will commence them tonight."

Emilio spoke no words, but his jaw dropped and his pale skin went even paler. After a few moments, he was finally able to say, "But…but we don't have time to move it."

"I know," Jason replied. "I hope your insurance is paid up."

"You…then you have to help me get these people out!" Emilio said, barely keeping his voice down. "If this happens while they're here—"

"Then there'll be more innocents for those fools to have on their conscience," Jason replied.

"So you plan to leave all those bodies here, and you think no one will notice?" Emilio retorted. "Even if no one escapes, this will be all over the news! It will draw attention to us!"

"I can cover it," Jason snarled. "Do not question my judgment."

"Your judgment could destroy us! I can't—"

But before Emilio could finish, the door to the bar flew open. His eyes turned to the doorway, where a group of men were visible in the dim light. Slowly they walked into the bar, revealing their white trench coats, their various belts covered with crosses and bottles and wooden spikes. But what was most frightening was the medallion each one wore, a crucifix. But instead of Jesus on the cross, a fanged, angry figure was writhing in pain from the stake that went through its chest. It was a symbol that made Jason's grin stretch wide, while it filled Emilio with fear—because that symbol meant two things.

It meant that the Vampire Hunters were standing before them. And it meant that the secrecy the vampires needed was completely screwed.

III

THE BAR FOLK STARED in disbelief, Emilio stared in panic, but Jason merely smiled and said, "Welcome friends. And what brings you here tonight?"

"You know damn well what, freak," one of the hunters snapped.

"Oh, I do? Please enlighten me."

"Don't bother answering, Tom," another voice said. Its bearer stepped forth from the ranks of the hunters, staring right at Jason. He was a tall, strong-looking man, with long, brown hair that had streaks of gray mixed in. His face was long and weathered, almost like he had been in a hundred storms on the high seas, one after the other. A long scar ran down his cheek and into his lip, as if someone had tried to give him a half grin.

Emilio knew that, years ago, someone had. Ever since the day he'd put on his cross, Hunst had been the most deadly and most feared hunter in the country. The Hunters had taken him in years ago, after vampires had slaughtered his parents in front of him as a child and given him his scar. The Hunters had taught him all the ways to destroy a vampire, and he had been an eager student. But he had not been so eager when they'd told him the rules that had been handed down by the highest of their order—that only a vampire who was proven to be evil could be killed and that the secrecy of their mission was to be protected at all costs. Hunst's anger and rage had nearly led to their secret being revealed a hundred times, and he was only to be used in extreme circumstances.

"I'm surprised, Hunst. I would've thought that you'd have brought a bigger force to deal with me," Jason said.

"I don't need it to deal with you," Hunst replied.

"Oh. So you're acting without the council's approval. How surprising of you!"

"And I suppose what you did was approved by your people?" Hunst snarled.

"Does it matter?"

"Not for long," Hunst replied, reaching into his coat and drawing out a long wooden stake. "Tonight I am finally going to put an end to you, and whatever of your kind is in here."

"Oh, I doubt it, Hunst," Jason said. "That's the one advantage we have over you—we don't wear our colors in the open."

Hunst's eyes narrowed, and he started to charge Jason. But he had barely taken two steps when, suddenly, one of the patrons leaped from his chair and tackled Hunst. The two wrestled along the floor, the other hunters drew their own weapons, and red eyes and fangs began appearing everywhere in the bar. The regular customers screamed and panicked as the two forces suddenly went to war, slamming each other across the room in rage.

"Time for you to do your job, Emilio!" Jason snarled as he popped his fangs and leaped after Hunst.

The hunter had gotten the upper hand on another vampire and was about to stake him, when Jason grabbed his hand, spun him around, and landed a blow to the back of his head. Hunst staggered back, and the vampires began to circle him. But Emilio just watched as the mortals tried to escape the bar, only to find the way blocked either by the battles or the injuries they'd caused. A man reaching for the door suddenly found a silver knife buried in his hand. A woman trying for a window screamed as a weakened vampire fed on her for strength.

And then, Emilio heard something that drew him away from the horror and forced him to act. He heard a scream, turned, and saw the vampire from the bar holding the dark-haired woman from before, using her as a shield against a hunter's crossbow. Emilio wasted no time then; moving across the bar with the speed only vampires have, he slammed his fist into the hunter's head, knocking him unconscious. Then, before the other vampire could react, he did the same to him, freeing the woman from his grasp. As the vampire hit the floor with a thud, Emilio turned to the woman and yelled, "There's another door in the back. Get out that way! Hurry!"

"But…but what about you?"

"*Go*!!" Emilio yelled as the woman suddenly backed away in horror and then took off for the door.

He wasn't surprised; after all, that was why he'd popped his fangs. Besides, he always felt better fighting like this, especially against his own kind. Speaking of which—

"Stupid, human-loving bastard!" the vampire roared as he got to his feet and charged at Emilio. He swiped at him, but the bartender was quickly able to move aside, dodging the blow while sending one of his own to the creature's face. As the crunch of a broken nose filled the air, the vampire howled in pain and Emilio threw another blow. But this time, it was the other vampire who dodged, landing a vicious kick to Emilio's side that threw him to the ground. He skidded for a few feet and then came to a halt as the other vampire advanced. He reached into his pocket and drew out a pair of brass knuckles, slipping them on with a grin.

But before the vampire could reach Emilio, a hand reached out and pulled him back. The vampire snarled and turned to see a tall, thin, black woman with long dreads standing there with a firm grip on him. The creature snarled and swung his free hand at her. But quick as lightning, the woman caught the vampire's hand in her own. The vampire grinned, but suddenly his face changed, becoming filled with pain and anguish, and he began to scream. Emilio looked at the vampire's captured hand and was amazed to see that it was smoking in the woman's grasp.

"Atomic number 47. Gets you guys every time," she said as she suddenly grabbed the vamp's head and slammed it into her knee. The vamp fell to the ground unconscious, and as the woman turned to Emilio, he saw the silver glinting in the skin of her palm. But instead of using it on him, she said, "Looks like you were right to call us."

"You… Thank God," Emilio said as the woman before him began to change.

Skin and clothes faded away like dust, to be replaced by a gray, tattered tunic and pants, thick boots, gauntlets, and a tattered trench coat. But the face was the most interesting, as the flesh twisted and changed. The woman's mouth stretched and bulged as two mandibles pushed their way through. Her hair stayed but was topped by a wide-brimmed, gray hat. And finally, the last change came; at her sides, four arms began to sprout out, until finally Emilio knew who stood before him—Forger the Elemental Spider-Knight of Metal.

"Thank God. We have to get these people out! And the basement… if they damage what Jason stole—"

"All being taken care of," Forger replied.

"Then the others are…?" Emilio said, as the spider helped him to his feet.

"Yes," Forger replied. "There were rumors Jason was adapting his plan. I felt it was better we hide and wait."

"Good call," Emilio said. "But where are—"

But the spider simply pointed behind him. Emilio turned and then understood. Within the two battling factions, new fighters had emerged—the Elemental Knights, the keepers of the balance and representatives of the Architects, the beings that had created all.

Emilio watched as one of the patrons held up his palms toward a battling vampire and hunter. The skin of his palms twisted, and then two long vines shot outward, wrapping themselves around the two and pulling them apart. Simultaneously, the human guise faded away to reveal Forester, the green-clad Squirrel-Knight of Forest. And behind him, the orange figure of Sandshifter, the Wolf-Knight of the Desert, battered down the front door, and then called out, "Move, people! Everybody get out!" And even as she spoke, two more knights—Firesprite, Lizard-Knight of Fire and Windrider, Falcon-Knight of Air, moved into place and used their collective power to first blow a path to the door and then burn any enemies who came close as the mortals quickly ran for the safety of the outside.

However, that still left a bar full of vampires and hunters, who were now beginning to turn their attention to the knights. The two groups began to advance, their hatreds temporarily forgotten against this new foe. But Firesprite simply pointed upward and sent a small tendril of flame into the sprinkler. Instantly the bar was awash in water. While the hunters looked up in confusion, the vampires began to scream, as the mere touch of the water burned their skin.

"Holy water?" Emilio asked, thankful for his choice of allegiance.

"We made a pit stop at St. John's," Forger said as the water on the ground began to collect together and rise up into a new form.

Within seconds, Wavecrasher, Cat-Knight of the Seas, stood before them. The hunters continued to advance on her, but she simply gave the grin that only cats can do and stepped back.

"You might want to stand on the bar now," Forger said as one of her arms reached over and grabbed the phone.

Emilio was confused, but when he saw the phone suddenly spark, he understood and frantically got onto the bar, just as Forger placed it into the water. Instantly, the water glowed with electricity that shot around the soaked bar until it reached the hunters and vampires, who let out new screams as their bodies coursed with energy. As Emilio watched, the two forces finally fell to the ground, and the electricity rose up from the ground and formed into the silver form of Thunderer, the Ram-Knight of the Storm.

He took a look at the downed hunters and vamps, turned, and said, "I think this was still a little much."

"If you've got a better way to stop them, I'd love to hear it," Sandshifter growled.

"'Sides, you never let volts get lethal. Though Ah think they could use it," Forester added.

"That holy water really got 'em, though," Windrider said, looking over the burns on the vampires. "Toldja gettin' blessed by the priest would work, Crash."

"And I'm not even Catholic," the cat answered as she looked over the bar at Forger and Emilio. "You two all right over there?"

"Wet but fine," Forger replied as she and Emilio stepped out.

"And you must be our informant," Wavecrasher said, looking at Emilio. "Appreciate the call. Place doesn't need any blood on the walls."

"Or extra publicity," Forger added.

"Publi— Lord, those people!" Emilio said. "If they talk—"

"Taken care of," Sandshifter said. "So let's get these sacks of crap up and talking, eh?"

Emilio nodded and moved over to help get Hunst and Jason upright. He had just gotten the lord into a sitting position when Jason's eyes popped open and he wrapped his hands around Emilio's throat.

"You...*traitor*! You ruined my plan!!" he hissed as Emilio choked. "We could've been rid of that bastard foreve— *Aaahhh!*"

Emilio felt the hands relax as Forger applied her silver hand to Jason. The vampire lay back in pain, while Sandshifter, who had just finished trapping Hunst in a rope of thick sand, growled at him to shut up. As Jason sat in pain, the lights inside the bar suddenly glowed brighter and then brighter still, until the whole room was awash in light. And when it faded, a voice spoke to Jason and said, "He saved people from your disgrace. Do shut up, Jason."

"All secure, Joe," Wavecrasher said to the gold-clad figure who now stood in the bar. Emilio just looked in amazement at the leader of the knights—Lightrider, the Knight of Light, and the only total human in the entire group. He was also one of the two most powerful knights, for his power gave him command over not only physical light but also half of the heart. Emilio wondered if he was using that power now as he looked at Jason and asked, "What are you doing here?"

"Protecting my race from this lunatic. What do you think?" Jason spat back, while glaring at Hunst.

"It stops being protection when you put your secrecy in danger," Lightrider said.

"That is my choice, not that of a human-loving traitor!"

"Traitors don't let people die for personal feuds," Emilio answered back. "And they don't risk revealing our existence to the world. This could've been the worst thing to happen to vampires—"

"Don't forget *Twilight*," Windrider interjected.

"This could've been the second worse thing to happen to vampires in our entire history! So I did what I had to do," Emilio answered. "And if I hadn't stopped you, the Eldeus would have!"

"True," Lightrider said. "But then again, this isn't completely his fault, is it?" With that, he walked over to Hunst. Looking down at the hunter, he said, "So, Hunst, what made you decide that coming here and slaughtering vampires in the open was a good idea?"

"You're actually defending them?" Hunst snapped. "After what they did to me?"

"What did they do? And not your parents again, please."

"That bastard took my children! He captured them and taunted me with how he was going to destroy them!"

"And why did you do that, Jason?" Lightrider asked the vampire.

"He killed Chantra!" Jason snarled.

"Chantra? Who is—"

"She was his consort," Emilio answered. "They killed her after they found she was preying on children in Central Park."

"I see," Lightrider said. "So you took his children in return. And you forced Emilio to keep them here."

"Yes. So that fool would have even more innocent blood on his hands when I decided to let him 'save' them," Jason answered.

Lightrider looked between the two of them and then shook his head in disbelief. "You two—how did you become leaders, being such fools? Chantra and the kids, I'm sorry any of them had to be put into this position, but, damn it, that is the way it works with you people! Vampires kill, hunters kill back, evil plans, etc. But I thought you at least understood that you could never be stupid enough to reveal yourselves to the mortals! Do you know what would've happened if they had learned about vampires and the war you two have? You'd have caused riots and hunts and bloodbaths that would've thrown the world into chaos!"

He sighed then and said, "And for that, and for the balance, I have to make you both suffer now."

"Do your worst. I'm not afraid of sunlight," Jason said. "I'll die happily knowing I made this bastard suffer."

"And there'll be others to take up after me," Hunst said.

But Lightrider didn't answer. Instead, he stood as footsteps could be heard from the doorway. Everyone looked toward the door, and Emilio gasped as he saw the only knight to rival Lightrider in power—Nightstalker, the Bat-Knight of Shadow. The second in command held power over the darkness and the other half of the heart, where all secrets were buried.

Lightrider looked at him, and asked, "Did you wipe them?"

"Yes," the bat nodded. "My shadow fell on everyone who left the bar."

"Good," Lightrider said. "But there is still one more job for you."

"Of course," Nightstalker said as he looked over at Jason. Staring at him in disgust, he said, "Well. I suppose we're going to need a new lord in this place, aren't we? Wonder who the Eldeus will pick? After all, you set a pretty high level of crazy, didn't you?"

"Please," Jason said with a laugh. "The others are far too weak for this job! Most of them actually fear for the humans! The Eldeus would never—"

But that was as far as he got, as Nightstalker placed a hand on the vampire's shoulder. Instantly, black mist began to drain out of Jason and into the bat. The vampire's body began to shrink, to grow small and weak, as Nightstalker spoke. "This is what I hate about your kind of vampire. You spend so much time preying on humans, thinking you're better than them, that you forget the most important things—that all a vampire is, is a corpse, animated by dark magic and kept alive with stolen blood. And guess what happens when you take away the magic?"

But Jason couldn't answer. When he opened his mouth, the dust that had been his tongue blew away. And as Nightstalker continued the drain, the rest of his body followed, until Jason's clothes fell to the floor, the dust billowing out from inside it.

"Well, that's one down," the bat said as he pushed the clothes aside with his foot. "Now, what about him?"

"The hunters will excommunicate him," Lightrider replied. "But he should still have his children back."

"Good," Emilio said.

"Let him know he can bring them up," Joe said.

"Way ahead a' ya," came a voice from behind the bar.

Emilio turned to see a door pop open and the final knight, Groundquake, Dog-Knight of Earth, emerge, followed by two dirty and tired-looking kids. One was a young boy, around twelve, who had his father's seriousness, and the same steely eyes glared at Emilio. The other was a girl of fourteen, with blond hair, dark eyes, and a strange look of calmness, even after everything she had been through.

"John! Emily!" Hunst said, struggling anew against his sandy bonds.

"Father!" John yelled, racing over to Hunst, beating at the sands that held his father captive. Emily however, stayed behind, eyeing her father cautiously, as if he was a lion about to strike.

"The vampires will leave you alone now," Lightrider said. "You and your children are free to go."

"Thank you, Lightrider," Hunst said begrudgingly as the sand fell away. "Come, Emily. Let's get out of here."

"No."

Emilio and everyone else stopped, turning to the girl in surprise and disbelief—everyone except Hunst. He looked at her in anger.

"I gave you an order. You will do what I say."

"No. I won't go back. Not with you," she stated.

"How dare you," the hunter hissed. "You are the daughter of a hunter! Don't you know what those freaks will do to you?"

"Yes, I know what you told me, but he was kind to us!" she insisted, pointing at Emilio. "He brought us food and kept us safe from the others. I heard him arguing with the other one about letting us go. He didn't beat me because I looked at an Ann Rice book!"

"His kind kidnapped us!" John yelled back. "They trapped us in a basement. How can you defend him?!"

"That's enough, Emily!" Hunst snarled.

"No, it isn't," Lightrider said, glaring at the ex-hunter. Turning to Nightstalker, he asked, "Is this true?"

The bat turned to Hunst and stared at him, his eyes going pitch-black. Slowly, Hunst's eyes also filled with blackness, as the bat searched his heart for the secrets he had locked away. After a few moments, he turned to Lightrider and said, "It's true. All of it."

"Emilio?"

"I had to make sure she and her brother were safe. She told me about Hunst, and I wasn't surprised."

"Yeah, that's why you left us to die—"

"Shut up, boy," Sandshifter snarled at John as Lightrider turned to Emilio.

"Do you still want what's best for her?"

"Yes."

Lightrider nodded and then turned to Emily and said, "Then you will be responsible for her now."

"*What*?!" Hunst howled. "She's *my* daughter! How dare—"

"You lost her a long time ago," Lightrider said as Emily moved over to Emilio. "The hunters have punished you. This will be your punishment from us. If you ever come near her again, we will find you, and you will wish for Jason's fate. Do you understand?"

"Think carefully," Nightstalker said, glaring at Hunst.

Hunst stared angrily at the bat and then shot an angry glance at everyone but his son. And then, the former hunter got to his feet, took one last look at his daughter, and walked away, his son following.

"Hmph," Nightstalker said. "Fun evening."

"Thank you for making sure it wasn't worse," Emilio said.

"Happy to," Lightrider said. "We'll drop off the hunters. Do you want to take care of the vamps?"

"I think I can handle that," Emilio replied.

"Good. We'll be watching you too, Emilio. Do a good job."

Emilio nodded, and then Lightrider vanished in a burst of golden light. The other knights followed one by one, in lights of their color, each taking a hunter with them. Within moments, the bar was empty, save for Emilio, Emily, and the group of vampires that were already starting to crawl to the door.

IV

EMILIO HAD ENCOUNTERED DIFFICULTY in contacting the knights because their home was a place only a few knew how to reach—the Obelisk, the dimensional lynchpin of the universe. Hidden in a dimension of darkness, it sent out its light to the worlds, mixing with all the shadows to create life. And because of its connection with all worlds, it was a great storehouse of knowledge and artifacts of magic.

But of all the secrets hidden within the Obelisk, the greatest was hidden away in the top of the great structure. It was a large room made of glass, into which many strange symbols had been carved. In the center of the room was a great glass spire, through which the magic of the room was realized. The symbols on the walls stood not for words or letters, but for places and times. Through them, the room could transport any person to any time and place he or she so desired. All the Knights had to do was to touch the spire and think of where and when they wanted to be. Returning took only thought of the room. There were also times when the spire, preset by some force that even the Knights did not fully understand, would send them to a place and time where they were needed. It was for that reason the Knights had named this room the Nexus of Worlds, the great knot in which all times and places were tied.

At the moment, the room was empty. But then the spire began to glow, its glass frame filling up with lights of red and orange, gold and green, more colors than could be counted. Those lights hovered within the spire for a moment and then floated outside the spire as orbs. They hovered a moment and then began to grow and change, until the Elemental Knights stood in the room once more.

"I think that's the first time we dealt with vamps and didn't get covered in blood," Groundquake said as he dusted off his shoulder.

"You were in the basement while we did the work," Sandshifter snapped.

"Hey, somebody had to get da kids," the dog snapped back.

"And be able to get underground quietly," Firesprite added.

"What's important is that we succeed and nobody got hurt who didn't need to be," Thunderer said.

Joe watched and smiled as the other knights nodded at that statement. He and the others began to walk out of the Nexus. No matter how many times he saw it, it was good to see his friends getting along. In the three years since the knights had been chosen for their mission, he had worked hard to make the group function as a unit, and it had not been easy. Between short tempers; button pushers; and the many, *many* different approaches that each of the knights had (all of which had worked at different times), Joe had often wanted to go and find a spell that would make him blind, deaf, and mute, just so the Architects would have to make Nightstalker the new leader. Hell, there had even been times where he had wished for his old job as a store manager back; he'd take people yelling about paper towels at half-off over Groundquake and Forester's complaints and Sandshifter's temper any day.

But ever since that day when they'd destroyed their first Chaos Demon in the gremlin caves under Miami, things had steadily improved. They all still disagreed and argued, but it was like simple sibling rivalry. Joe knew his own growth as leader had helped, but he wasn't sure what to credit all of the new dynamic to—maybe seeing the enemy that would emerge if they didn't work together, the fact they were the only ones of their kind, or the realization that they were simply going to have to get along. Or maybe it was all of those things.

But whatever the reason, he had been able to watch as the group began to, at least, tolerate the differences they each had and be smart enough to use them to their advantage when the time came. Joe could remember Sandshifter actually listening quietly to one of Wavecrasher's lengthy explanations on a type of demon or trying to help Forester learn to use his powers with more effectiveness and less show. And he had watched Groundquake accept the many jokes made at his expense, even laughing at a few of them. But most of all, Joe had seen the other knights treat him with respect and even admiration in the field, listening to his orders without question and even asking his advice.

The camaraderie was a good feeling, and for all his power, he still needed that from time to time. He touched the gold rings that hung around his neck, the last symbol of the marriage and life he'd been forced to leave. Despite all the wonders he found in his new life, simple thoughts of his old life still came. Usually it was when he came to the dirty parts of his job—the death and destruction that was sometimes needed to keep the balance—or the lives forever changed by his words, like Hunst's. But after three years, he had learned to accept what he had to do for the greater purpose. Thinking on his old life now simply gave him a healthy nostalgia, and a reminder of the people he fought for.

"Joe? Gotta a second?" Wavecrasher asked, drawing Joe out of his thoughts.

"Huh? Is something wrong, Crash?" Joe replied, noticing that Stalker had stayed behind as well.

"Apparently, the Coral Queen thinks there's more to this vampire thing," the bat said.

"And what would that be?" Joe asked, reminding himself to take things with a grain of salt. Wavecrasher was the group's resident expert on the supernatural; she had studied every book on demons and angels in the library, obsessed with letting nothing slip by her. But the downside was that she often saw things that simply weren't there and would loudly argue her case to the others.

"So what do you think it is?" Joe asked. "Do the Eldeus or the hunters have some sort of evil plan? Or are they both being used to wipe themselves out and make room for someone else?"

"I can't say for sure, but … something just doesn't feel right about this whole thing," the cat said.

"We deal with weird things day in and day out," Joe said. "We're gonna need some specifics."

"Well, don't you think that a vampire behaving with such disobedience to the rules is a bit off?" Wavecrasher began. "The only thing that the Eldeus punish more fiercely then betrayal is exposure. It's why they've been able to keep things quiet for so long."

"From what the Eldeus told us, Jason was unstable for a long time," Joe said. "Even they were worried about what he might do."

"The hunters said the same thing about Hunst," Stalker said.

"Still, I can't believe that a vampire or a hunter, even an unstable one would risk this much," Wavecrasher said. "I'd like to take a closer look at things, maybe talk to the Eldeus and the hunters."

"The ones so secretive we had to force them to give us any info," Nightstalker muttered. "Crash, the two of them had suffered great losses. That can easily cloud judgment, especially with people who aren't very sane to begin with."

"I agree, and I don't see either side swallowing their pride and letting us do things for them," Joe said. "But Crash's feelings have saved us before. Stalker, I want you to keep an eye on them."

"Full surveillance?"

"Yes. Check into their lairs as much as you can. Look for anything that would indicate something amiss. And report back first thing if you see anything that even hints at Chaos."

Wavecrasher thanked Joe and turned toward the door. The Knights of Light and Dark waited until she was gone, and then Nightstalker asked, "So you think she's right?"

"She makes a good argument," Joe replied. "And she was right before. But it may just be coincidence."

"Better safe than sorry though."

"Absolutely."

"I think she just needs to be right after what happened with that 'possessed' guy last month. Though it was pretty funny to watch her hitting the guy with her trident yelling, 'Out demon, *out!*'"

"Thank God she didn't try the rite with the lamb's blood again."

"Whatever happened to that guy, anyway?"

*   *   *

As the two knights spoke, in a plane high above the realm of the Obelisk, Ruta, one of the Architects of Creation, watched them through a sphere of water. Her face narrowed as she heard them speak and then she shivered and dissipated the sphere.

"Strange as it sounds, I too, hope that Wavecrasher is wrong," the Architect of Water said, her pale, clammy hands clutching the sleeves of her blue robes.

"It is wiser to hope that she is wrong but prepare if she is right," whispered a rich, feminine voice.

Ruta turned to see her sister, Rastla, the Architect of Shadow walking over in her dark robes, her face a pale moon in her dark hood.

"The demons have been dormant for too long. It troubles me to think of what they could have planned with so much time," Rastla said as another form appeared behind her.

"I agree. But surely, we are prepared," said Demtia, the Architect of Forest, each word sending a rustle through the vines that entrenched his robes. "The knights are far stronger than they were when they fought the demons before."

"I am simply being prudent, brother," Rastla hissed softly. "Unlike you, I am well aware of how easily things can fall apart, no matter how strong they seem at first."

"And you think we are not?" Ruta snapped, her stringy blond hair swinging about as she turned to face Rastla. "We have all faced the Chaos Demons, Rastla. That is why I fear them and why I pray that I shall not see them again!"

"I hope for that as well. But I do not let my fear prevent me from acting," Rastla answered. "You might deign to think upon that, rather than gaze into your puddles and wring your hands."

"Forgive me if I cannot bury the past in the blackness as you do! I remember the time before the Chaos Demons and why that time ended."

Rastla's face grew even darker then as she started to move toward Ruta. But Demtia stepped between them.

"Sisters, be calm," the Architect of Forest insisted as water and shadowfire bristled about them. "Ruta, we cannot let fear control us. And, Rastla, you must remember the law that allowed all of us to banish the demons."

"I remember the law, brother," Rastla whispered. "And I am prepared to defend it if the knights fall. As we should all be."

"Not all of us look at the dark side," Ruta replied.

But before Rastla or Demtia could say anything, a new voice entered the conversation, along with a flash of golden light. "I have heard that there may be more Chaos Demons on the mortal plane. Is this true?" asked Ralin, Architect of Light, his robes giving off a slight glow, save for the spot where his long white beard flowed down.

"Wavecrasher believes it may be possible," Rastla answered, facing her brother. "But it may be coincidence, as I hope it is."

"Nightstalker will be observing for any signs of the demons—a wise precaution," Ruta said.

"I see," Ralin said. "I, too, hope for coincidence. Still, this may shed some light on another matter."

"What has happened?" Demtia asked.

"I have been summoned to an audience."

Ruta and Demtia gasped in unison, while Rastla's eyes narrowed.

"Only you, Ralin?" the dark Architect asked.

"I do not know what will be said or why it must only be said to me. But whatever the reason, it must be of strictest importance."

"Agreed. When are you to go?"

"Immediately. Only the mention of the Chaos Demons slowed me."

"Understandable. Go quickly then, Ralin, and tell us of what you learn."

Ralin nodded and then vanished in a burst of light. The other Architects watched him go and then vanished as well, Rastla muttering, "Chaos Demons and now a summoning. Preparations are wise indeed."

V

"So should I keep my search to New York, or should keep tabs on the other nests?" Stalker asked as he and Lightrider walked down the stairs.

"New York's the only one with this sort of trouble so far, so I'd keep to that," Joe replied. "I'm going to try to monitor for other outbreaks. But first, I want to go and try to get a little rest before something else goes wrong."

"Does something go wrong often? I never see it," the bat said.

"I guess you're getting bored with things going right again?" Joe asked back.

"Well you know, the beat downs and frightening monologues are nice, but a little change doesn't hurt, right?"

"I thought you liked the frightening monologues and beat downs."

"Well it's not like you can do them," the bat replied.

Joe started to answer the bat, but as he looked at him, he saw a strange, almost melancholy expression come into his into his friend's eyes for a brief second. Joe almost asked him about it, but then a familiar impulse ran through his brain—the voice of the Obelisk, telling him that something was wrong with the balance and the time had come for the knights to act once again.

Apparently Nightstalker had heard it too, as he said, "Well, guess you can forget that rest, huh?"

"Guess so," Joe said as he watched the bat turn and head back up to the Nexus. Joe followed, but not without wondering what it was that had troubled his friend.

*　　*　　*

The duo reached the Nexus in moments, thanks to the inherent magic of the Obelisk stairs. They found the other knights already inside, all waiting to head out.

"Never ends, does it?" Forester muttered.

"The job or you complaining?" Sandshifter growled.

"Guys, I know it's a busy day, but that doesn't matter," Joe said. "Did anyone check to find out where we're headed?"

"I took the liberty," Forger replied. "The Nexus has instructions to send us to Hoboken. It says something about an innocent to save."

"Anything a tad more specific?" Firesprite asked.

"Not much. Just that it's an innocent in New Jersey," Forger said.

"Lucky us," Quake muttered.

"But what are we going down there to fight? Goblins? Angry ghosts? Demons? The Archangel Gabriel?" Windrider asked.

"Well, if you keep going, I'm sure you'll come up with it," Forger said. "But ... I can't really tell what we're going down there for."

"What?! Lemme see that thing," Groundquake snapped, making his way up to the Nexus. Placing his hand on it, the dog waited a few moments and then asked, "Is there a magic bill we didn't pay?"

"We'll worry about that later," Joe said. "Let's just go down there and try to figure things out. Hopefully, it will be something obvious that we can deal with quickly. And without destruction."

"Taking the fun out of the job again, I see," Sandshifter muttered as she reached over and touched the spire. Instantly, she was transformed into orange light, which sped through the spire, through the ceiling, to be sent off to the mortal world.

"She's just mad because she didn't get to kill any vampires in the bar," Thunderer said as he and Forester moved toward the spire.

"We should let 'er have a few licks at whatever this thing is then," Forester replied.

"Yeah but—" Thunderer began, but his words were cut off as the two knights touched the spire and were quickly drawn away.

The other knights followed, and the spire filled with different lights and then returned to transparency, leaving the room barren once again.

*   *   *

As always, Joe found himself surrounded by bright lights, felt a brief sensation of weightlessness, and then he was back on solid ground. The smells of his new environment came rushing at him in a wave—concrete, exhaust, garbage, and a hundred other city odors. He took a moment to adjust and then turned to make sure the others had also gotten through safely.

As always, he saw them behind him in a group, making the same adjustments. And as always, Sandshifter was the first to come out of it. "So, now what?" the wolf growled. "I don't see any major fiery doom raining down, do you?"

"Only you would complain we're not in a fiery inferno surrounded by demons," Stalker said, looking around.

The knights had appeared in an alleyway, just overlooking a city street. Cars whizzed by them, their headlights leaving trails of radiance in the dark night. But as Sandshifter had pointed out, that was the only thing they could see.

"Forger, are you sure this wasn't a false alarm?" Joe asked. "I know the spire didn't give you any specifics—"

"I agree," the spider cut in. "But it was a genuine alert. Perhaps the event we need to halt hasn't occurred yet. We may need to search."

Joe nodded and glanced at Wavecrasher. The cat nodded and whispered the ancient words under her breath. Joe's vision shimmered for a moment as he felt the magic of the glamour wrap around him like a well-worn blanket. This spell had been one of the best discoveries of Wavecrasher's mass reading sessions in the library. It was simple, but effective; the user was covered in a magic shell that cast the image of a normal person to any non-magical person who saw him or her. The cat had spent months trying to perfect the spell, with many broken results, before she finally perfected it for all the knights.

Joe watched as the other glamours fell into place and then motioned for the group to head out toward the street. As they joined the mass of humanity, the lights of the buildings and the streetlight covered them in their cold, electric blanket. The streets were crowded, but no noticed their unmasked faces as they walked by. One man, talking on his cell phone and oblivious in more ways than one, actually bumped into Windrider, jarring him from his conversation. He looked at the falcon dead on, muttered an apology, and moved on without so much as another glance.

Joe took no notice of this; he had worked with the glamour long enough to become used to the mortal's normal reaction. He still remembered the pale-skinned Goth, dressed in black and pierced in every place imaginable, who had bumped into him, looked back in anger, and told him to watch where he was going.

But Joe tried to focus on the strangeness of the mission at hand. Joe could not remember a time when they had not been given at least the name of the creature or event they had been sent to deal with. What kind of problem could exist that the Nexus could not tell them details about?

At the thought of hidden problems, Joe briefly glanced at Nightstalker, who was walking undeterred by the people around him. Joe's mind kept drifting back to the look in the bat's eyes in the Obelisk. That glimmer of weary resignation—it had been brief but certainly real. And in the years that Joe had known the bat, Nightstalker had always maintained a calm acceptance about his life and everything that came with it. It had been Nightstalker who had convinced him to give up his attempt at regaining his old life. It had been Nightstalker who had made him understand the importance of death in their business but that he did not have to enjoy it. And the bat had been his only counsel as the two of them had struggled to control the "berserkers"—those moments of anger or fear, where their powers, drawn from the emotional spectrum as well as the spectrum of light and shadow, overwhelmed them. They were moments that could end in a successful attack or a long bloodbath; Joe had awoken from those massacres sickened, but Stalker had been able to rationalize those violent breaks, saying that the attacks were against those who deserved it. Stalker's words did not make the guilt vanish, but they did make it easier to withstand, and the help of another person who had learned to control them was invaluable.

But if he stops caring, Joe thought, *things could get bad quickly.* Joe tried to imagine someone with the bat's power, in the throes of a berserker with nothing guiding him and could not even come close to what could happen. He was going to have to watch the bat closely, he decided. A look could just be a look, but if there was more to this then …

"*Ummph!*"

Joe was suddenly dashed out of his thoughts as a random shoulder bumped into his, knocking him off balance. He tried to right himself, but Joe found himself slipping quickly and then hitting the ground in a heap. He groaned but still managed to turn and see the figure that had hit him, a slim one dressed in a leather coat, run through the crowd and then turn into the very alley that he and the knights had just been in.

"You all right, buddy?" said a man on the street, who stretched out his hand to help Joe up as the knights approached.

"Yeah, thanks," Joe said, taking the man's hand and pulling himself up. "Wonder what that was about."

"Crazy people in this city. Nobody cares what they do anymore," the man replied, glancing at the alley with a look of disgust.

"I suppose," Joe said. But then, his eyes narrowed as he looked past the man and back at the alley's entrance. A group of about six men, dressed in dark clothing and with hard, angry faces, stopped in front of the alley and began to argue among themselves. Finally, one of them pointed down the alley, and they ran down, their angry expressions becoming even more frightening, almost predatory.

"Excuse me. I'm late for an appointment. Thanks again," Joe said as he moved past the man and headed toward the alley.

The other knights followed him, each one slowly moving their hands to their weapons.

*   *   *

"There you are," Donnie said as he and the rest of the boys came into the alley. Donnie was tall and thick, his pale white biceps bulging out of his black shirt. His face, marked by a scar on his forehead and a slightly misshapen jaw (the result of a high school football accident), shifted into a twisted smile as he looked down the alley. He could see their prey huddled at the back of the alley, its face obscured in the shadows. "We coulda had this over back on Third, you know."

"Like I give a shit," the prey said. "Why don't you boys just go back to your pond and play with the rest of the scum?"

"The right answer back there was, 'Sure, take it,' not ... What was it again, Dom? I can't seem to remember."

"Screw off, jerk wads," snorted Dom, a short, chubby kid dressed in way too much leather and chains.

Donnie took a moment to nod, remembering to beat Dom if he didn't stop dressing like such a frigging tool and then turned back to the prey and said, "And if you'd just done that, you could be home right now."

"Gee, why do I not believe you?" the prey replied.

Donnie smiled again and took a step forward. But before he could put his foot down, a voice said, "I wouldn't. Just a suggestion."

Surprised, Donnie almost lost his balance but then turned around to see who this new smartass was. All he saw was what looked like a weird cosplayer, completely wrapped in a long, gold coat, who leaned on a big stick and wore a hat over a face wrapped in cloth.

"What the hell are you? This is our business, and I got no problems cutting you out of it."

"Yeah … Listen, that's not really gonna work on me. Why don't you and the rest of the boys let this person go on her way? Simple plan?"

"Yeah. Except there's six of us saying we stay," Donnie replied as the others stood by him. "I think majority rule counts for something, don't you?"

"Oh, absolutely," Joe said, "except you aren't in the majority."

The others laughed at this, but Donnie was smart enough to quickly look around, for whatever it was that this guy was talking about. But no one was behind them, save their intended victim, and no one was positioned in the fire escapes above.

Donnie laughed then, and turned his attention back to the gold hobo they were about to obliterate. But Donnie had neglected to look down, so he missed the cracks forming around himself and his cohorts, cracks that allowed the ground below to suddenly rise up and dump them backward like a garbage truck. The six of them tumbled back, hitting the ground and each other with a thud. As the piece of ground shifted back into place, Donnie looked over and saw another hobo standing there, this one dressed in brown and carrying a hammer.

"Anybody else like a ride?" the brown man asked.

"Get 'em!" Donnie yelled, struggling back up to his feet. The others quickly followed, temporarily forgetting about their prey in their anger and humiliation. But the gold-coated man raised up his staff, and suddenly a blinding light swept over them. Donnie and his boys came to a halt, screaming and covering their eyes against the blinding glare. And that proved to be their mistake.

Donnie stumbled about, trying to clear his eyes. But even as he moved around, he could hear sounds like metal being thrown about and a weird shifting noise, like sand being poured through a sieve. He could smell something like open flames, along with the salty brine of ocean water and even the smell of wood. And he could feel strong winds rush by him as he struggled to see. How could two men do all this? And where were all these damn smells and sounds coming from?

Finally, Donnie saw the colors begin to fade, and he opened his eyes once again. But the second he looked out into the alley, he wished he were blind again. Dom was chained up to the fire escape, and next to him, Tino was frozen in ice up to his head. Lee was stuck in a huge block of what looked like sand, and Johnny and Kwame were stuck on the wall, trapped in the mouths of what looked like giant Venus flytraps. Donnie stared at his friends in disbelief and then looked back at the two men, only to see them joined by seven other figures, each in a different color.

"Are you going to leave?" the gold man asked as he held up his staff once again.

But Donnie, unable to even attempt thinking clearly, turned from these strange, powerful men and ran back to the prey, who was also staring in utter disbelief. Before she could even think enough to react to him, Donnie had grabbed her, spun her around, and then pulled her close, pulling out his knife and holding it to her throat.

"Stay back! Get away from me, you goddamn freaks!" Donnie screamed out in a panic-filled voice.

But the men didn't move, and at that moment, Donnie was so grateful to the prey, he almost considered letting her go. But then he felt something cold wrap around his wrist, something so frozen and dead that he dropped the knife in shock. Turning his head, Donnie screamed again as he saw a man dressed in black glaring at him as he said, "That was a very stupid decision."

Donnie continued to scream as the black man raised a fist. But then, Donnie bent over as the prey delivered a hard blow to his gut. It didn't stop there; she grabbed Donnie's collar and spun him around headfirst into the wall. Donnie bounced off, clutching his head in pain, as the prey grabbed a stray trash can lid and gave him one final blow upside the head. He staggered backward, standing upright a few moments, and then finally fell to the ground with a thud, the prey standing over him.

"So, you still want me to give it to you?" the prey snapped, holding the trash can lid over her head.

Donnie didn't give a response this time, save to frantically backpedal on his hands until he was able to turn over, get to his feet, and run like hell away from the prey, as the colored figures cleared a way to let him pass. Donnie ran down that block and the next and the next, thinking only that this might be an excellent time to visit his cousin in California, who only had to deal with gangs and drug dealers.

VI

"HE RUNS FAST," GROUNDQUAKE said as he looked past the alley and watched Donnie speed down the street. "Should we go after 'im?"

"What for?" Forger asked. "No one ever believes the runners."

"Yeah, but my way's more fun," Quake grumbled.

"If ya want something ta do, ya can help us get these guys down," Wavecrasher said, moving over to where she'd frozen the one thug. He stood within the ice, teeth chattering and skin rapidly going blue. Wavecrasher moved before him and raised her hand. Joining her thumb, ring, and pinky fingers, the cat pointed with her remaining fingers and gestured downward. Instantly, the ice first unfroze, and then the water spilled down onto the pavement as the thug inside fell to his knees, curling his frozen body into a ball.

"Easy, kid, you'll be all right in a few," Wavecrasher said as she removed her coat and draped it over him.

Glancing over, the cat saw Forester opening the mouths of the flytraps, dropping the men inside into Firesprite and Joe's waiting arms. The men were covered in green liquid, some sort of plant 'saliva.' As nasty as they looked, though, they looked unbelievably relieved just to be out of the plants. But they were still plenty afraid, as a simple look from both knights was enough to make them stand still against the wall.

Wavecrasher nodded in approval and then turned back to Nightstalker, to see the reason they'd been through all this trouble. But when she looked, the cat didn't get an immediate answer. The person they had been sent to save was a woman, about twenty-five or so by Crash's reckoning, dressed in a Colorado Avalanche shirt and wearing a worn-looking backpack. She wasn't bad-looking—a slim body but not one that didn't understand curves and a pretty face with high cheekbones and a small but full mouth. Still, certain details that stuck out most—the long and fiery red hair that fell to her shoulders and the bright green eyes that Wavecrasher could see blazing even in the dark.

Still, the cat hadn't been pulled away from her work in the Obelisk for nothing, and she intended to find out what it was. Taking one last look at the thug to make sure he was warming up, Wavecrasher moved over to where the girl stood, still talking to Nightstalker.

"Are you sure you're all right?" the bat asked under the cover of his mask.

"You did hear the trash can lid hit that guy right?" the girl asked, crossing her arms and giving the bat a quizzical look.

"I'm pretty sure he's still hearing it."

"He just likes being the 'dark avenger,' miss," Wavecrasher said as she approached. "Are you all right?"

"If it'll make you guys stop asking me that, then yes, I'm fine," the girl said. "Does that I mean I get to ask a question or two now?"

"Not yet," Wavecrasher said. "We'd like your name too."

"Why, are you guys some sort of medieval police?"

"In a way."

"It might be useful," Nightstalker added. "You can trust us."

"Well, you did beat the hell out of those guys," the girl answered. "It's Sara Dalle."

"Hmm, nothing obvious there," Wavecrasher said. "Now then—"

"Nothing obvious?" the newly named Sara said, sticking out a finger in the cat's face. "You guys show up out of nowhere, do ... whatever it was to them, and then you start asking me questions that clearly need a specific answer, and you think I won't notice? I want to know how the hell you found me and why you did all this."

"We can't answer that," Wavecrasher said. "But this isn't about us. We need—"

"Wait a second," Nightstalker interrupted. "You aren't freaked out by what we did?"

"Tying up some perverts who were trying to rob and God knows what else to me ... no, I'm not really bothered by that," Sara replied. "Is that how you usually spend your nights?"

"For the most part, yes," Nightstalker replied.

"Hmm," Sara said.

"Hey, look, I know this is weird, but these answers are important," Wavecrasher said firmly. "Now, have you ever been involved in spiritual possessions, magical battles or history, have a family with mystical lineage, had contact with mystical creatures, demons, the Loch Ness Monster, and do you have strong belief in the theory of Atlantis?"

Both Sara and Nightstalker stared at the cat in disbelief, until she finally said, "What? Standard questions."

"Atlantis?" Stalker asked.

"Most of the big ones on both sides think it's real. And it's a sign of belief, which can be a good indicator of—"

"Why don't you let me talk now?" the bat said. Turning to Sara, he said, "We seem to have been sent here to help you."

"Why me?" Sara asked.

"We're not sure. Have you any sort of experiences like what my friend described?"

"I don't come from a family of wizards, I don't know any demons, and I've never seen Bigfoot."

"Atlantis! Come on, Bigfoot's just a myth," Wavecrasher grumbled.

Nightstalker chuckled under his mask at that but then noticed something out of the corner of his eye. Turning, he saw Joe motioning him over to one of the thugs. The bat nodded and then turned back and said, "Pardon me. My friends apparently need my assistance."

"If they need me to hit someone again," Sara said.

"I'll let you know," the bat replied, nodding to her as he moved over to his friends.

*　　*　　*

— 41 —

"How's the girl?" Joe asked, as Stalker moved over to them.

"Fine," Stalker replied. "Seems like a real fighter."

"Apparently," Joe answered. "I saw that stunt with the can lid."

"Hell of a dent too," Stalker replied. "So what do we have here?" he asked, looking down at the slime-covered thug.

"Something I'm hoping you can answer," Joe said. "Would you mind taking a look at this guy?"

"Oh, of course," the bat replied as he stretched out his gloved hand. The thug tried to pull his face away, but the hand was too quick, and it clutched his face, pressing it back against the wall.

Joe watched as the thug first struggled and then slowed, an inky blackness falling over his eyes. The same blackness also came over Stalker's as the bat's powers inched their way into the man's heart. Joe watched as the bat's eyes stared endlessly at the thug's, until finally, Stalker said, "This guy's a stupid, ignorant, waste of skin."

"And?" Joe asked.

"But that's all he is," the bat finished, his eyes beginning to clear. "He has no ulterior motive, no secret demon plot or angel scheme. They weren't going after Sara for any other reason than to steal and—"

"So it's a good thing that we were here."

"But it doesn't make sense," Quake said. "Why would we get sent out here just to save her from some thugs?"

"I don't know," Joe answered. "Was there anything special about the girl?"

"No, she seems normal," the bat said.

"She might not know," Joe replied. "I think you should examine her."

Groundquake snickered at that, but a sharp glance from Nightstalker silenced him. Turning back to Joe, the bat said, "Look, Joe, I really think that this is a normal girl. She certainly doesn't know anything about our line of work—"

"And how many times have we encountered people unaware of their destiny?" Forger argued. "Joe's logic is sound, Stalker. There must be some greater reason for her being rescued than simply the danger of a few thugs. It might even be a trap."

"No, the Obelisk would've told us," Stalker said.

"And you know this how?" Forger asked. "This isn't something new for you. Just scan her so we can see exactly why we came here. Besides," the spider whispered, "it's not beyond imagining that she could be a Chaos—"

"All right," Stalker said sharply and slowly walked back over to Sara.

"You and your friends have a nice chat?" Sara asked as the bat approached.

"For the most part. I'm going to … need to do something with you."

"Hmmph."

"Yeah, the brown guy over there thought the same thing," Stalker said. "No I need to … well … I need to see if what you're telling us is true."

"They think I'm lying?"

"I don't. But they want to make sure. We've been tricked before in this line of work."

"And what exactly is that, anyway?" Sara asked with a wry smile.

"I'd tell you if I could," the bat replied. "I promise, though, we're not here to do you any harm."

"I figured that much," Sara replied. "Fine, do what you need to."

"All right," Nightstalker said. He stretched out his hand and placed it on her face.

Sara started a moment but then went still as her eyes clouded over. Stalker's eyes followed, and the bat looked through the secrets of her heart. As he worked his power through the girl, Joe moved to his side, waiting for some sign that his friend was seeing something useful.

Finally, after a moment, the Shadow Knight spoke. "I've discovered her biggest secret."

"What have you got?" Joe asked.

"Once, in second grade, she played with matches and burned up her mother's picture of her dead grandma. She hid the ashes, and her mom assumed she lost the photo.

"Not quite what I was looking for," Joe said.

"I told you she wasn't lying."

"I didn't think you were wrong, but better to be safe. Wipe her mind of this so we can get back to the Obelisk."

"Uh … right," Stalker said, narrowing his black eyes. The hand on Sara's face suddenly began to leak black shadow, the darkness creeping across her face like fog over a riverbed.

Sara stood still, even as the shadow began to force its way into her black eyes.

Joe watched without comment; but he took note that until today, Stalker had never displayed any kind of ignorance toward the task that was always his and his alone.

"Okay, it's done," Stalker said, pulling his hands away as his eyes returned to normal.

Sara's, however, remained black.

"How much time did you give her?" Joe asked.

"About five minutes. Plenty of time for us to get out, and she'll think she made a wrong turn."

"Good. Now let's take care of the final detail," Joe said as he turned to the thugs that the other knights had finally finished removing from their trappings. Quake, Firesprite, Sandshifter, Forger, and Forester held each of them in place as Joe walked over to them.

"Are we going to do this again?" he asked.

The five of them shook their heads in unison.

"Very good," Joe said. "Now, I'm not the guy who tells you that, if you *ever* do this again, I'll come after you and haunt your dreams."

The thugs sighed in relief, until Stalker moved into view, pulled off his wrappings and said in a low, ground-tearing voice, "Because I don't give warnings!"

The thugs immediately began to scream and push away from the mere sight of the bat before them. But in their struggles, they got turned around and saw the animal heads of their captors (especially the teeth-filled mouth of Sandshifter, who grinned at her thug as saliva dripped from her jaws). The Knights held them a moment more and then released the thugs, who ran off into the street as if their sneakers were on fire and the devil was chasing them with lighter fluid. But that

"God, I love that part!" Shifter said gleefully.

"The drooling makes that clear," Forester commented.

"You're just unhappy because nobody's scared of the cute little squirrel."

"Guys, now's really not the time," Stalker said, gesturing to Sara, who was slowly beginning to stir.

"Head for the territories," Joe said.

One by one, the knights quickly vanished, each in a halo of his or her own light, until Sara was finally alone in the alley.

*　　*　　*

Joe felt the usual sensation of dislocation and nausea, and then his body reformed within the confines of the Nexus. He opened his eyes, blinking rapidly to eliminate the blurriness.

"So. Was anybody else confused by dat whole thing?" Groundquake asked.

"Perhaps it was a sort of a balancing mission," Forger suggested. "With all the strange events that have been happening as of late, saving an innocent may have helped to even things out somewhat."

"Then why weren't we sent on a mission for the other side?" Sandshifter argued. "The last time we had two, and Firesprite, Stalker, and I got sent to take care of those eco-freaks who wanted to blow up the construction guys tearing down the rainforest."

"Even so," Firesprite said, "I'm inclined ta go with Forger. We've done a lotta jobs with killing lately. Saving somebody sounds like a swing a' the pendulum to me."

"Or maybe it's a sign of what I've been saying," Wavecrasher said, glaring at Stalker and Joe. "You know it could be!"

"What are we seeing signs of this time, Mulder?" Windrider said with a sigh.

"Give her a chance," Thunderer insisted. "Crash's been right in the past, and we've benefited from it."

"So what is it this time?" Groundquake asked.

Joe rubbed his forehead and then said, "Crash has … theorized … that we might be … seeing a resurgence of the Chaos Demons."

The knights fell silent at that. None of them had seen head or tail of the Chaos Demons since their battle with the gremlins. But they all remembered the power the last Demon had had—how it had changed its shape, how it had poisoned the air, how it had come back from a liquid state, the way it had nearly been able to rip them apart. Had it not been for Joe and Stalker, they wouldn't have survived the battle.

This was especially true for one knight, who swallowed and then said softly, "And why do you think that?"

"Like Joe said, it's just a theory right now, Forester," the cat replied. "But after seeing the hunters and the vampires breaking their sacred laws, even with all the strictness of their codes … I'm worried."

"I don't know," Forger said. "Both of them were crazed. Sometimes things are just coincidence, Crash."

"But with crazies like Hunst and Jason involved now … yeah, coincidence could be the case," Firesprite mused.

"We'll find out soon enough," Stalker said. "I'm going to monitor them for a while, get some hard proof before doing anything."

"The rest of us will try to prepare," Joe said. "It never hurts to be careful."

"And how do we prepare for a Chaos Demon?" Forester asked.

"We're years better than we were then. We've got the library that can give us information and magic that can be of use," Joe said. "Crash,

I want you to keep studying and see if there's anything else we can use for an edge, or something that might indicate why they'd be interested in the vampires and hunters. Forger, I want you to help her."

"Right."

"Everyone else, just keep your eyes open. There could be more to this then we thought, and we need to look for anything that might give us a clue."

*   *   *

"Indeed you do, Lightrider. But what will you find? And can you stop it?" Rastla whispered aloud as she gazed at the Light Knight.

"He has stopped the demons before, sister," said Darya, the Fire Architect, as he moved his thin frame over to Rastla's side. "But Ruta said you have been in a gloomy mood of late."

"And that surprises you?"

"Truthfully, no," Darya replied. "But then again, I am aware of your worry toward Ralin's audience."

"And you think I should not be?" Rastla asked, turning to face her fiery brother. "How many times, in all the history of creation, has only one been summoned?"

"I was around long before you, Rastla," Darya said. "I am aware of the significance."

"We are all the maintainers of the world. What events do not concern us all?" Rastla snapped back.

"Hmmph. Perhaps the better question is, what event does not concern *you*? Come now, sister, do you think I cannot see the source of your burning anger?" Darya said, as Rastla glared. "Since you came here, you have always feared that Ralin shall overpower you some day."

"I care not. Right now, I fear only for what may endanger the world—"

"I am not blind, Rastla. You feared him once and with good reason. It is why you were placed here, for the balance."

"He could not exist with me. Nor I without him."

"And yet you fear anyway. Sister, I dare not tell you what to do. But remember that you brought here because you were deemed worthy—and because, for all your dark nature, I would not want to look over a world with only Ralin to guide it."

"Why is it, out of all of them, that only you see into my darkness?" Rastla asked slowly.

"Remember, I can illuminate as well," Darya said, a slight grin on his face. "And I know the weight of carrying a power that can destroy and keep life at the same time."

From within the folds of her hood, Rastla gave a small grin. But it had no sooner crept across her face than a blue light shined into view behind them.

The two Architects turned, to see Ruta standing there, her face lined with urgency.

"Ralin has returned. He has brought a message he wishes to share. But with Rastla alone," the Architect of Water said.

"Then I should not keep our brother waiting," Rastla said, and Darya nodded in agreement. There were three flashes of red, blue, and black light, and then the space the Architects had occupied was empty once more.

*　　*　　*

The door swung as Sara walked into her small apartment, her body aching from the day's work and the long walk home. Dropping her purse onto an armchair, Sara turned and plopped onto her couch with a groan of exhaustion and pleasure at finally being able to sit. Her day had been another long mess of work—stocking the new Stephen King book that seemed to weigh at least ten pounds, while getting asked constantly about other new books.

Sara grimaced as she thought of the one guy who had been shopping for a last-minute gift for his son. 'Is there a new Harry Potter book? Are you sure? Can you find one?" It had taken all her will not to reach over and bash the man's head in with one of the new books. And of course, no sooner than that guy had finally gotten the hint, a damn posse of tweens had strolled in for the *Twilight* movie adaptation graphic. Sara didn't know which was worse—that they didn't know it had been a book first or that they actually wanted to read it.

I have to get out of that place before I'm arrested for homicide, Sara thought as she stretched out on the couch and pressed the play button on her answering machine.

The first message played, and Sara already groaned. "Sara? Honey, it's Mom. Listen, I know you said you'd call if you need us, but we were just wondering how things are. Your dad heard that Tim was working on a play in New York. Maybe you can help him? He was always so nice to you …"

"Yeah, Mom, the fact we broke up doesn't matter at all," Sara muttered as she stopped the machine. Even if she did want to work with her ex again, Sara knew there was no way she could get him a good play; Tim tried to force his political views into everything he wrote, with all the subtlety of a sledgehammer. She could still remember the screenplay he'd written where Clinton was revealed to be a brain-eating alien. But for some reason, her mom loved Tim and kept on her about what he was doing, looking for any chance to push them back together.

But it was better than her mom's usual nagging calls about work. Since she'd graduated, Sara had been searching and plodding away at the bookstore, while her parents called and she steered clear from their offers of money and ignored their suggestions about coming back and working for "one of our friends." Whatever it was Sara was going to do, she'd find it on her own. And when she found it, she'd be damn good at it. But until she did, she would get along on her own, without having to run home to Mommy and Daddy, begging for money.

"Hmph, I keep thinking like this for much longer, I'm going to have to write an emo album," Sara snorted aloud as she slowly pulled herself off the couch and moved toward her kitchen. As she pulled out the evening's major culinary experiment (a Lean Cuisine pasta dinner with a side of frozen French fries), Sara reminded herself that things could be worse; most of her old classmates were struggling to pay off student loans and credit card debt from drunken college endeavors. Sara was a hard worker and had never had a taste for throwing large piles of money into a toilet and pulling the handle, so her savings were taking care of her, and her loans—

She shivered suddenly, the cold driving her out of her thoughts momentarily. Turning her head, she saw that the kitchen window was open—not by much, but just enough to let in the cold air.

"What the …? I closed that thing this morning. God, was Jimmy doing one of his 'safety checks' again?" Sara muttered as she reached over to close the window. Did he really think that she'd let the only way to the fire escape rust shut or something? To prove him wrong, before Sara closed the window, she opened it wide and stuck her head out. Snorting in the cold air, she said aloud, "See, Jimmy? I'm still perfectly capable of opening a window without your help."

Sara began to pull her head back inside. But she had barely gotten in, when she was struck with another burst of cold. This time, though, it wasn't from the window; it came from inside, a feeling like she was being watched. Sara looked all around, checking the upper levels of the fire escape, the windows of the nearby apartment, even glancing across the street to see if any light were on in the building on the other side. But finally, Sara had to conclude nothing was out there. Still, as she closed her window, she hoped to get rid of her inner chill.

VII

ON THE ETHEREAL PLANE, Ralin stood alone on the platform on which the Architects called council. His face was heavy with concern; his audience with the High God had been a discomforting experience. Since he had been alone, Ralin had briefly entertained the notion that the High God was going to say the balance had become weak and that it would be his task to correct Rastla. But the Architect of Light had quickly dismissed that thought. Though he did not always agree with or even trust his sister, he had learned not to doubt her dedication to keeping the balance. Besides, much had changed from the early days, and all because of the "never-ending battle" between himself and Rastla. Ralin shook his head at that; he never understood why the mortals cast everything in such black and white terms, ignoring the spots where the black and white mixed.

Speaking of which, Ralin thought as the spot on the dais for Shadow began to glow. The Architect of Light watched as the black smoke rose from the platform and then began to coalesce, until Rastla stood before him.

"This seems to be a day for secrets, Ralin," Rastla said, staring at him. "First, a secret meeting for you; now one for me."

"There was reason, sister," Ralin said. "The High God told me of a great crisis that is building in the world."

"And why would he tell only you? Surely we are all meant to stop this," Rastla asked.

"No, we are not. And I was told because I am to have a great part in what happens to restore it," Ralin replied. "It said ... that our knights ... are not perfect—that we have erred in our selection."

"What? Did It ... speak of Joe?" Rastla asked, her voice empty of sarcasm, only surprise. "Was there something wrong with him? But even I have grown to accept him, brother."

"No. Joseph was the proper choice, but he is meant for a greater destiny then the title of Lightrider. In the uproar to come, it will be Joe who will be the anchor that swings us back to normalcy. But when it is over, Light and Dark will have changed, sister."

"What do you mean? Surely not you and I—"

"No, Rastla. Let me tell you."

And so Ralin shared with his sister all that the High God had told him. And as Rastla listened, her eyes grew wide in astonishment. Even as Ralin spoke of things that would benefit her, all Rastla could focus on was the great crisis and what had to be done to solve it. As Ralin finished speaking, the Architect of Shadow found herself unable to speak.

"I felt the same," Ralin said, seeing his sister's troubled silence. "But if all we have created is to survive, we must play our part and let the rest progress as it must."

"I," Rastla began, as she shook her head in disbelief. "I never expected this, Ralin. I admit, I feared what you and the High God might discuss—"

"As I would have, had it been you."

"Still, I never imagined things happening this way. Nor would I have wanted them to. The repercussions of it …"

"True. And I appreciate your candor. But there is nothing for us to gain by questioning it. We must work now, to save all we hold dear."

"When … when should I prepare for …"

"He said you would know. Watch Nightstalker, as you always have, and you will see the time to move. But you must be ready."

"I will. And Ralin?"

"Yes?"

"I … am sorry things must work out this way. I realized long ago I was wrong to doubt Joe."

"Thank you, sister. Though I know this is destiny, I shall be sad to see him leave us."

VIII

He felt himself floating through space, emptiness all around. The stars were gone, the sun unlit, all hidden with a great curtain of blackness. Joe looked about, looking for some sort of familiar sign, something that might turn him toward safety. But only emptiness stretched across the vast plane.

Suddenly, he heard something—a great explosion, far off in the distance. Joe looked up, toward the noise. Something was in the distance, something that seemed to glow as bright as the sun in this darkness. Joe pushed himself forward, toward the light, trying to see it what it was.

The light grew brighter as he got closer, but as he pushed through the space, Joe felt nothing from it—no warmth, no strength flowing into his body, only a strange brightness that blurred his eyes. Still he pushed toward it, now from need as well as curiosity. And as he got closer, Joe began to see something in the light, forms that were moving about within it. He could not see them clearly at first, but as he grew closer, he noticed glowing scales and pasty white skin. Joe tried to halt, but he was already too close to the light when the Chaos Demons marched out of it.

Joe reached for his staff, ready to fight, only to realize it was gone. As the demons came closer, he began to summon the light from deep within him. But though he reached into himself with all his strength, he could not draw the power forth. Joe frantically called for the light as the demons prepared to stampede onto him. A shadow fell upon him as a huge clawed foot appeared, ready to stomp him into nothing.

Joe pushed himself out of the way, but even as he moved, he saw another demon block his path. He tried to bring himself to a halt, but it was too late; Joe went face-first into the demon ... and passed through it.

Joe came to a halt just outside the creature, thoroughly confused, as the demons continued to move forward, plowing through him as if he was not there and leaving just as much impact.

Joe watched as the great herd moved on, taking its strange light with it. But as the demons left, Joe felt something pull at him. He turned back to where the demons had come from and saw he was not alone. A lone figure stood there, floating in the nothingness. His clothing was like that of an Architect—a long robe and a hooded face. But he did not wear a single color. Instead, his robe was dark but covered with moving stars with splotches of the colors of the Architects and others. As Joe watched, the figure pulled up his hood ...

*   *   *

"*Gah!*"

Joe sat up in his bed, breathing hard and sweat pouring down his body. He shook his head, trying to throw off the feelings of shock and panic that were coursing through his system.

"What the hell?" he said as he threw back the covers and shambled toward the sink in his room. Turning the faucet, he splashed cold water on his face, the shock of the water forcing the panic away. He gripped the sink and began to breathe slowly, forcing his body to calm down. As his heart slowed, he was able to release the sink and make his way back to the bed, trying to remember what had happened.

He remembered the weightlessness and the Chaos Demons; they were nothing new. So what had shocked him awake like this?

He went over what he could remember of the dream—the floating, the flash of weird light, the demons racing toward him. All of that he could remember clearly. But he knew that hadn't been what had woken him up. Joe strained his mind, trying to push past the clouds of sleepiness and his own memory, trying to remember what it was.

"A man ... it was a man. Some guy in ... in robes. Ralin?" he asked himself. "No, this guy's robes were ... different. He looked at me and ..."

But that was where the dream had ended. Try as he might, Joe couldn't remember anything past that. Joe shook his head once more and then lay back on the bed, closed his eyes, and tried to sleep. For a moment, he thought he was going to dream of the robed man again. But this time, nothing came, and slowly, Joe drifted off to sleep, his dream forgotten for the moment.

*　　*　　*

"You're late again," Bob said, folding his arms across his chest.

"I know, I know. Traffic was hell," Sara said as she pinned her name tag onto her vest and finished tying her hair into a ponytail.

"Sara, I know this place isn't Barnes and Noble," Bob said as both he and Sara headed out onto the floor. "But it's been in my family for years, ever since my grandfather came off the boat—"

And here we go, Sara groaned inwardly, as Bob told, for the umpteenth time, the story of his grandfather coming over from Wales with only a few books to his name and turned his business into one of the longest-running independent bookstores in Northern New Jersey. He also took the time to mention how his granddad had devoted all his time to the store, even starting a family in the apartment above.

Sara listened to this story about as long as she could and then said, with as much humility as she could muster, "Bob, I'm really sorry I was late. I promise, it won't happen again."

"Just make sure of it," Bob snapped, irked at the interruption of his family history. "Now go over to the centerpiece. I'm having Tina work on a *Twilight* display for the latest movie, and I want you to help her put it up."

"Right," Sara said, waiting until Bob was well out of the way to roll her eyes and groan. Still, she walked over to the middle of the store, where she found Tina sitting amid a pile of books, some posters, and a ladder. There was a single tall display rack in front of her, and Tina was trying to figure out how to carry up two massive posters at the same time. Sara watched for a minute as Tina got up a step and then had to stop and readjust her grip as the posters started to fall.

"Need a hand there?" Sara asked after a few minutes.

"Sara! Oh yeah, completely," Tina said, hopping down from the ladder, which caused her to lose her grip and dump all the posters on the floor. She grinned sheepishly at Sara, who said nothing as she watched the girl kneel down, her long, brown hair falling around her as she picked them up. Tina was working at the store part-time, trying to earn some money while she was in high school. Unfortunately, she was a bad mix of clumsy and eager-to-please, which meant she was always cracking her oversized glasses trying to balance too many books or frightening the customers by knocking down a bookshelf when someone called her name. But Bob needed the help, and to her credit, Tina never stopped trying.

"Sorry about that," Tina said, grabbing the last of the posters. "I've been trying to figure out the fastest way to do this."

"Lemme guess, because Bob told you to?" Sara asked.

"Uh-huh."

"For someone so concerned with time and work, he doesn't seem to mind keeping me from it for his history lessons," Sara said.

"Oh, are you in trouble?" Tina asked.

"No more than usual," Sara replied. "Now, how's about I get on the ladder and do some stacking up top, while you stack the books on the bottom?"

"Sure. I don't like heights anyway," Tina said, handing Sara her pile.

Sara groaned under the weight but managed to reach the display, slip her hand around, and get a few books into the middle to lighten the load. Once she felt like she could move, she turned to the ladder and started to climb, slowing making her way up. She reached the highest display and slowly began to attach the posters. They were already pretty crumpled, so Sara took her time to smooth them out, using the flat of the front display board. Plus, it gave her the chance to feel like she was crushing the face of that pretty boy vampire. Sara didn't care about literary vampires, but she hated the idea that anyone was stupid enough to fall in love because of somebody's eyes or any of that crap.

Of course, a navel-gazing seventeen-year-old might think differentl—

"Hey, Sara, should I stack them...? *Ooww!*" Tina said as she turned to ask her question and knocked into the ladder.

The ladder shook, and Sara tried to grab it. But her hand slipped, and Sara felt herself fall over the ladder, turn around mid fall, and land on something.

"Uhh ... Tina, get out from under me, so I can hit you," Sara muttered.

"I don't think I can."

"Oh, don't start. I'm not that ... wha?" Sara said as she started to get up, only to see Tina standing by the ladder. Sara turned around, to see that she'd landed on a young man instead.

"Hi. Sorry I'm not Tina," the man groaned, even as he kept a smile on his face.

"Sorry! Are you okay?" Sara said, quickly getting to her feet and helping the man up.

"It's all right," the man said, dusting off his dark blue jacket. "It's not everyday women fall from the sky."

"I ...I'm sorry too," Tina said. "It was my fault. But that was a good catch though."

"Catch?" Sara asked.

"Yeah. As you fell, he ran over and got under you. I saw the whole thing," Tina said.

"Really?" Sara asked, turning to the man again.

"I'd hope most people would," he replied.

"Not that many," Sara said, looking over the man. He was an average build, dressed in a jacket and jeans that added a little more mass but not much. His face was long with a black beard and shaggy black hair. His eyes were a striking blue, but that was about his only interesting feature.

"Still, I hope you're all right," the man said.

"I'm fine; it hurts more looking at that stuff all day," Sara said, motioning to the *Twilight* books.

"I can imagine," the man said with a laugh. "But from what I hear of it, I think you might be a bit too old for those books."

"Without a doubt," Sara said.

"Well, as much as I'd like to keep you two from work, I think your boss is glaring at us," the man said, pointing across the room to where Bob stood.

"Yeah, he's in a mood with me today," Sara said.

"I've been there. Good luck to you," the man said as he turned and walked off.

"Thanks again," Sara called out.

The man turned and smiled back at her.

Sara turned to the ladder and slowly started to climb back up, even as Tina watched the man walk away.

"Sara, you should've at least gotten his name," Tina moaned. "He had *such* gorgeous eyes."

"Tina, I like you, but if you turn into Bella on me, I will drop this ladder on you," Sara said. "Now please, stack the books."

Tina quickly did what she was told as Sara kept flattening the poster. *Nice eyes*, she thought. *Tina'd probably marry him for that.*

IX

"Hmm ... maybe there ... damn it!" Wavecrasher muttered as she shut the book, running her fingers through her fur. She sighed at the latest failed link between the vampires, hunters, and Chaos Demons. It had been like this all night (or so the knight could reckon in a place that existed outside time). Granted, Crash hadn't really expected to find much. The hunters' history was already well-documented, and nothing had indicated demon involvement. And the demons and vampires were both exiles from the crowds; too many vampires were convinced of their complete superiority over other life, and the demons' goal made it impossible for them to form an alliance with anyone on this plane.

Still, Crash had hoped to find something, a grudge or stolen power, which might link the trio. It would've helped her offset the fact that she hadn't found any information on the demons that the knights didn't already know (Forger had already called it a night, but Crash had kept looking). It seemed impossible that they could've gone through all the information in the library, but then again, the demons might not be that complex.

The cat yawned and stretched out. It was late, and she wasn't getting anywhere. She should call it a night, get some sleep, and be rested for whatever might come their way tomorrow.

"Wait, missed one," she muttered as she took another book from the pile and began to paw through it.

"Doing some light reading?"

Crash turned to see Joe entering the room, dressed in a blue robe.

"Isn't that my color?" the cat asked.

"I'll pay you for gimmick infringement later," Joe said as he pulled back a chair and sat down. "How's the search going?"

"Badly," Crash answered. "I'm not finding anything new on the vamps, the hunters, or the demons."

"Then you should take a break," Joe said. "But wait," he added, raising an eyebrow. "Let me guess. There's still a book you haven't gone through."

"Just one," Crash replied. "Then I'm done, I swear."

"Maybe I can give you a hand."

"No, I'll get this myself. Thanks though."

"All right. Then can you recommend anything particularly boring from your search?"

"Why? Having trouble sleeping?"

"Yeah. And with Windy asleep, I can't conk out listening to his recap of *Battlestar Galactica*."

"God, how does he remember all that crap?" Crash said, shaking her head.

"Says someone who memorized how many books?" Joe answered grinning.

"Yeah, but at least that's useful," Crash said. "For example, I can think of a few ways to put you back to sleep medically."

"I'll just take a long book, thanks," Joe said.

"Hmm … well, I guess I could recommend that one there," Crash said, gesturing toward a thick book on the pile next to her. "It's about vampire history in the Americas, circa the very first bloodsucker on the continent. Lots of names and lists and family feuds. You'd love it."

"Sounds good," Joe said, grabbing the book and popping it open. He had just begun the first page when Crash asked, "So what's keeping you up?"

"Um?"

"I spend more than a few nights in the library, and this is the first time I've seen you come in this late," the cat replied. "So why are you here?"

"The mustiness and smell of paper?"

"Joe."

With a sigh, Joe closed the book and said, "I had a dream."

"A nightmare?" Crash asked. "That's not so strange."

"No, it wasn't that. It was ... well, it was just weird."

"Do you remember it?"

"Yeah," Joe said, "which is even weirder, since I never remember my dreams."

"So what happened?"

"Why, do you remember psych info too?"

"I'm curious," Crash replied.

"Fine," Joe said. "I was in space, floating around. But there was nothing around me—no stars, no planets, no kind of light at all. It must be what it's like to be deep underwater or something."

"Go on."

"Anyway, there was this big flash of light, and then I saw a bunch of Chaos Demons running toward me. I tried to use my powers, but nothing worked. But then they all just ran through me, like I didn't exist. And then ..."

"Yes?"

"There ... there was someone behind them," Joe said. "I couldn't see him until after they all left, but it was a figure, all dressed in robes and a hood."

"One of the Architects?" Crash asked. "Ralin, or maybe Rastla, talking to you in your dreams?"

"No. Whoever this was, he was dressed in a robe that ... I don't know, it was like darkness, but it had part of the rainbow in it. It kept shifting between all the colors, not just the Architect's but every color. And there were things moving around on the robe too, images that I couldn't see."

"Did you see his face?"

"No. He looked at me and started to pull up his hood, and that's when I woke up," Joe said. "And I was all wired, like I'd had a nightmare."

"Well, were you afraid of this guy?"

"No. I don't remember any strong feelings," Joe said. "Except confusion."

"From a guy in robes? Like the ones we work for?"

"Yeah, but this one … I don't know. There was just something really strange about him. Like he was too powerful to even look at or something."

Crash leaned back in her chair, put her hands together, and said, "Well, a shrink would probably say that the figure represents eternity, since it came after the demons had passed you, signifying that you are uncertain about what you are going to do with your immortality beyond battling the demons."

"That makes sense," Joe said.

"But there is the possibility that maybe you're being contacted."

"You mean that the figure is real?"

"Yes and that the dream is his way of trying to tell you something."

"Like what?"

"I don't know; it's your dream," Crash said. "Look, if you have it again, we can tell something by whether it's different or not. And I'll try to find something in the books, okay? I could use the change of materials."

"All right, but …" Joe paused and then said, "I thought I had accepted all this. I don't want to have to start questioning myself again. Or have the others—"

"I know how to keep my mouth shut," Crash said. "Besides, it may just be some lingering doubt. I don't know if we ever totally accept something like this."

"Yeah, I guess that's true," Joe said. "You know, maybe I'll go take the book back to my room, try to sleep there."

"Cool with me. Just bring it back," Crash said.

"No problem. And thanks for listening."

"Like I said, I was happy for the change in topic. And you don't bother me much anyway."

"Yeah, I usually talk with Stalker about my problems most of the time."

"Actually, you just missed him a while ago," Crash said.

"He came back?"

"Just for a minute. He wanted to drop off his report."

"What did he say?"

"Yeah. So far, both vampires and hunters are quiet."

"He came all the way back here for that? He usually only comes when something's wrong," Joe said.

"Said he needed a break," Crash said. "After all, he's been there about a day or so."

"I guess," Joe said. "He's back there now?"

"Yep, popped right back into the Nexus after he dropped off the message."

"Well, I guess we all need a break sometimes," Joe said. "Thanks for passing it on, Crash. See you in the morning."

"See you," Crash said as Joe picked up the book and walked out the door.

*　　*　　*

They walked the hallways together, their footsteps clicking along with each step. The marble around them gleamed but not as brightly as their long, white coats, which trailed about their feet. Together, the two men had fought against the evil vampires and had stemmed that evil enough to rise up within their order. One, a bespectacled young man, dark haired and tall, was named Kurt and commanded this branch of the hunters. He answered to only one other man—the older man with a stern face and salt-and-pepper hair who walked behind him. He was Nelson, Grand Master of the Eastern Hunters, the group that patrolled the northeastern United States. He was one of six such men who governed the country. Nelson normally made his home in Boston, but he had come to the New York complex when news of Hunst had reached him.

"But he destroyed so many!" Kurt said. "Shouldn't we at least consider—"

"What he did was unauthorized and dangerous," answered Nelson, a look of sternness on his squat face. "Hunst could have brought them all down upon us, and we have a hard enough time with the vampires that we know want us dead."

"But Master Nelson," the younger man said, "we've had several dealings with vampires like the one Hunst killed—ones who use their positions in the vampire bureaucracy to hide their true evil intentions."

"And have you forgotten how many of us have misused the hunter's emblem, Kurt?" Nelson asked, turning toward his companion's thin face. "Our organization is rife with men who have used our cause to indulge in bloodbaths. We changed our ways so that we could be sure we were only hunting the ones who were a threat to humanity—unlike the one that alerted the Elementals to what Lord Jason was doing and prevented further bloodshed."

"But he still went along with it!" Kurt yelled.

"He was following orders, until he realized the right course of action. The vampires do have some honor. I've already received apologies from the Eldeus for what's happened."

"Apologies?" Kurt said in disbelief. "Master, Hunst nearly lost his children because of those things! His daughter—"

"Hunst lost his daughter because he was obsessed," Nelson said angrily. "Or do you want to go against the Elemental Knights and their proclamation?"

"They still don't understand what we do, why do we listen to—"

"Because they have greater power than we or the vampires do, and they use it to maintain balance and order!" Nelson said. "We both know that Hunst was trouble before all this went down. Can you imagine what he would do if we let him back out there? How many might die because of his blind obsession?!"

Kurt was quiet then as Nelson continued. "Many of the vampires are our enemies. But the moment we turn on the ones who do no evil is the moment we've become worse than them. I've worked very hard to keep those words, and I will not have them undone. Do you understand, Kurt?"

Kurt swallowed hard, then answered, "Yes."

"Good. Then I trust you will not spring Hunst from his confinement?"

"Master, I would never do such a thing! Not without—"

"My permission. Which is where you were headed with this conversation," Nelson said. "But I will not risk further exposure. Hunst will remain confined in the barracks until I can decide the proper way to punish him."

"As you wish. But, sir," Nelson said, "at the very least, I worry about leaving him alone like that. If he starts rambling again—"

"Yes. I worry too," Nelson said. "The reports indicate he doesn't even seem aware of what he says when he does it. And when he awakens, he is so full of rage and anger."

"I've stationed double guards around his room, but I don't know how well they can hold him should the worst happen," Kurt said. "I thought that maybe letting him out would help him deal with this."

"No, Kurt, Hunst's anger was strong even before this," Nelson said. "I will try to help him, but I feel it may be safer if he does not remain with us."

"He won't like that."

"Indeed. And he would be a dangerous rogue," Nelson said. "That is the only reason I keep him here. But I don't even know how long we can continue to hold him."

Kurt nodded, and the two of them walked away, their shadows trailing behind them. As they walked, Kurt's shadow began to ripple as a part of it slowly broke away. It slithered away from the two, until they were far out of sight. Then it slowly rose up, growing and changing until it had become a familiar black-coated figure, with red eyes blazing.

So Hunst was worse than we believed, Nightstalker thought as he glanced around. *I picked the right shadow. Now then, where are the barracks?*

The bat looked about and smiled as he saw an open grate above him. Once more, he let the blackness overtake him; his body faded away, and his shadow form flowed up the wall, through the ceiling, and into the darkness of the grate. He flowed through the open ducts of the Hunters' complex, twisting about as he sensed for the dark heart of Hunst and the secrets it held. As he sensed the darkness of the hearts within the complex, Stalker honed his mind, waiting for the familiar voice of Hunst to appear.

Ba-bum
Ba-bum
Hate-them
Took-Emily
Kill-knights
Kill-vamps

There it was. The shadow took a left, growing closer to the sound of Hunst's heartspeech, until Stalker could hear it directly beneath him. No grate was below him, but this time, it didn't matter. As Hunst's heartspeech grew louder and louder, Stalker felt it drawing him, like a siren taking a sailor. He allowed the call to take control as his shadowy essence began to fade. For a brief second, there was blindness, and then, the shadow reformed, with Hunst directly below it. The hunter was laid out on a cot, his body askew as he snored.

Above him, the shadow swirled about, slowly shifting back into solid form. Within moments, Nightstalker stood next to Hunst, his arrival as silent as a draft. The bat glanced around, making sure no one else was about. Other than a table, a toilet, and a large locked door in the wall, the room was bare. The bat nodded in silent approval and then turned back to Hunst. He watched in disgust as the Hunter snorted in his sleep, throwing a long line of drool from his mouth.

"*This* is the one we're worried about?" the bat muttered to himself. Still, he reached out with his hand, ready to look into Hunst's heart and report what he had found. Or he would have, until he heard Hunst mutter, "Why wasn't it there?"

Stalker pulled back. For a moment, he thought Hunst was just muttering in his sleep, until he yelled out, "He took my children, that golden bastard!" Either Hunst was in a deep dream about what had happened, or he was carrying on some sort of subconscious rant. The bat knew either was possible, so he watched and waited. Sure enough, Hunst continued to speak, saying, "If they killed him first." He cringed in pain then; apparently just the memory caused him pain. As Stalker kept watching, the hunter's face relaxed and he said, "Yes, I will. Afterward. And then?"

Silence held a moment, and then Hunst's face broke into a smile. "Then they'll all be gone."

The bat had seen enough. He laid his palm down on Hunst's head, trying to find his heartspeech, hoping to use it to get inside the conversation. The bat's eyes closed as he began to feel about.

Ba-bum

...

Ba-bum

Yes. Stalker pressed on, trying to go deeper into Hunst's mind and learn. But as he pushed further, Stalker could feel something pushing back. It felt as though he was moving through a huge rubber band, trying to gain steps even as he was resisted. Still, Stalker pushed deeper, trying to find Hunst's deepest secrets and read them.

Ba-bum

...

.... Bum

Stalker redoubled his efforts. His probe began to push through more and more; the rubber band began to weaken.

Rebirth

...

Ba ... darkness

...

Will-destroy

He was almost through the barrier. But then, there was the sound of metal scraping, the heavy noise of the door opening. Stalker instantly broke contact and moved backward, toward the shadow of the table. As the door swung open, the bat fell into it, vanishing from sight as two hunters entered the room.

"Jeez, he's still out?" said one, shaking his red bearded face at the sight of Hunst.

"The doctor gave him a heavy dose," replied his companion, a bearded man with dark hair and darker eyes, who bore a strong resemblance to Abe Lincoln. "He should be out for a while."

"I still don't know why we have to do this," said Red Beard as he and Lincoln moved to either side of Hunst's bed. As they grabbed the man's arms and legs and hoisted him up, Red-Hair continued. "I mean, he still took down most of those evil vamps, right?"

"Yeah, but in a bar? With people to see? That's just sloppy," Lincoln replied.

"But it must've gone over okay. Why else are they moving him into the sunlight room?"

"I did hear Kurt doesn't trust the vamps to leave him alone," Lincoln answered. "But stupid is stupid. Let's just get him onto the table and move him out."

Red Hair nodded, and he and Lincoln carried Hunst out of the room. The door shut behind them. Stalker waited until he heard the sound of wheels rolling and then stepped out of the shadow. He considered following the two but shook his head. It was unlikely they'd leave Hunst alone, and he couldn't wait all night. But he needed another shot at the hunter. Something was clearly protecting the hunter, and right now it seemed any number of the Hunters could be behind it.

"And that sunlight room ..." the bat murmured. He hadn't heard of it before, but it sounded like some sort of panic room against vampires, which would most likely make it difficult, if not impossible, for Stalker to enter. Stalker needed to know more about this, especially what the sunlight room was. And there was only one place he could do that. The shadows swirled about him, and the bat vanished, already on his way to the Obelisk.

*   *   *

He felt the tug of his body, pulling him out of sleep. For a moment, he fought it, and then he succumbed and opened his eyes. And again, he found himself floating out into the nothing of space. He tried again to awaken, until he heard an all-too-familiar noise just in front of him. Joe looked up and saw just how bad a dream this was.

Like before, he saw Chaos Demons. But this time, there were more of them—hundreds more, all screaming and howling as if in some mad orgy. But as Joe looked on, he saw this might be something far more dangerous. Demons were jumping past each other, pushing and shoving as they tried to get onto a single point. Joe saw flashes of their scales, saw energy move back and forth as they moved onto their unseen target. As they writhed, Joe saw bits of dark color and something that looked like star patterns shoot through the mass of demons. Images of the robed figure moved though Joe's head, and he began to glide forward, hoping that, even in his incorporeal state, he could help somehow.

But as Joe came closer, there was a sudden burst of light, only it was of a kind stronger than Joe had ever seen before. The demons went flying backward in mass, toward Joe. He halted and tried to shield himself, but as before, the demons flew past him, as if he didn't even exist. Joe even felt some fly through him. But even as they flew, Joe looked ahead and saw the robed figure once more.

He stood there without a single mark, as if the demon's attacks were nothing but bug bites to him. The figure raised his hand up and pointed to Joe.

The Knight was confused but then heard something move into place behind him. Joe turned and froze. Standing behind him, with all the Chaos Demons behind him, was a monstrous demon, huge and tall and glowing with power. The High Chaos stood there, looking as terrifying as that long-ago day in the Architect's pocket dimension.

Joe sweated, despite his invisibility, as the monster above him howled and shrieked at the figure, hurling out curses that Joe couldn't comprehend and didn't want to. Behind him, the other demons added their own voices to the hellish choir. But the figure stood silent, his finger pointed solely at the High Chaos.

Suddenly, the demons' howls of mockery turned to shock and horror. Joe turned and watched in shock as the demons literally began to fade away, their bodies becoming slowly transparent and then vanishing altogether. Joe saw even the High Chaos writhing under the power that had overtaken it. The process moved swiftly, as more and more demons began to vanish. As its troops vanished around it, the High Chaos let loose a final scream and pointed back at the figure, in both challenge and accusation, as it finally faded away.

Joe looked back at the figure, whose hand had slumped back down. The figure turned away from the scene, his body hunched over as if in sadness. He began to move away, but then the figure came to a halt. His body straightened up, and he turned around, looking determined. He glanced at his robes, seeing the colors dance about. He nodded, and his hands came up once more. He began to move them about in the air. Joe could see energy of gold, red, blue, white, and brown coalescing around the figure as he drew the power to himself. He continued his motions, and the energy began to form around his arms and hands.

Suddenly, as Joe watched, the figure swirled his right hand around, creating a sphere of brown energy in its wake. He then repeated the motion thrice more, leaving spheres of red, white, and blue about him. Then he drew his hands together and slammed them down in front of himself, creating a huge burst of gold.

With all the colors about him, the figure held his hands up to the heavens; Joe watched the spheres grow brighter and brighter. Suddenly, the gold one erupted like a geyser, spraying brilliant light all around. The others shot off as well, creating pillars of colored light. But Joe noticed how the figure was still moving his hands; and as he did, the lights began to bend and change. They seemed to grow in width and dimension, taking on forms as Joe watched. The figure stopped moving his hands, and a burst of light came from each of the colors. Joe was forced to cover his eyes, but when he looked again, he gasped in shock.

Five beings stood before the robed figure. They were each dressed in a robe identical to his, but each was one of the five colors summoned. They stood there, unmoving, until the figure relaxed his hands. It was then they moved. They gazed at themselves and each other, before finally settling their gazes upon the robed figure.

He looked at each of them in turn, as if inspecting his work. Then he clapped his hands together, and a ball of energy appeared between them. As he held it, he glanced at the figures and then back to the ball. Slowly, the others moved their hands together as well, as each created his or her own ball of energy. The figure looked at each one, dissipating his own orb, and then ran his hands across his robes, streaks of energy following his fingertips. He withdrew his hands to show streams of colored energy, one for each of the previous colors, glistening from his fingertips. As the new figures watched, the streams hung in the air and then bent themselves downward, each one moving to a different figure. Each reached its corresponding figure and then dove inside the energy ball that figure had created, turning it a specific color.

Joe observed all of it in complete silence. He was too confused to speak. For the beings that stood around the figure were Ralin, Ruta, Chirron, Aeris, and Darya, younger looking, but undeniably themselves. As they looked at the glowing spheres, the energy inside danced and twirled. They were completely entranced, as though they had never seen anything like it before. Whatever this was, it seemed to be some sort of vision of the past. But that did nothing to ease Joe's confusion. The Architects had never said anything of their creation, nor of a being having made them. And where were the others—Rastla, Zeuia, and the rest? Hadn't they been created as well?

Joe hoped that watching this progression before him would answer those questions. The young Architects continued to look at their orbs. Suddenly each one gasped as the balls passed from their hands into their very bodies, *which now glowed with light. But as before, the figure suddenly looked over at Joe, his eyes burning into Joe's very being …*

*   *   *

And just like before, Joe awoke with a gasp and a yell back in his room. But he wasn't alone this time; as he awoke, he saw a dark figure before him suddenly jump back in surprise, trip over the trails of his coat, and fall upon the floor.

"Jesus, Joe, do you always wake up like this?" Stalker asked as the Light Knight sat up on the bed.

"S-Sorry, Stalker," Joe said, still breathing hard. "Just some … bad dreams."

"Looks like it," the bat said as he got to his feet. "Crash said something about you not sleeping well."

"Well, if you've got something I need to hear, it's good I'm up," Joe said, getting out of bed.

"The vampires are clean. But not the hunters," Stalker said. "They're still not sure what to do with Hunst. They've got him locked up in a cell right now."

"Do they want to let him go?"

"Their leaders are arguing about it now. But there's something else keeping them from letting him out. I don't think he's acting alone."

"Has he formed some kind of faction in the hunters?" Joe asked as he took his staff from the side of the bed.

"No. But he does have an ally. The leaders said how he was talking in his sleep. I saw him myself, and he was doing more than that. He was having a full rant, about destroying everything."

"How?" Joe asked.

"I don't know. I tried to look into his heart for answers, but there was something … blocking me."

"Blocking you?" Joe gaped. "That's not possible."

"I know. But getting into his heart was like swimming against caramel. I couldn't get in there before the guards came. They moved him somewhere else in the compound."

"This is serious," Joe said. "And if they're moving him to keep him safe, he certainly could have an ally in the hunters."

"Either way, it's bad. He muttered about you, his kids, and a sort of promise that 'they'll all be gone.' And my gut tells me he wants us, the vamps, and anything else that stands in his way."

"Then it sounds like the time for secrecy might be over," Joe said. "We have to get another crack at his psyche. Maybe the two of us together can—"

Suddenly, Joe grabbed his head, as he was racked with pain. Stalker moved to help, but then he grabbed his own skull in agony. The two of them heard the call of the Nexus, warning them of danger. It was like huge church bells, amplified through giant Marshall amps, ringing inside their brains—once, twice, then three, then four times. The two knights stood there in agony, until finally, the mental bells became but an echo that faded away.

"Wha … what was *that*?" Stalker said, rubbing his temples against the fading pain.

"It … it sounded like the Nexus," Joe replied.

"The Nexus never called us like that," the bat responded. "It must be some kind of malfunction."

"A malfunction in the heart of all worlds?" Joe asked.

'Stalker took a breath, and said "We should go look then, shouldn't we?"

"What do you think?" Joe asked as his staff began to glow. For a second, light washed over Joe and then it faded, leaving him in his knight uniform.

"C'mon," Joe said, moving to the door without waiting for Stalker. He swung it open and, as he got onto the stairway, concentrated on the Nexus as he walked upward. Joe heard the door shut and the sound of footsteps behind him but didn't stop as he moved up. But a few seconds later, he had to come to a halt, as he saw a group moving up ahead of him.

"Guys!" Joe yelled, causing Sandshifter, Thunderer, and Firesprite to halt. The three of them looked back at Joe, who said, "I assume you all felt that too?"

"You mean the *clavo* being driven through my head?" Sandshifter asked. "Kinda hard not to."

"This has to mean a bigger problem than usual," Thunderer stated. "I mean, why else would we get such a strong alarm?"

"Any number of reasons," said Stalker, with the remaining knights coming up behind him.

As they caught up, Forger came to the front and spoke. "What makes the most sense is that whatever happened with the hunters and vampires probably has led to this," the spider explained, "or that someone is tampering with the Nexus."

"That's impossible. No one has the power to control the Nexus," Wavecrasher said. "It's connected to every world and time in creation."

"Ah have a thought here," Forester said. "What if we just go up and see what the hell is going on instead of sitting here debating?"

"I'm with Fuzzy Tail. If something's messing around with the Nexus, we're getting *nada* done like this," Sandshifter said as she turned back to the stairs.

The others glanced at each other and then followed, each one making sure his or her weapon was in reach, just in case. Within minutes, they reached the doorway to the Nexus room. Sandshifter moved toward the door and then paused and motioned for Joe and Stalker to come up as well. The two of them quickly moved their way up, standing right behind Sandshifter, their hands on their weapons as she reached for the door handle. The wolf gripped it, turned back to the others, nodded, and then pulled it open as both Joe and Stalker leaped into the room, weapons drawn, as they saw that something was in the room. They looked at it, and it spoke to them.

"Timely as always, knights."

X

"RALIN?" JOE SAID IN disbelief, lowering his staff as he looked at the gold-clad Architect. Stalker just stared, as did the other knights as they entered the room.

"What's going on?" Joe asked. "Why have you come to us?"

"Because of what the Nexus has seen," the Architect answered.

"So this wasn't a fluke," Wavecrasher said.

"I only wish it were," Ralin said. "The last call of the Nexus was a special signal, one that would be heard not only in the Obelisk, but in my realm as well."

"What is it? What's happened?" Stalker asked.

"That call, a call made with four times the power the Nexus usually has, was warning that the Equites are in danger. They are mystic items of great power, which neither good nor evil has any hope of stopping if they are united."

"If they're so powerful, how would anyone get to them?" Groundquake asked. "I know you guys. You'd keep something like this with you."

"The last of the Equites is with us," Ralin said. "But the other three are on Earth, buried and kept safe by forces of both good and evil. They are dangerous but cannot reach their full potential unless united."

"And you never thought telling us about them was a good idea?" Sandshifter snapped.

"They are the greatest secret we hold," Ralin answered. "Not even the races that guard them know what they truly are. You have seen one of them before, in the lair of the gremlins."

"That door—that was what was behind it?!" the wolf snapped. "Those mischief makers have one of the most destructive powers in the universe, and they don't even know it?!"

"Which helps keep it that way," Forger said. "Who would suspect them of having something so dangerous?"

"Someone does," Stalker said. "The Demons went after it once, and I'm betting they're doing it again."

"That is what the Nexus has called you for," Ralin said. "You must separate and safeguard the remaining Equites from the demons."

"I agree. But I may know something else to help us," Stalker said. "I have reason to believe that a vampire hunter is being influenced by some force; it may be a demon."

"We have suspected as much from Hunst as well," Ralin said. "He has long been a source of unbalance. Continue your observation on him; he may lead us to whatever threatens the Equites. Lightrider, I will also require you to remain here and coordinate the effort."

"Ralin, this is something I need to be with them for," Joe said. "Stalker and I are the only ones who can stop them. We need to be there."

"Nightstalker will be helping in another way," Ralin continued. "We may be able to use this connection between the demons and Hunst, if he can find it. But the main goal is the Equites."

"How?"

"The Equites are buried under special doors, like the one in the gremlins' lair," Ralin explained. "They are sealed so that the Demons cannot open them by themselves, but the doors can be opened. And with Demons about, it is best to keep at least one of you away from Earth, lest the demons capture either Light or Shadow."

Joe and Stalker were silent then, and Ralin said, "You two are on paths to ending this already. If you continue along them and keep steady in all your efforts, you will be able to end this."

Joe sighed and said, "All right."

Stalker just nodded.

"Good. You must depart as soon as possible. The Nexus shall send each of you to the place best suited for you. We shall always be watching, Knights of the Elements."

With that, Ralin began to shimmer and then faded away into nothing, leaving the knights alone in the room, with nothing but their mission … and their fears.

INTERLUDE

Joe put his pen down as his mind wandered over that moment. It had been so like the Architects, really—to give them a cryptic story with no real answers and then expect them to figure it out. More than once, Joe had thought this strategy was their way of getting around free will— make them curious enough to solve problems on their own.

But that time was long buried in the past, and as with so many other things, Joe had lost his passion for those old suspicions. Looking back, he actually saw the wisdom in what the Architects had done and how much they really had told them. He wondered what would've happened if they had been told everything point-blank. Would the knights, would he, have gone forward with it all? Or would they have been forced to do it against their will?

Joe didn't have to think hard on the answer.

As the memories kept moving in his mind, he re-dipped his pen and began to chronicle what had happened after the knights had spoken with Ralin—how they had begun their last great adventure together, the one where not all of them had returned …

BOOK TWO

THE SEARCH FOR
THE EQUITES

XI

"*EQUITES*?" SANDSHIFTER SPAT OUT. "Does anyone have any idea what that means?"

"I ... I've actually never heard of them," Wavecrasher said. "None of the books—"

"Oh, just great," Sandshifter said.

"This smells too weird, even for the Architects," Groundquake agreed. "If there's always been something this important, wouldn't they have told us by now?"

"Not to mention takin' away our best weapons," Forester added.

"It isn't that simple," Forger said. "For one thing, I know something about what Equites is."

Everyone turned to the spider then, with Crash looking very curious.

Forger answered, "It's a Latin word. It means..." Forger hung on the word, snapping her fingers in concentration

"Come on, we're all waiting," Sandshifter said.

"I ... I can't remember. But we can find it."

"Normally, I'd agree," Joe said. "But knowing what they are shouldn't be what we're focusing on."

"How do you know that?" Groundquake said. "It could be the main—"

"Ralin said that the Equites are locked behind doors that have some kind of key," Windrider said. "It's like Gannondorf in *Ocarina of Time*—the demons need to figure out the keys to get the power."

"And that worries me," Firesprite said. "If they're powerful enough the Architects need to guard one themselves, then they could be too much for anyone."

"Exactly!" Sandshifter exclaimed. "That's why we should have known about them! Hell, at the very least knowing could tell us what these 'keys' are."

"Maybe the creatures guarding the doors might know?" Thunderer asked.

Sandshifter growled but nodded her head. Turning to face the Nexus, she muttered, "This had better work." She walked to the crystal and placed her hand upon it. Instantly, she teleported away. The other knights nodded and then looked at Joe one last time.

"I'll keep everyone in the loop through the Nexus," Joe said. "If anything happens or needs to happen, you'll know. Good luck."

"We'll need it," Forester grumbled. But even with that, the squirrel walked up the stairs, slapped his hand on the crystal, and teleported away.

The others followed, until only Joe and Nightstalker were left standing in the room.

"There is something weird about this, Joe," Stalker said.

"I know. But Ralin wouldn't do all this without a reason. So for now, we do what he says."

"All right," Stalker said. "I may call for help. Hunst is supposed to be in a place called a 'sunlight room.'"

"I'll do what I can. But you'd better have a backup plan," Joe said.

"That's what I'll be working on now," Stalker said. He moved up to the Nexus and teleported.

As the black spark moved and then vanished through the crystal, Joe moved to the crystal himself. But he did not follow his friends. Rather, he reached out for a long extension of the crystal and snapped it off. The stump gleamed and then regrew itself. Joe watched and then looked down into the crystal he now held. It glimmered, and then images of the knights returning to Earth filled it. Joe nodded and slipped the crystal into a pouch on his belt. He then headed for the door, ready to spend time in another part of the Obelisk.

"Well, a little below profit tonight, but not too bad," Bob said as he flipped the sign in the door from Open to Closed.

"Are you kidding? That display Tina and I set up got taken out in an hour," Sara said as she hung up her vest and headed for the door.

"It would've been more if we could restock, but that shipment was late again," Bob said. "I swear, the UPS men hate me. All they want is a fat tip; they don't care if their deliveries are on time."

"Bob, it could also be because you always make them wait before you sign for their packages."

"Well, at least we sold what we had. See you tomorrow, right?"

"Bob, tomorrow's Saturday," Sara said.

"And?"

"That's my day off, remember?"

"But … but the shipment!" Bob said. "If you don't come in, Tina will be the only one here to help me!"

"Well maybe you should've asked earlier," Sara said as she headed for the door. "Besides, I'm busy tomorrow."

"Please Sara, I meant to ask you, but I needed to check on the shipment and—"

"Sorry, Bob. I can't get out of it. Besides, Tina needs to learn these things too. I've already helped with the last four shipments. Anyway, isn't Saturday Jim's day here?"

"I … uh … hmm, yes fine," Bob said as he grabbed the door and flung it open and then stepped out into the night.

Sara shook her head and then put on her coat and headed for the door, remembering to turn the lock just before closing it. Standing outside, she took a breath of the night air and turned to head toward the parking lot nearby. At least, that's what she planned to do. Instead, Sara slammed into a coat, which reared up as she tumbled back in surprise. She looked up, a "Watch it!" forming on her lips, until she saw who it was.

"I guess I should announce myself beforehand, huh?" the man from this afternoon said as he extended his hand to Sara.

"I'd appreciate it," Sara said, taking his hand.

The man pulled her up and then reached under his free arm and withdrew a book. "I was hoping I could get more of this guy," the man said, holding out a copy of Ray Bradbury's *The Illustrated Man*. "But it looks like I'm a little late."

"Ten thirty's a bit much for bookstores," Sara said. "At least you have good taste. Bradbury's always been a favorite."

"I try to pick the good ones," the man said.

"Well, if you wanna prove it, I'll be back at the store on Sunday," Sara said as she started back toward the parking lot.

But she hadn't taken more than two steps before the man said, "Why wait?"

"Excuse me?" Sara asked, turning around.

"Well, I know it's late for bookstores, but is it too late for their employees to grab a coffee and talk sci-fi with potential customers?" the man said.

"Actually, yes," Sara said.

"Then a chance to discuss good literature?" the man asked.

"Look, I appreciate the offer, but I've had a long day, and I don't need a guy I don't know hitting on me," Sara answered.

The man shook his head at that and said, "True. But you do owe me one."

"Oh, you're trying to guilt me now?" Sara said.

"Is it working?"

Sara thought, and replied, "A little."

"How about you pick the place? One cup, that's it, I swear," the man said, even getting on his knee to demonstrate.

Sara tried to keep a straight face, but seeing him kneeling like that was just too much. She smirked and said, "Fine. There's a coffee shop on the next block. But there is one thing I need first."

"Whatever you want," the man said, getting to his feet.

"Your name. I refuse to drink with anyone who doesn't have a name."

"Name, name," the man said, scratching his head. "Okay, then. My name is Mark."

"And mine is Sara. Now follow me, Mark, and be prepared to open your mind and spend five dollars."

XII

"WHERE THE HELL AM I now?" Groundquake asked as the lights finished shimmering around him.

"You tell me. Ah think this is your area," Forester said, looking about the huge stone cavern lit only by a few torches that he and the dog had appeared in.

The dog took one look around and groaned. "Damn it, we got the gremlins again," he moaned.

"Is it just you and me against 'em?" Forester asked.

"Nope," said Thunderer. The ram suddenly stepped out from behind a rock formation.

"Think we're alone?" the squirrel asked.

"Look around," Thunderer said, motioning to the walls and the rocks. "You see what's different?"

"No, just a bunch of rocks—"

"A buncha *clean* rocks," Quake said, holding a few in his hand. "They were covered with gremlin slime the last time."

"Which tells us they haven't been here in a while," Thunderer said. "And we know they move through these caves all the time, so we may need help finding them. Quake?"

The dog nodded and took a whiff of the air. He moved about, taking in deep breaths as he moved toward the left wall.

"This way," the dog said suddenly, pointing ahead.

Thunderer and Forester followed as the dog led them to an opening inside the cave wall. The three knights walked through slowly, as the little light they had dimmed even further. Thunderer created a ball of lightning to light their way, and Groundquake's nose kept them on track.

"We must be getting closer," Thunderer said. "I'm starting to smell the slime again."

"Why do you think I brought us here?" Quake asked. "It's like they painted the walls with it."

"But why is it so strong here?" Forester retorted. "They clearly aren't coming into the cavern back there."

"It could be— *Thunderer! Duck!*"

"Wha— *Gah!!*" The ram cried out as something popped out of the wall and swung toward him. Thunderer ducked down as Forester pulled his ax and swung it in the opposite direction. There was a clang as the two forces met and were then torn asunder. The attacking object clanged against the wall. Thunderer brought the lightning ball over to reveal a long, slender blade sticking out of a now broken spring trap.

"Good … save," Thunderer panted as he got to his feet.

"When did they change things here?" Forester asked as he sheathed his ax.

"I think you can ask them," Groundquake answered, pointing ahead.

The two knights turned their heads to the sounds of footsteps coming toward them.

"I'll handle it," Quake said. He moved toward the sound. But he had barely gotten a few steps before green flame filled the tunnel and slammed into him. The dog went flying backward, right into Forester, knocking the squirrel down.

"Gremlins," Thunderer said as he drew his rod and stood in front of the others.

The footsteps stopped. A spark flashed, and then a smaller green flame lit the tunnel, showing Thunderer the two gremlin guards who stood with their crude spears at the ready.

"Who dares invade the gremlins' lair?!" the one holding the flame sneered. "Answer!"

"I am Thunderer, Elemental Knight of Zeuia," the ram answered smoothly. "My comrades and I were sent here to—"

"An Elemental!" the younger guard, short and chubby with trembling hands, spat out. "I'm so sorry we attacked you. Please don't tell the king! We were just following orders with what's happened and all—"

"Shut *up!*" the other guard, a tall and gangly gremlin with dark hair, snapped. "This could be some sort of trick! They could be those damn radicals again, trying to get in and kill us all!"

"I assure you, we are not," Thunderer replied smoothly. "The Architects sent us here because they believe your city is in danger from the Chaos Demons. We need to speak with your king."

"And how do we know you aren't one of them?" the spear guard said. "Cause a problem, come down in a friendly form, tell us that you can make it all better if we let you see the king! You either prove to me you're who you say you are, or I'll— Gahh!"

The gremlin screamed as the ground under him suddenly trembled and then raised up and flung him backward. As he skidded down the tunnel, the younger guard looked up to see Quake and Forester standing next to Thunderer.

"Ah assume you believe us now?" Forester asked.

"Yes, I'm sorry, it's just … Well, everything's gone wrong, and we don't know what to do, and—"

"It's all right," the ram said. "Can you take us to the king then, …?"

"Hazari," the gremlin said. "Of course."

The gremlin turned and started back down the tunnel. As the knights followed, Thunderer asked, "Hazari, what is it that's happened here?"

"You'll understand when you see," the gremlin said as he moved on ahead.

"Does anyone else think that sounds like a trap?" Forester said.

"Yes, but I don't think it is," Thunderer said. "You saw how paranoid they were of us."

"And we get to stop whatever it is," Quake sighed.

"Hey, are you coming?" Hazari called from down the tunnel.

The three of them looked at each other. Then sighing, they followed their guide down the tunnel.

*　　*　　*

Joe pushed open the doors to the library. The table before him was still covered with Wavecrasher's findings on the vampires, demons, and hunters. Normally, the mess would have bothered Joe, but he thought little of it as he moved past the table and onto the ladder that was connected to the library walls. Holding onto it, he thought about what he wanted, and the ladder whirled away, moving to the left of the room as it pushed him upward. Joe held on tightly as the floor moved away from him. He rose higher and higher, until finally he came to where he needed to be, the binding of the needed tome glowing in the dim light. Joe reached forward and grabbed the book and then held it close as the ladder swung back around and lowered him to the ground.

He stepped off and returned to the table where Crash had been. Moving quickly, Joe took all the books and moved them to the side in a pile, leaving only the books on Chaos Demons. When the books were properly organized, he placed the one he had taken down on the table, and looked at its title—*The Gods of the Cosmos*.

"This has to have his name," Joe said as he sat. He placed the book on the table. Then he reached over and grabbed the thickest tome he saw on the Chaos Demons. Opening it, he scanned the first few lines:

> The Chaos Demons have existed since the dawn of creation. They are the first race of beings created and roamed free in the nothingness for thousands of years, until they were sealed away in a pocket dimension by a great and powerful force. While unconfirmed, it is believed that this force was also what created the Architects and, in turn, existence. However, as the Architects have not spoken of it, and there is little evidence of this power, it must remain a theory.

"Says you," Joe said, closing the book. He'd seen the force that had created the Architects. That had to be what visited his dream- they were too intense, too weird, and took up too much space in Joe's mind for them to be anything else. But knowing that didn't answer the question of what they meant. He needed more answers, and the answers had to be here.

Turning in the chair, Joe opened the book he'd taken and scanned the first entry. Emblazoned on the page was the image of a group of ten figures. Surrounded by clouds and positioned next to the sun, they looked down upon a huge city. The text identified them as the *Anunnaki*, the Sumerian gods. Joe looked over each figure, scanning for anything that might even remotely resemble the robed figure of his dreams. But none of the ancient deities came close.

Joe turned the page and, this time, came across the Egyptian Gods. These took less time; many of the gods had animal heads, and nothing in Ra or Osiris reminded Joe of the figure.

He looked at the pantheons for a moment, and Joe wondered briefly if he was overthinking this. The pantheons were endlessly varied, and the current God had so many variations that Joe had no idea what the "correct" appearance would be. Maybe what he was seeing was something that looked different to everyone who saw it, which would make his searching pointless.

"But I have to know," Joe said, turning back to the book and flipping to the next page. He grinned a little, seeing he had opened to the Shinto gods of Japan. He was about to start going through them when he suddenly felt a great warmth in his coat pocket. Reaching into it, he pulled out the chunk of crystal he'd taken from the Nexus and looked into it. Slowly, images began to form inside it—images of the others apparently having a very interesting time.

XIII

"GOD DAMN IT, GET off me!" Sandshifter swore, grabbing Windrider and tossing him to the side.

"You couldn't have just waited a sec? I wasn't exactly thrilled landing on you," the falcon replied as, next to them, Forger stood up and looked about.

"Wherever we are, there's a lot of forestation," the spider said, looking around at the trees that surrounded them in the dark night.

"You do remember we came here to stop the end of the world from happening?" Sandshifter said. "Not look at the scenery?"

"The scenery might help tell us where we are," Forger replied.

"Fine, look at the trees," Sandshifter growled back. "I've got another idea. Windy, fly up and— Windy? Damn it, he's gone already?"

"Not for long," the birdman said suddenly, stepping out from behind a bush. "I heard some noise by the trees in the back and went to check it out. It was just a deer, but I found a sign post—written in German."

"How can you read in this darkness?" Forger asked.

"Dude, I do keep a light," Windrider said, pulling a small flashlight from his coat. "And I learned a little German from the dialogue in *Indiana Jones*."

"Only you can make a film marathon into something useful," Forger said with a grin.

"Did it say where we are?" Sandshifter asked.

"About a half a mile or so from a town," the falcon answered. "I couldn't figure the name though."

"Then we should get there as soon as possible," Forger said.

"Yeah, because people who don't speak English are always fun," Sandshifter muttered.

"Are you *ever* optimistic? I mean seriously," Windrider said.

"Sandy, let's just do our job here," Forger said.

"No, something's wrong," the wolf said, breathing in deeply as she turned to the west. "I can smell smoke."

"That's not so bad," Windrider said.

"And burning flesh."

"Windy, which direction was that town in?" Forger asked.

"That way," the falcon replied, pointing in the direction the wolf was sniffing.

"Then we need to get there now," Forger said as both she and Sandshifter started toward the scent.

But they had barely taken a few steps when both knights felt something push up their backs, stick in their coats, and then lift them up off the ground. The two of them panicked, kicking wildly, until Windrider said, "This would be a lot easier if you two could grab my belt."

"Wha— You couldn't have given us some warning?" Sandshifter snarled as she realized that the falcon had each of the knights' coats pushed over his boots, his wings unfurled from his sleeves and pumping hard.

"You said we needed to hurry. Now grab my belt before you two throw me off balance," Windrider said.

The wolf growled, but both she and the spider reached over and grabbed onto the bird's belt. The three of them immediately soared higher, the trees below becoming smaller and smaller every second as they sped onward. All of them kept their eyes open, looking for any sight of the flames that Sandshifter had smelled, until …

"*There*!!" Forger yelled, using a free hand to point to a bright spot just in front of them.

But Windrider had already begun his descent toward the fiery spot. As he got close, he yelled, "Let go! I'll get you down there!"

The two knights did as bidden, releasing their grips and falling toward the ground. But as they came closer, they found themselves slowing, their descent halted by the gathering winds. Windrider's power gently lowered his companions down to the ground, and he descended with them.

The three of them touched ground, pulled up their masks, and drew their weapons, looking about the ruined village. Squat white houses with brown lines racing down them blackened in the grip of flames. The cobbles of the street were black with soot, and the wreckage of cars, walls, and some broken weapons littered the streets. There were no bodies, but there were more than a few bloodstains on the walls around the knights.

"What on Earth did this?" Forger asked. "The demons would just wipe it out, leave nothing."

"I don't— *Wait!*" Sandshifter said, spotting a boy emerging from the side of the street.

The boy ran toward them in a panic, his clothes ragged and covered in blood. He didn't even seem to notice the knights, until Windrider reached out and grabbed him.

"It's all right," the falcon said as the boy struggled against his grasp. "We can help you. Just tell us what's going on."

"*Sie kommen! Die monster, werden sie uns alle töten!*" the boy yelled, doing all he could to pull away from the trio.

"Windy, how much German did you get from that movie?" Sandshifter asked.

"Not enough for this," the falcon answered. "Um … *Sprechen sie englisch?*

"*Die monster! Böse werwolf!*"

"I did get werewolf out of that," Forger said.

"Uh, I think I see why," Windrider said.

Sandshifter turned to see three large, black forms pounce into the street. They came to a halt before the group and then stood back on their hind legs, revealing their giant black lupine forms. They growled at the foursome, the sound like a rusty engine warming up, and the leader pointed at the boy.

"Well, now we know what burned the town," Windrider said as he held out his staff.

"Windy, take the kid. Get him someplace safe," Sandshifter said. "Forger and I will take care of them."

"No way. You're outnumbered—"

"No, she's right. Get him to safety," Forger echoed. "You can come back after that. I'm packing silver, remember?"

Windrider looked from one knight to the other and then grabbed the boy, unfurled his wings, and took off, leaving his companions with the three wolves.

"All right, *culos*," Sandshifter said as she and Forger faced the trio. "Come and get us."

XIV

"So, what is this place?" Firesprite asked as she looked about the countryside. All about the lizard were a lush forest and an open, but well-farmed meadow, with mountainous terrain in the distance behind her. The weather was cool, with a great deal of humidity in the air.

"There are a lot of options. Maybe Japan; the scenery's right," Wavecrasher replied.

"Okay. Any idea where we should start looking?"

"First step is to find out where we are," the cat answered. "There must be a town around here somewhere."

"Don't you know? I figured you'd have the whole planet memorized."

"I don't read that much," Crash said. "Besides, my focus is monsters and magic."

"Mm," the lizard said. "Well, we don't seem to have any here, so— Wait, look over there."

The lizard pointed to the east, and Wavecrasher followed her gaze and saw smoke, seeming to rise from behind a nearby hill. The two looked at each other, and with only a nod, headed toward it.

"What do you think we're in for?" Firesprite asked.

"No idea," Crash replied. "I never saw anything about these Equites in the books in the library. And that worries me more than anything."

"For once, I agree," Firesprite said as they reached the foot of the hill.

Pausing a moment, the cat whispered the words of the glamour, cloaking herself in its protective veil. "You'd better suit up," she said to the lizard.

"Already on it," Firesprite replied as she pulled her mask up over her face.

"Oh, very subtle," Crash said. "No one would ever suspect you."

"We should try to assert ourselves; it could make things go faster."

"So we should alert people to our presence?"

"If these people guard one of the Equites, they already know about us," Firesprite said. "But look, why don't you go first then, if you're so worried?"

"Fine. But don't come to me if someone screams," Crash said, starting up the hill.

The Water Knight reached the top and looked out in surprise. She had expected to see a village, or perhaps even a farm. But instead, she saw a large, square building, with the cornered, multileveled roofs and stark colors of a Buddhist temple. As Crash watched, the doors opened and three men in robes appeared.

"Monks? Out here?" the cat wondered aloud.

The men in the distance all seemed to be middle-aged, though they were strong-looking under their robes. One seemed a little older, and Crash caught how the other two walked behind him. But something was odd about their movements—they were looking about like rabbits, their gazes never stopping for a second. Nevertheless, Crash moved down the hill. Moving down the hill, she whistled and then waved at the small band. They turned to see her, stopped, and watched as she descended down the hill, coming closer to them with each step.

When she was close enough, she said, "Pardon me, but can one of you please tell me where we are?"

But the monks gave no reply. They simply stared at the cat, until one of them took a medallion from his robe and held it up to the cat. It was small but made of gold, and the sun reflected from it, right into the knight's eyes. Crash felt her eyes burn from the brightness, and she turned away, saying, "Sorry, it's just the light—"

"*Akuma!*" yelled the monk, holding the medallion as the two behind him suddenly drew daggers from their robes.

Still half-blind, Crash managed to pull out her trident as the monks charged. She heard their footsteps and stuck out her weapon as the monks drove their daggers down. Their arms caught in between the trident's spikes; Crash felt the impact and threw the weapon to the side, bringing the monks down with it. As they fell, Crash turned back to the remaining monk, only to be met with a kick to the side of her face. She staggered to the side, holding her jaw as the monk moved into a fighting stance.

"I thought ... you guys ... were peaceful." Crash breathed heavily as she turned back to the monk. There was a click as the cat moved her jaw back into place, and then the monk charged once again.

But this time, Crash was ready and let loose with a stream of water that knocked the monk back. He fell to the ground, just as the cat heard a whistling noise approaching. Without a second's hesitation, she reached out her hand and caught her trident as it moved through the air. Spinning around, she found herself face to face with the two other monks, still armed with their knives. They moved to strike, but the cat just held up the trident, and the two suddenly stopped, frozen in ice.

"Look, I don't want to hurt anyone, so will you please listen to ... *Uhh!*"

The cat fell to one knee, and the third monk stood behind her with a rock. The other two unfroze, first falling to their knees and then rushing the cat, knocking her down and holding her to the ground. The third monk raised the rock again. But before he could bring it down, there was an explosion of fire, and the rock flew from his hands. The monks started and then turned to see a red figure coming down the hill, her hands still ablaze. As they watched, Firesprite pulled down her mask. The effect was instanteous; the monks gasped and then released Crash and bowed to the lizard.

Firesprite just nodded, held up her hand in a halting gesture, and then asked, "*Eigo o hanashimasu ka?*"

"*Hai,*" the third monk said. "We are pleased to see you, Fire Knight. We were just about to deal with this—"

"That's the Water Knight. If you would be so kind as to let her up."

"What? But the medallion—"

"It just blinded me," Crash said, muttering the words that undid the glamour. The two monks gasped and then backed off and helped her up.

"We apologize," the head monk said. "The medallion is an anathema to all those who come here with evil intent. When you reacted to it—"

"Don't worry. You didn't hurt her too badly," the lizard replied as Crash slowly got to her feet.

"We apologize again for the mistake, but these are dangerous times," the monk said.

"We heard as much. You're the guardians of one of the Equites?" Firesprite asked. "Can you take us to it?"

"We can take you to the room where it is guarded," the monk said, "and tell you of the evil that threatens it."

"Thank you," the lizard said as the monks turned and walked to the temple. She followed and then paused as she came to Wavecrasher. "Told you we didn't need the glamour."

"Fine, they knew who we were," the cat snapped. "Most people just freak and run when we aren't covered."

"Not the ones who are expecting us, mate," Firesprite answered.

"Whatever," the cat growled back.

"At least you were right about the region."

Crash muttered something, then asked, "How did you know to say that?"

"You said the region was right for Japan. And I know how to say, 'Do you speak English,' in six languages."

"Wha— How?"

"I can read too, you know. Figured it would be important somewhere down the line," Firesprite said.

"Oh. Good call."

"Thanks."

*   *   *

Joe watched as Crash, Firesprite and the monks began to march toward the temple. Glancing away from the crystal, he turned back to his book and took a look at the newest pantheon. This time, it was less work; his text was from the Torah, and it was simply a picture of God bestowing the commandments upon Moses. And just as in the other books Joe saw nothing here of what he'd seen in his dreams. Groaning, he flipped the book closed and rubbed his eyes. He looked over the pile of books he still had to look through—Shinto, Hindu, Greek, Norse, Egyptian, and even a couple of religions from the demons—and he had no idea what he was seeing. All he was getting was a massive case of eye strain and a heavy head.

"There must be another book. Something." Joe yawned. "Something that'll give me a clue. Just gotta stay awake."

Sleep.

"This isn't working," Joe muttered. "I have to find another— Wait."

It was right in front of him. The only thing that had given him any clues was the dream. Hell, what did he really expect to find in books with just a mental image of a being minus the face? If Joe was going to solve this, he needed more info. But there was still one thing that he needed to do first.

"I can't leave the others alone," Joe said as he looked at the crystal. If something happened, he'd need to get down there. He needed a plan to—

They can handle it. Their calls will awaken you.

"The guys can handle things down there," Joe said to himself. "And the staff will alert me if they need me. I can spare a little time."

Joe yawned again and leaned back in his chair. He pulled his staff close, to make sure he'd hear the signal, and then tipped his head back and began to doze.

After all the books he'd read, sleep came quickly, and Joe's steady breathing became the only sound in the library.

XV

"HE ACTUALLY WROTE THAT kind of story back then?" Mark asked as Sara sipped her coffee.

"Oh yeah," Sara answered. She finished her drink. "I would've loved to see people's faces at the idea of black people ruling Mars back in the '50s. And maybe after you finish, I can introduce you to *Dandelion Wine*," Sara said.

"Is that another drink here?" Mark asked, gesturing to the warmly lit walls of the small shop Sara had brought them to.

"Oh, please, that would be a terrible name for coffee," Sara said with a shudder. "No, it's a book all about the summer."

"And?"

"That's it."

"Well, after Mars and evil hologram nurseries, a book like that might be what I need."

"And after a hard day of … What do you do?" Sara asked.

"Accounting. It's all about checks and balances and not screwing up."

"Too bad. A little imagination is what keeps me sane at work," Sara said. "Usually it's shoving my foot down someone's throat."

"Your boss didn't seem like much fun," Mark added.

"I can deal with Bob, believe me," Sara said. "And I get to see the newest books; keep things organized; and, on occasion, start someone out on some good literature."

"Really?" Mark said.

"Ha, ha," Sara said back. "But I just can't work at that place forever. It's just … well it's just a job."

"You need something that makes you happy; I can relate," Mark said. "So what do you want to do?"

"I don't know," Sara replied. "When I was in school, I thought I could teach English—show kids good stories, get them to like reading. But when I got into it, I realized it just didn't work for me."

She snorted suddenly, saying, "God, what am I doing, dumping all this on you? You barely know me."

"I don't mind," Mark said. "I think it's great you were able to get out. I work with way too many people stuck in a job they hate. At least you like part of yours."

"For now."

"You seem like a smart enough girl to be able to get a better job when it comes along."

"Thanks."

"No prob— Oh," Mark said, noticing the lights going off. "Well, thanks for the evening. Do you want a ride home?"

"No, I can walk," Sara said as she got her things. "Frankly, I enjoy it."

"Are you sure? Lotta crazy people out at night."

"Most of them are on the other side of the river."

"Good point," Mark admitted as they headed to the door. "But be careful anyway."

"Aren't you protective?" Sara asked.

"I have to be. Otherwise, I might get off track and read *Twilight*," Mark said as he opened the door.

"You don't seem dumb enough to do that," Sara said. "But stop by again. I'll show you some other good reads."

"I will. Get home safe," Mark said as Sara turned down the street, stopping to wave.

Mark returned the wave and then left the shop, heading the other way. As he did, he took one last glance at Sara walking away and then turned his head away. He shook it slowly as he whispered to himself, "I must be out of my mind."

XVI

He found himself back in the same spot—the strange figure and the young Architects all around him. They stood in the shape of a star, the Architects on the points with the figure in the middle. Joe watched as the figure looked at each of the Architects and then pointed to Ralin. The young Architect of Light turned as the figure spoke to him in a low voice Joe could barely hear. But it seemed that, to Ralin, the message was as clear as day. He nodded, turning his attention to the emptiness in front of him. Ralin rubbed his hands together and then held them out, fingers extended. The tips began to glow brightly, and as Joe watched, Ralin flung his hands about in the air, the light breaking off as he did so. It flew all about him, embedding itself in the darkness as small white glowing dots. Joe was confused for a moment, and then understanding hit—Ralin had just created stars.

The figure nodded in approval and then turned to Darya. The red-robed Architect turned to his teacher, as the figure spoke to both Darya and Ralin this time. Joe still couldn't make out the instructions, but again, the Architects nodded, this time with both of them turning to the side. Ralin was the first to act. He grew a light ball inside his hands and then tossed it out, far from the group. It floated through the empty space and then came to a halt, hovering there quietly. Darya then unleashed streams of fire that streaked across the empty space and into the ball. The ball held the fire for a moment, and then began to swell, growing larger and brighter with every second. Joe realized it was getting hotter too, as the ball swelled to the size of a building, and still Darya poured in his power. The ball of fire and light swelled, glowing as hot and bright as …

The sun.

Joe was seeing what had been debated for more years then he could fathom—the beginning of the universe. That's why these Architects had been summoned. Fire, Water, Earth, and Air—the main building blocks of the physical world—with Light to bring them substance. It all fit, but it didn't explain why the other Architects, especially Rastla, weren't here.

Joe focused on Chirron then, who came up to Darya. They acknowledged each other, and the cloaked figure motioned to them. The two of them stood apart from each other, their hands held upright, palm outs. They closed their eyes, and slowly a brown and red sphere grew between them. The two sweated as the sphere slowly grew brighter and brighter, pushing the Architects further and further apart. But still, they worked to hold the energy together, their faces straining with the mighty effort. As the sphere grew and grew, Joe stared at it in complete confusion. He could feel massive heat emanating from the sphere, but this wasn't a sun. Fire and earth. What could they form together? What would have this sort of heat? And what need would they have for it?

Suddenly, the cloaked figure called for them to stop. Darya and Chirron backed away, the sphere floating between them. It was huge now, at least twelve times larger than a bus. The cloaked figure looked over the sphere, nodded, and then turned to Chirron. Again, words passed between them, and Chirron, looking nervous, stepped toward the sphere. He brought his hands in close, holding his hands a few inches apart near his chest. As he did this, the sphere began to glow once more, this time the brown light overtaking the red. The brown stretched everywhere, overtaking the sun, seeming to touch every corner of this empty realm. But Chirron continued to gather it and place it into the sphere, until finally, he threw apart his hands.

The brown light exploded, turning the entire cosmos into the inside of a mud pile. Joe shut his eyes, the dull color still managing to blind him with its intensity. But even through his eyelids, Joe could see the color seep through, as sounds began to emerge—gnashing, grinding, tearing sounds, as if something was being ripped apart, crunched up, spit out, and fused together all at once. Joe covered his ears against it, but then, just as quickly as it had appeared, the sound stopped. The light dimmed as well, as though someone had simultaneously turned off the lights and the stereo.

Joe carefully opened his eyes, not sure of what he was going to see. But even then, he was shocked by what lay before him. What had been an empty cosmos was now … land. A brown, rocky landscape now stretched before him in all directions. It was barren and harsh looking, but it was the first familiar thing Joe had seen in these dreams, the first earthly thing.

Joe's jaw dropped. The ball of fire and earth had been for this—the core of the first planet to be formed. And if that was the case …

Joe turned to see the cloaked figure and the Architects standing behind him, amazed at what they were seeing. Chirron looked especially proud, as the cloaked arm patted him on the shoulder.

The figure then turned to Aeris, speaking softly to her and then pointing upward. The pale Architect followed his gaze and then nodded. She breathed deeply, turned her head up, and released her breath into the heavens. As she did, Joe heard a "pop," and his ears followed suit. Shaking his head to combat the feeling, Joe still managed to see Aeris pour her seemingly never-ending breath up, creating the blanket of the atmosphere to wrap around this planet. She finally stopped, barely winded at all by the effort.

The figure again nodded his approval and then spoke to Chirron once more. As the Architect of Earth brought up both hands, the earth they were standing on rose up, elevating them toward the heavens. They stopped after a few feet, and then the figure turned to the last Architect.

Ruta listened intently as the figure whispered his instructions to her. As had the others, she nodded. Then she glanced up to the sky. Joe wasn't sure what would happen here; there was no water around for the Architect to manipulate. Perhaps she was to draw it from her body as Wavecrasher had done before. But for the whole planet? Even for the Architect, it seemed too great a task.

Plink.

Joe started at the impact and then glanced up. The sky, a bright blue with the sun blazing in the distance, had begun to darken. As Joe looked up, another drop splashed down upon his head. This was followed by another and then another, until the sky was alive with rain. It splashed down around him, first soaking into the earth and then overflowing above it. Joe was amazed, but he knew this meant it was time to wake up; he had no intention of drowning in his dreams.

Still, he felt he should take one last look at the young Architects. But when he turned to them, Joe saw something that surprised him. Ralin was glancing up at the darkened sky, a displeased look on his face. Joe glanced up as well and saw that the sun had been blocked out. Was Joe seeing jealousy on the face of his Architect? He moved to take another look, only to see the cloaked figure stare at him and begin to remove his hood ...

＊　　＊　　＊

Joe snapped awake, the newly created world falling away to be replaced by the confines of the library. He shook his head as he thought about what he had seen. Despite the amazing scene, Joe kept remembering that displeased look on Ralin's face. It hadn't seemed to be the rain that bothered him, but something else in the sky that—

"Sleep well?"

Joe turned toward the voice to see Nightstalker standing by the door.

"I didn't think monitor duty would be that boring," the bat said as he came toward Joe.

"Well ... I didn't sleep well last night. And the others seem to be taking care of themselves," Joe answered, glancing back at the unlit crystal.

"I'll take your word for it," Stalker said. "Right now, I have a problem."

"You can't find this sunlight room where Hunst is?"

"Not yet," the bat said. "I need to borrow your staff."

"Why?"

"Once they moved him in, I lost the ability to sense him, and the hunters' fortress is way too vast for me to find it alone."

"And you need a way to sense the light," Joe said.

"I just assumed the room would be one where I couldn't sense any shadows. Apparently, it's more than that."

"But there's one hitch; the staff won't work for you," Joe said.

"It will if you tell it to," Stalker said.

"I told the light to avoid you last time," Joe said. "I don't know if I can make the staff obey you."

"I just need something that can sense light and let me move in it if need be."

Joe stared at 'Stalker, then said, "I'll try. Give me a moment."

Joe drew his staff from its holster. Holding it before him, he closed his eyes and concentrated on the image of the staff in his mind. Stalker watched calmly as the staff began to glow with light. The light held for a moment and then began to dim. But Joe grimaced, and the light returned. The glow held for a few moments and then finally faded as Joe opened his eyes.

"All right," he said, turning back to Nightstalker. "The staff will obey you. But only in sensing light. Otherwise, it's useless."

"That'll be enough," the bat said as he held out his hand. Joe placed the staff into it, and Stalker took the weapon and looked it over.

"This really is a strong weapon," he said. "But I never thought I'd be the one to use it."

"Stranger things have happened," Joe said.

"Than Shadow using Light?"

"Okay, not many," Joe answered. "But we always have the same goal; we just argue about the route there."

"You truly believe that?"

"If I didn't, I wouldn't keep doing this."

"Thanks."

"I know you will use the staff well."

"No, the speech; it may come in handy. I have a feeling using this thing won't be easy, even with your command."

"It'll be fine," Joe said as Stalker waved his hand over the staff, causing it to vanish into the shadows. "If there is anyone I know with enough blind, stupid determination to work the staff, it's you."

"Thanks ... I think," Stalker said. He turned to get to the Nexus. "Although Sandy might come close. You think that she's doing all right out there?"

"Forger and Windrider are with her. I'm sure things are fine."

XVII

"*YEARGH!*" FORGER SCREAMED AS the werewolf dug its teeth into her left shoulder, holding her off the ground in a deadly bear hug. The spider gritted her jaw and then wiggled free her second left arm, reforming the hand into a large metal sphere. Ignoring the pain as best she could, Forger brought the sphere forward and, with all her strength, slammed it directly into the monster's side.

She heard an audible crack and then a second howl of pain, as the monster released some of its grip to hold its ribs.

"You're really not going to like this, then," Forger said. She freed her second right arm, its hand already remade into a second sphere.

Before the werewolf could react, Forger brought both spheres into its side; this time, there were dual cracks, and the wolf finally let go of the spider. As it cradled its sides, Forger crouched on the ground and took a moment to glance at her shoulder. The flesh and cloth were already sealing up as fluidly as melted steel. But in that second, the werewolf had already turned its attention back to her. Growling, it lunged at her, ready to take another bite. This time, though, when its jaws reached her, Forger held up her arm and caught its teeth with her first right forearm. The werewolf bit down hard, but instead of flesh, it tasted a strange metal. Then its howls began anew as smoke began to rise from between its teeth. The monster let go, and backed away. Forger raised up all six of her arms, their silver armguards glinting in the moonlight.

The werewolf turned to run, but Forger merely brought two arms to bear, and silvery chains shot forth from her palms. They stretched forth, wrapping themselves around the body of the werewolf. It fell to the ground and screamed in pain as its body smoked and burned. But Forger took no notice. She drew her mace and quickly made her way to the front of the creature. As it twisted on the ground, the spider held the mace high above her head. Then, taking a second to withdraw the spikes from her weapon, Forger brought the mace down onto the wolf's head. The howls stopped immediately, though the werewolf's breathing did not.

"One less problem," Forger said. "But where did Sandshifter go. *Merde!*"

The spider ducked down as a werewolf flew over her head and crashed through a nearby building. Forger quickly turned her gaze over to where Sandshifter was still battling the remaining werewolf. The two of them were literally locked tooth and claw, as the werewolf tore at Sandshifter's face, only for the wolf to bite back at him.

Sandshifter pushed the werewolf away, snarling at him as he hit a nearby wall. The werewolf bounced back and howled at her, but this time, Sandshifter just grinned and held out her hands at her side. A flash of orange lit up her palms, and then two streams of sand were flying out of the wolf's hands, pressing her adversary back against the wall. The werewolf, held back by countless pounds of sand, struggled and howled. But as more and more of its body vanished under the grains, its struggles stopped. Finally, Sandshifter stopped the streams, only to bring her hands together and press them tightly against each other; as she did so, the sand surrounding the werewolf followed her example. The creature screamed as the sands crushed its body; Forger could even hear bones breaking and see blood seeping out of the sands. But as the wolf's howls finally reached a fever pitch, Sandshifter unlocked her hands, and the sands broke away. The werewolf fell to the ground, broken and bloody.

"Was that necessary?" Forger asked as she approached Sandshifter.

"He'll heal up," Sandshifter said.

"And the biting?"

"That was just fun."

"Hmph."

"What did you do to yours?"

"Knocked him unconscious … aw, crap," Forger said as she saw the werewolf that Sandy had thrown through the building shakily getting to its feet. It shook its head; saw them; and with a howl, began to charge.

The wolf and the spider went for their weapons. But before the werewolf had gotten even halfway to them, it suddenly went flying backward, as if it had been launched from a cannon, right through another building. The two Knights looked for a moment and then glanced up as they saw Windrider flying down to them.

"Wow," the falcon said as he landed before them. He looked at the two werewolves his companions had captured. "You guys really tore it up here."

"Coulda done more," Sandshifter said, glaring behind the falcon.

"What happened with the boy?" Forger asked.

"Well, he fought me at first, but I think he figured out that I wasn't about to kill him. Then he pointed me west, to this area of the forest the villagers went to."

"Can you get us back there?" Sandshifter asked.

"No problem."

"Then let's get going," Forger said. "*After* I wrap up our friend there in silver."

*   *   *

The point Windrider had pointed to was a large hill that rose up through the trees, just before a ravine cut away the woods. The landscape was dotted with rocky ground and a steep rise that gave no footholds. The top of the hill was large and flat, however, and if one knew how to get to the top, it would allow him or her to see all around for miles, even to the nearby village.

It was here that the people of the village had come when the wolves attacked. The hill was a refuge they hadn't used for generations, but they had wisely maintained it. The secret ways to climb it safely were maintained, and small amounts of supplies had been left under the ground. The villagers had already dug them up and were feeding and healing their people, while men kept guard on the entrance from the forest, armed with guns and silver bullets.

As the others tended to themselves, two men were speaking. One was a young man with stringy, dark hair and an angry expression on his thin face. His body was thin but strong, and he waved his arms about as he spoke. The other man was older, with a trim, white beard and a plump body. His face was stern yet serene. He barely moved as he spoke, providing the calm to his opposite's anger.

"I can't believe you just let him go!" the younger man said.

"And how would you have trapped him, Paul?" the older man asked. "Did you really expect us to hold someone who can fly?"

"He's not natural!" Paul yelled back. "I'm telling you; he's the same type as those wolves, Johan! He probably knows about what they've been doing!"

"Is that why he saved Hans?" Johan countered. "Is that why he brought him back and promised us help?"

"And how do you know he will—"

"Listen to me, boy," Johan said. "This is not a horror film, and we will not start a mob for no reason." Johan looked out over the rest of the villagers. Some families clung to each other, weeping over the loss of their homes. Others tended to the injured and tried to eat what rations they had. The only ones who seemed halfway unaffected were young Hans's family, who kept a close watch on the boy.

"Blast those wolves!" Paul muttered.

"Yes, but we—" Johan began and then stopped, as cries of surprise and horror began to rise from the crowd. Both men looked about for any sign of trouble, but it was another's cries that caused them to look up and then quickly move to the sides. A werewolf, bound in silver chains fell to the ground, followed by Windrider, his face wrapped in a cloth mask.

"*Gott im Himmel!*" Johan cried out.

"You see!" Paul yelled. "I told he would betray us!"

"Whoa, calm down," Windrider said, holding up his hands for calm as his wings folded into his sleeves. "This wolf isn't going to cause you any trouble. I just brought him here—"

"To destroy us!"

"Shut up, Paul," Johan said, regaining his composure. Turning to the crowd, he held up his hands and said, "It is all right! The creature is unconscious and chained in silver!"

As Johan's voice traveled over the crowd, the people slowly began to calm down and stared in amazement at the sight of Windrider and the chained werewolf.

"How did this happen?" Johan asked, turning to the knight. "You said you were going to the village again to search—"

"I did, Mayor," Windrider said. "No one was left there, except for this guy and two of his friends."

"How bad was the damage?" Johan asked.

"I didn't really get a chance to examine it, but only a few buildings are totally gone," the knight said. "I think you can rebuild."

"Where … where on Earth did you get all this?" Paul asked, glancing at the massive chains holding the werewolf. The creature was wrapped head to toe in silver, but even as steam rose from its body at the metal's touch, it stayed motionless.

"My friends were there too," Windrider said. "It was great. We took them out like the Defenders taking down Yandroth … Uh, but I guess you don't care about that," he said sheepishly.

"Where are your friends then?" Johan asked.

"Hold on one second, Mayor," Windrider said. He reached into his coat and pulled out a metal sphere the size of a baseball. As Johan and Paul watched in confusion, he placed the ball on the ground before him, tapped it, and said, "We're here, guys."

The effect was instantaneous. The sphere split open, its very form becoming almost liquid as it shifted and grew in the air. From the inside of the sphere, sand also rose up, moving to the side of the changing metal. As Johan, Paul, and the villagers watched in disbelief, the two substances began to coalesce, slowly taking forms, until finally, two women stood before them. Both were dressed as Windrider, but in clothes and masks of orange and gray respectively. The gray woman was tall, and the orange one had long, dark hair spilling from under her hat.

"Mayor Johan, Councilman Paul, allow me to introduce Forger and Sandshifter," Windrider said, gesturing to each woman in turn.

"Greetings," Forger said. "I apologize for our entrance, but time is of the essence here."

"Of course," Johan said, finally regaining his breath. "We appreciate what you have been able to do for us."

"Stopping rogue monsters is always worthwhile," Sandshifter said. "So what were they going after in the village?"

"We have nothing those monsters would want," Paul snapped.

"And you're sure of this how?"

"Sandy," Forger said, glaring at the wolf. Turning back to the two men, she asked, "I know the wolves are generally animals, but you sure you can't think of anything they might want from your village?"

"Not that I know of," Johan said. "But this attack may explain something else."

"What?"

"We had a truce with them, to stay off each other's lands. It's lasted …"

"Until tonight."

"Yes. And there have been other disturbances. The … the children of our village are going missing."

"Children? And you think the wolves are responsible?" Forger asked.

"Who else?" Paul sneered.

"Yes, because kidnappers and lunatics certainly don't exist in this part of the world," Sandshifter snarled.

"Paul suspects the wolves, but we could find no proof," Johan said. "But after tonight…"

"There may be a way to find out," Forger said. "But I'll need the werewolf to be awake."

"And endanger the people?" Paul asked.

"With all that silver we wrapped him in?" Windrider said.

"Johan, my … associates and I deal with monsters like this all the time," Forger said. "I should be able to make this wolf more talkative, without freeing him."

"What do you have in mind?" the mayor asked.

Forger drew in breath through her teeth, and said,"It's probably better I don't describe it to you just yet," Forger said. "It won't be pleasant."

"Very well, Forger," Johan said. "Do what you must."

"Thank you," Forger said as Paul fumed in the background. "Who wants to wake up the wolf?"

At that, the townsfolk all moved back from the wolf even further. Men stepped in front of women and children, and a few grabbed rocks and heavy sticks. Johan motioned for calm, but he told no one to disarm themselves.

"I've got it," Windrider said. He bent down to the ground. Holding his hand over the werewolf's head, he suddenly clenched his fist. There was a brief sucking noise; the wolf twitched and then snapped awake, gasping like a fish out of water. Seeing him awake, Windrider unclenched his fist. The wolf immediately began to take great, gulping gasps of air, which made more then a few villagers get ready to throw.

"He's all yours," Windrider said.

Forger nodded and moved over to the wolf. Bending down, she extended a single finger that began to lengthen and grow thin, the skin changing into silver. When it had reached six inches, she reached out with her other hand and gripped the wolf's head. It snarled in her grasp, but Forger held it firm as Windrider and Sandshifter took hold of the chains. Forger took a breath, and then, her hands steady, jammed the metal finger into the wolf's temple.

The creature howled in agony, straining against its bonds even as Windrider and Sandshifter held the chains tight. And as Johan and Paul watched, the wolf's body began to shudder and then to shrink. Its hair retracted, the claws and tail vanished, and its muzzle head began to draw in on itself. Within moments, the wolf had vanished, leaving only a young man, naked and wrapped in silver.

"I'll take it from here," Sandshifter said. She released the chains and walked over to the spider. Leaning down, she said to the man, "Isn't it amazing what a little silver in a few nerves can do?"

"W-What... d-do you ... want?" the man sputtered.

"Answers," Sandshifter said. "Why did you attack this village and break your truce? And don't lie; or I'll have my friend wiggle her finger."

"To ... get back ... w-what they ... stole."

"You stole from us!" Paul said. "Where are our children?"

"How ... should ... we ... know?"

"You didn't take their kids?" Sandshifter asked. "I don't quite believe you."

"We ... attacked ... searching for ... *our* children."

"What?"

"Our ... cubs ... missing ... for weeks."

"As long as our children have been gone," Johan said.

"We ... we thought ... the humans ... had done this ... so ..."

"So you attacked without warning or proof?" Sandshifter snarled. "No wonder you've got a spike in your head."

Leaning in closer, the knight said, "Here's the deal. We will let you go. You go back to your pack and tell them that something else has both your children. And you tell them that both sides will stay their hands and that the children will be found. And you tell them that the Elemental Knights say so."

The man's eyes went wide, but he nodded his acceptance. Sandshifter stood up, even as the man stared at her orange clothes and a look of recognition came onto his face. Looking at the knight, he whispered, "Thank ... you ... sister."

"Get that thing out of him," Sandshifter snarled.

Forger nodded and quickly removed her finger. The man let out a sigh of relief as the wound began to heal, and his body swelled, returning to its wolf form. Forger glanced at the wolf and then placed her hands onto the silver chains. There was a clunk, and the chains began to retract into the spider's body. Within seconds, they had vanished, leaving the wolf free. It leaped to its feet, and the villagers backed away in fear. It looked about, growled, and then ran off into the woods, leaving the people and the knights alone.

XVIII

"How much further do we have to go?" Forester asked as Hazari led them down the dim and seemingly unending tunnel. "Feels like we've been going for weeks."

"It's been ten minutes," Groundquake answered.

"*Ow!*"

"Will you *please* watch in front of you?!" Groundquake muttered as Forester jumped up, holding his boot. "That's the third stalagmite you've hit! I—"

Forester turned, surprised to hear no retort but then realized that he could actually see the dog. He turned back around to find Thunderer and Hazari looking out at the end of the tunnel, which had opened directly in the center of the city. Without another word, the dog and squirrel caught up with the ram and the gremlin and looked out into the main hub of the gremlins' underground home. As they exited, Hazari grabbed the handle of a door and slid it over the hole. It was new, but the knights were more concerned with what they saw in front of them. Instead of the usual bustling, slime-ridden metropolis they had seen before, they saw something that actually drove a stake of pity into Groundquake's heart.

"What ... what happened here?" Forester asked, his annoyance forgotten as he looked out into the city.

"I was hoping you could tell us," Hazari said sadly.

He looked out at the mass of his people, collapsed onto the stone, wheezing and struggling just to draw breath. Their skin was a pale green and covered with sores that cracked open and bled as the knights watched. As they looked out at the gremlins closest to them, they saw that their eyes had been covered with a milky film, blinding them to everything. The gremlins moaned and sniffed at the air, trying to gain some sense of what was around them. A gremlin child hacked and coughed into her fist, covering it with blood even as her mother tried to place a sore-covered hand on the child's back.

"It started only two days ago, but it spread quickly," Hazari said. "No one knows what caused it."

"Dear God," Quake said. "How many?"

"The doctors estimated half of the city was infected," Hazari answered. "They are all too sick to move, and the king has no space to keep this many infected quarantined."

"Did he order the tunnels sealed off?" Thunderer asked.

Hazari nodded. "It was the first thing we did after the plague was found."

"God, this …" Quake said.

"We can fix it," Thunderer said, his voice suddenly steely. He moved over to the sick gremlin child. The young one looked at the sound of the silver-clad figure as he knelt down.

"Who are you?" the child hacked out.

"Someone who can help you," Thunderer said. He reached out, his hand glowing, and placed it on the child's head.

The child breathed in sharply and then calmed as the ram began to use his power to heal her.

"By the first gremlin," Hazari breathed as he watched.

The very air around the two seemed to spark as the sores on the child's body shrunk, her skin already darkening.

"It's working!" Hazari called out in joy.

But then a young scream cut through his words. The gremlin turned back to see Thunderer forcing more power into the child, his body trembling as sweat began to pour from his horns. The sores continued to shrink, but slowly, despite all the energy the ram was pouring in.

"Should … should it be happening like this?" Hazari asked Forester.

"No, it shouldn't," the squirrel answered.

"Screw it, I'm going in there before he uses up all he has," Quake said, his hands beginning to glow as he moved over. But before he had come within a few feet of the two, Thunderer suddenly threw back his head and let out a yell, his eyes and even his horns crackling with energy.

Quake stopped and backed away, and Hazari and Forester also moved back. The energy crackled around the ram for a moment, and then a thunderclap shook the walls and the energy blew off him in a ring, striking Quake and the others with the force of a speeding car and the electricity of a downed power line. The stone structures around them cracked, and the sick gremlins cried out in pain and confusion. But then, the energy dissipated, its force spent.

"Uhh ... the hell ... was that?" Forester asked as he slowly pulled himself up. The squirrel's body and clothes were covered in charred marks, but as he sat up, they began to heal with bursts of green light. He turned and saw Hazari lying on the ground, his charred body twitching in pain and shock. Without a word, the squirrel laid his hand down on the gremlin, allowing the green light to pass onto him as well. The twitching stopped instantly, and the burned flesh returned to normal. The gremlin looked up, his wounds healed, and said, "Wh-what happened?"

"Damn good question," the squirrel replied.

He stood back up, helping the gremlin up as he did so, and looked for his fellows. Groundquake was already shakily getting to his feet, his body healing in brown light. The dog glanced about and then stopped and quickly made his way over to where Thunderer's body lay, his hands still on the gremlin child. Forester and Hazari followed. The dog reached the ram's unconscious frame and pulled him up from the ground. The ram was covered in sweat, his fur matted and his breathing shallow. His eyes were closed, his face gaunt and skeletal.

"Christ, man, all this for a—" Quake began but then stopped as he looked over and saw the gremlin child sitting up, her body healed of the sickness.

"Is he all right?" she asked as she looked at the ram.

"Uh ... he will be," Quake said, placing one hand on the stone floor and another on the ram. The energy of the earth immediately began to pulse through the dog and into Thunderer as his breathing eased and his eyes fluttered open.

"Did … did I … help… the child?"

"Yeah, she's fine," Groundquake said, turning the ram so he could see.

Thunderer looked at the child and smiled; she returned the grin.

"What was that?" Forester asked. "Ah felt like Ah was being hit by an electrified bus."

"I can't explain it," Thunderer said. "When I tried to heal her, it was like there was some sort of blockage. I kept putting more and more power in, trying to get past it."

"There's no way we can heal these guys if this is what it takes," Groundquake said.

"Do you have a better idea?" Thunderer asked. "We have to help them."

"No, our job is keeping the balance. We can't do that if we destroy this place."

"You can do it then. You're in a cave; use the earth as a power source."

"You caused a power burst getting around it; do you want me to cause an earthquake and shake this city to pieces?"

"A city means nothing without the people in it."

"Guys," Forester said, "much as Ah'd like to see you two argue, didn't Ralin say that there was some way that the doors could be opened? Maybe this is what he meant?"

"He's got a point, Quake. And if that's the case—"

"It means that getting to that door and keeping it shut is the way to end this," Quake answered.

"Ah'm for that," Forester said.

"If we go to the palace, we may learn more that can help us," Hazari said.

"All right," Thunderer said. "But if we find some sort of cure there—"

"I'll come down here and administer it myself," Groundquake said. "Now get up and let's get moving before you find a puppy with a broken leg."

*　　*　　*

"This is worse than I thought," Thunderer said as the group made its way into the palace, Hazari and the healed gremlin child leading the way. The gremlin guards still stood at attention, but they were leaning heavily on their spears, their bodies awash with sores. Others, still healthy, ran about, applying water and, in some cases, slime to their sickened brethren, but those caretakers were few and far between.

"They will not be able to survive for much longer," Hazari said as he led them to the throne room.

"What about you?" Forester asked. "Why aren't you sick?"

"I … I don't know," Hazari said. "A few of us seem immune, but the healers haven't been able to determine why. Our blood is normally toxic, but—"

"Gee, wouldn't immunity be a tad important to understand?" Quake asked as they crossed into the throne room.

"It has … been hard enough … keeping my people … alive," a deep, wheezing uttered.

"Nerbino!" Thunderer cried in shock. The young king was seated upon his throne, but he was far from a powerful king at the moment. His skin was pale, and there were sores scattered across his body.

"You have come … good," he wheezed. "I was about to … send word to the Architects."

"When did you get this?" Quake asked, a note of actual concern in his voice.

"A few hours ago. I had been … trying to help the healers … find a cure."

"My king, no!" Hazari said. "You have enough to do; you cannot tire your body this way—"

"I know that, fool!" Nerbino snapped. "But I cannot let them die."

"Nerbino, we were sent here because the Architects believe that something is going after the door again," Thunderer said.

"Another Chaos Demon? How?" Nerbino said. "The Lightrider ... sealed the door with his magic."

"We know, but it looks like it might happen anyway," the ram said. "They said that the door holds one of these four things called Equites. You're the king; do you know what that is?"

"We gremlins were never ... told what lies behind the door," Nerbino said. "We were only told ... that it was a great power and could never be released."

"Blood magic. Wait a minute," Forester said. "Everyone out there is sick, right?"

"Yeah, we established that," Groundquake said.

"Well, don't you think it's strange that the door can only be opened by blood that's normally toxic? And that every gremlin is sick and even more toxic right now?"

"You think that ... this sickness is somehow linked ... to opening the door?" Nerbino asked

"No," Groundquake said. "It has to be royal blood."

"Which is nothing more than a name," Thunderer said.

"Then ... we must make safe the door," Nerbino said, slowly getting up. "Guards ... remain here ... as I escort the knights."

XIX

"My name is Hiro. My order has guarded the item for many centuries," the head monk said as he led Firesprite and Wavecrasher into the temple (the others quickly left for other sections).

"Did they tell you what it was?" Wavecrasher asked.

"No. We only know it is behind a—"

"Another huge door," Firesprite finished.

"Yes. There are others?" the monk said in shock.

"Three, apparently," the lizard said.

"We … had no idea," the monk replied.

"We didn't even know about them," Wavecrasher said. "So why do the vampires want yours?"

"I do not know," Hiro said. "They have been kept away by the sacred nature of the grounds until now. But now they can come after us, as long as they do not touch the ground," Hiro explained. "But I have an idea as to why."

"Good, because I'm— *Gahhh*!" Crash yelled. She whipped around, drew her trident, and pointed it at … a small fox that had its tail on her leg.

"Calm down, mate. I don't think you need to drown it," Firesprite said.

"It … startled me, that's all. And why is there a fox here anyway?"

"A stray that wondered in a few years ago," Hiro said as he reached into his robes and withdrew a small piece of food. The fox's ears perked up, and it came over to the monk, who tossed the food into its mouth.

"Does she have a name?" Crash asked.

"No. Nothing seemed to fit," Hiro said.

"Very nice, but you said you had something to show us," Crash said.

"Yes, of course. This way," Hiro said, moving toward a large door to their right.

As the monk pushed the door open, the knights gasped in astonishment. The room was full of cots, and on each one was a person moaning in pain.

"What happened to them?" Firesprite asked as Crash rushed in. Kneeling next to the closest person, the cat looked over the pale body as Hiro spoke.

"They said that something had gotten into their food, destroyed all of it. And then the vampires came."

"And drained them dry," Firesprite said.

"We have tried to contact help, but all our phones lines are down. We have given them what food we can and hoped their blood will regenerate."

"It won't; they haven't lost any blood," Crash answered. "Look."

Hiro and the lizard quickly came over. Crash was pointing to two holes on the man's neck. "Here's the bite marks from a vampire," the cat said. "But there's no blood trails, no signs of healing or draining, nothing. And I can sense from his water levels that the right amount of blood is still in his body."

"So what does that mean?"

"It means that a vampire bit this person but took no blood. And yet, as far as I can tell, this man is suffering from some kind of anemia."

"But you said the vamps got nothing out of these people?"

"Not a drop. Which means we can't heal them, because it isn't actual blood loss."

"How can these people have anemia without losing any blood?" Firesprite said as she gazed at the man lying on the cot.

"The best I can figure is that something is keeping their bodies from getting the nutrients blood carries," Wavecrasher replied.

"But why would the vamps hang around?" the lizard asked.

"We have given shelter to those they would feed on," Hiro replied.

"Then we have got to get these people well and then get them out of here," Firesprite said. "Any ideas on that, doc?"

"I'd need to get a closer look at their blood to know," Wavecrasher said. "Where's the nearest hospital?"

"Aiiku Hospital is the closest major one," the monk replied. "It is several miles away, however."

"Just give me the directions and I'll get there," Crash said.

"Sounds good to me," Firesprite said.

"No, it's best I go alo…what?"

"You know more about medical equipment and if we both leave, then this place is unprotected. Besides, vampires hate fire a lot more then they hate water."

"I will give you the directions from here," Hiro said.

Crash nodded as she gave the lizard a look of surprise. Hiro recited the directions, placing the temple about fifteen miles south of Aiiku.

"Good. Now I just need some blood," the cat said. She knelt near one of the people on the cots. She drew her trident and placed one of the spines on the man's arm. Moving carefully, she made a small but deep cut. Blood began to well up instantly, and the cat reached into her pockets and withdrew a small beaker.

"You carry that around with you all the time?" Firesprite asked.

"Always be prepared," Crash answered as she collected some of the man's blood. Placing it back into her coat, she then closed her eyes. Her body began to evaporate and she rose up into the air and then vanished from sight.

A second later, she reappeared a second later in a Tokyo alley. The cat quickly pulled up her mask, went up to the wall, and peered out. The huge orange outline of a building greeted her at the end of the alley, the word *Aiiku* glaring out in huge red letters on a nearby signpost.

"Now I just have to get in," 'Crash muttered as she looked around.

The street was fairly quiet, but she couldn't take the risk of being seen. The glamour wouldn't let her just walk into the hospital rooms looking for the equipment. Evaporating could work, but she could only do it for a few seconds with her teleport. If it had been raining, she might've been able to change into water and cling to someone's coat, but now she needed to improvise. Crash quickly glanced back into the alley, looking for anything that might be of use to her. But there was no manhole cover, and while there was a pipeline here, it didn't connect to the hospital network. Muttering further under her mask, the cat then glanced into the street, but the sewers were closed to her there as well. At this rate, she would have to risk turning into a puddle and slithering across the street.

Suddenly, Crash noticed a strong scent coming from the building nearby. She breathed in deeply, taking the odor in. She could smell jasmine and honey and … steam. And in Japan, that could only mean one thing—a tea shop. The cat smiled then as she looked at the pipeline once more, examining it for the slightest crack. After a few moments, she found one—a hairline fracture in the pipe, one so small that no one would have seen it. It was tight, but it would do.

Her entry secure, Wavecrasher turned over to the street. Sure enough, she could see a pair of nurses walking to the shop, a list in the male nurse's hand. Crash smiled, even as her body began to turn translucent. When she had completely shifted, the cat stopped holding her form and poured her liquid body into the crack in the pipe. She flowed inside the pipe, merging with the water inside, (which was tremendously clean after the water systems she'd encountered in New York). Her consciousness spread out through the liquid, and Crash followed as it moved through the building's waterlines. She could sense the water in every direction, pulling her as water was poured out. Crash followed the pull, and a sliver of light began to grow in the distance. When it was almost all consuming, she halted her flow, and tentatively sent a tendril of water out, along with a large piece of her consciousness. Once it passed the light, Crash was looking at a room filled with men and women, porcelain and Styrofoam cups, the smell of herbs, and several strips of paper being handed off. She'd reached the kitchen.

Crash pulled the tendril back just as one of the employees reached above her and turned a knob. The water around Crash flowed down, and she went with it, through a filtering device and then collected into a teapot. She felt the sensation of being moved and then of being placed upon something. Crash knew what was coming next, as the temperature began to rise. The water swiftly began to boil, but even as much of it turned to steam, Crash kept her essence intact, allowing her temperature to rise but keeping her form liquid. There was a piercing whistle, and then the heat abated as the kettle was moved again. Crash moved around with the water. The light came again, and she felt herself being poured outward. There was a brief second of freefall, and then she collected herself again as she felt and smelled jasmine mixing with her being. As the water level rose, she was moved again, and she carefully sent out the tendril again. She was in a paper container with other cups of teas. She saw the front of the shop and the counter where the two nurses were waiting.

Crash counted herself lucky; the two nurses paid for their tea, picked up her container, and then turned and started to walk back to the hospital. Now it was just a matter of getting to the lab.

XX

"SO WHAT HAPPENED? COME on, tell me!"

"Tina, there's nothing more to tell. Just like yesterday," Sara said as she put on her name tag.

"I don't get it," Tina said. "A guy like that comes here, catches you, takes you out on a date, and then doesn't call back. What's going on?"

"First off, it wasn't a date," Sara said as they walked out onto the floor. "We just talked about Ray Bradbury books and had coffee. Second, I didn't leave him my number. Third, I have no reason to hold my breath yet."

"Too bad. He seems really cool and … unique."

"Don't you mean mysterious?" Sara smirked.

"Well, that too," Tina said. "But come on, aren't you a little curious about him?"

"A little, sure," Sara answered as they reached a cart full of books. She began to push it over to the nearby shelf. "But I have other things to do."

"Come on, this even feels like something out of a story," Tina said. "The guy saves you at work, takes you out—"

"Those stories *are* just stories. They never happen in real life, and I have too much to worry about as it is."

"Oh, so romances never happen, but all those sci-fi stories you read have so much more weight?" Tina asked.

"No, but at least some of them can make some kind of message."

"Like black people on Mars."

"Right, Mark, like black people …" Sara said, suddenly turning around to see Mark standing before her.

"Sorry, didn't mean to startle you," he said with a grin.

"No, no, that's okay," Sara said.

"Hi, Mark," Tina said. "We met the other day, I'm—"

"Tina, I remember," Mark said. "Sara thought that she'd fallen on you."

"Right. So did you come here to make sure she's okay and everything?"

"Uh, the truth is, I was hoping she could help me find a new Bradbury to read. I pretty much burned through the last one."

"They're this way," Sara said.

"I'll help you!" Tina said.

"Uh, thanks, but I think that we can handle it. Besides, I think you might be needed elsewhere," Mark said, pointing behind her. As Tina turned to see an old man waving a hand holding a James Patterson novel, Mark and Sara quickly headed off in the opposite direction.

"Nice job," Sara said.

"I could tell you weren't in the mood for her to come along. Was the other night a problem with her?"

"Oh, no, that was fine," Sara said as they reached the sci-fi section. "It was you not coming back until today that made her keeping asking about it."

"Oh. Sorry."

"Hey, don't feel bad," Sara said as she scanned the shelf for the B's. "I wasn't sitting around waiting for you to come back."

"No, you don't strike me as the kind of woman that would."

"Too bad Tina doesn't get that. Probably thought that after having coffee we'd be moving in together … Ah, here we go."

"And what do we have here?" Mark said as Sara handed him the book. "*Golden Apples of the Sun?*"

"It's a collection of his short stories from magazines and everything else," Sara said. "I think a few of his *Twilight Zone* episodes are in there too."

"He got that far with his stories?"

"Mm-hm."

"Then I will be enjoying this," Mark said. He tucked the book under his arm. "And now, I was hoping you could help me with something else."

"Yes?"

"I'm looking to talk about Bradbury with an expert, in someplace that might serve more than coffee. You think you can help me with that?"

Sara raised her eyebrow and said, "Take you this long to script that?"

"Well, I did want to finish the book," Mark said.

"Uh-huh."

"Is that a yes?"

"I'm not convinced."

Mark was quiet then and said, "Fair enough. But I would like to talk to you again, at the very least. It's just food, I promise."

Sara was quiet for a second, which made Mark open his mouth to speak again. But before he could get a word out, Sara said, "I'm off Thursday night. Do you know what restaurant this will be at? Or do you need me to pick one for you?"

"I have a few ideas, but I don't know what you like," Mark said.

"Then we meet at The Carpe Diem. Think you can make time for it?"

"Yes."

"Good. Then you'll find me there at six," Sara said. "Just do two things."

"Name them."

"Don't be late. And if you see Tina, keep quiet about this."

"Yes, ma'am."

"Then have a good day and enjoy your book sir."

"I shall," Mark said as he tipped an imaginary hat and walked away. Sara watched him move through the store (taking care to avoid Tina) and smiled a little.

XXI

THE RAIN CONTINUED TO *fall. The Architects and the being watched in silence. Joe watched as the ground became mud, and Ralin continued to look up with annoyance at the dark skies. Finally, the being tapped Ruta on the shoulder and motioned to the heavens. The Architect snapped her fingers, and instantly, the waters stopped, the clouds vanishing. Ralin's expression improved as the Being walked onto the muddy ground and knelt. It motioned for Chirron to come forth. The Architect did so and, following instruction from the being, held out his hand before the ground, his fingertips beginning to glow. The being then moved over and drove Chirron's fingers into the muddy ground.*

For a moment, nothing happened. Joe and the Architects both looked on. Then suddenly, the ground began to shake as a ring of energy pulsed through the ground from Chirron's hand. The energy spread across the entire landscape, and more rings began to pulse. Joe waited for something to happen, but all he saw before him was the same empty land. But then he felt something pushing under his feet. He raised one foot and gasped; new grass pushed its way out of the ground.

Cries from the Architects then filled the air; all around them, grass and plants sprang up out of the ground. Trees erupted from the earth, their branches growing out and sprouting leaves within seconds. Flowers bloomed in an ocean of color. And the grass covered the land with a burst of green. Joe looked around dumbfounded as, all around him, the Garden of Eden bloomed into life.

The Architects were no less shocked. Ralin and all the others looked around like children. The being turned back to them. It called for their attention, and their chatter ceased instantly. The being walked over to a large patch of flowers, wading into them as carefully if it was walking onto a floor of glass. Gently, the being reached down and grasped the head of one of the flowers. The bloom shuddered a moment at the being's touch, and then something emerged. The being took it, released the flower, and then held up the object, motioning for the Architects to come closer. They did so, making sure to stay on the outskirts of the flower bed. Joe came over as well, just as the being lowered its hand and gave the Architects a look. The flower had produced a small golden orb, no bigger than a marble. The being motioned for the Architects to pluck a flower, though he gestured for Ralin to hold off. The other four looked at each other but quickly did as bidden, each one gently grasping a flower as the Being had done. And as had the one the being had touched, each flower produced a golden orb.

The being looked over each of them and then pointed to Chirron's orb. As the Architect of Earth watched, the orb began to glow with multicolored light. Startled, Chirron released his hold, but the orb stayed suspended in midair. Chirron looked up in surprise, but the being motioned for him to touch the orb again. Chirron paused but then rubbed his hands together and reached up, placing his hands around the orb. The multicolored lights stopped, to be replaced by a single flash of brown light. The orb then split apart, and the light spewed outward, traveling to the ground and slowly taking a form. Something large began to form, a form of power and strength. The light began to change, becoming more solid and material, until it had achieved its final form—a great bear that took its first breath, snorted, and then looked around while Chirron stared in amazement.

The being smiled and then gestured to Ruta, Aeris, and Darya. The three Architects quickly followed suit, and bursts of blue, white, and red light flashed and reformed into a fish (which Ruta quickly placed into a sphere of water she summoned), a bird, and a lizard. The animals began to move around the land, the bird finding solace in the treetops, the bear by rolling in the dirt, and the lizard stretching on a warm piece of rock. Ruta held the fish steady however, until the being pointed to a small pit in the ground nearby. Ruta nodded and willed the water to flow from her hands into the pit, taking the fish with it. As the fish swam in the new pond, the being took not one but two flowers. Ralin, assuming they were for him started to reach for them, but the being stopped him with a gesture *as it activated the flowers. Again, there were orbs and bursts of light, but when the burst faded, even Joe felt his jaw drop.*

Two creations stood there. Their bodies were covered in dark hair, and they slumped forward, leaning on their great knuckles. Their faces were free of hair, but dark and wrinkled, with flat noses and large teeth. Ralin stared at the creature with a mix of surprise and disgust, even as the apes looked around with what appeared to be curiosity, unlike the other animals.

But while Ralin was confused and disgusted by the apes, the being had no such reservations. He walked over to the two apes, holding both his hands out. They paused in their search, and upon seeing the being, shambled over to him. It smiled at them and gestured for them to take its hands. The apes hesitated a moment and then gingerly reached out and took the hands offered. The being held them a moment and then gestured for Ralin to come take them.

The Architect was slow to move, but did make his way over and, slowly stretching out his hands, took each hand from the being. But the touch was enough. Both apes began to glow. Their bodies began to contract, shrinking on themselves even as their legs began to lengthen. Their dark hair vanished, their faces smoothed out, and hair began to grow atop their heads. Within moments, the two apes, their bodies now smooth and tan, stood atop their two legs and turned to face the Architects.

Joe had no words to speak. He now knew man and woman had been willed to life from the power of the being, evolved by the power of Light. He watched as the first humans looked upon the Architects, who stared back in wonder at what their master and Ralin had made. The Light Architect's revulsion was gone; now he stared at the humans with pride. Joe moved in to look closer, but then he felt the eyes of the being upon him once more ...

*   *   *

Joe snapped awake with a gasp. He breathed in deeply, trying to think about what he had seen. If this dream was even the slightest hint of the truth, then what it did mean about man? And what of the

Architects? Why had Rastla not been present at humanity's birth? What was the being's purpose in even bringing that race to life?

The Being. That was the real question. Joe's breathing slowed as he focused on it. He'd always assumed after meeting the Architects that they were the end all, the gods people prayed to. But now, he'd seen a power that more than dwarfed them; it had created them. And he and the others had never heard even a word about it. Why? Did the being no longer exist? And if it didn't, where had it gone? Had it faded away? Or had the Architects somehow overpowered it, and taken the world for themselves?

Joe shook his head at that; he doubted that something capable of destroying the Chaos Demons and creating existence could be dethroned so easily. The Architects had seemed worshipful of the being anyway. But speculating on it wasn't going to help anything. The books were of no help, and if the Architects hadn't spoken by now, it seemed unlikely they would.

But before he resumed his dreaming, Joe needed to do his duty and check up on the others. Taking the crystal from his pocket, he peered into it, focusing on the knights. Everything seemed in order. Stalker was moving through the hunters' headquarters, Quake was making his way through the hobgoblin kingdom, Forger was speaking with a man in the forest, and Firesprite was inside a stone temple. Joe paused, and then took a closer look at the bat.

XXII

"Hunst's move to the sunlight room has been finalized then?" Nelson asked as he looked over the assignments on the desk before him.

"Yes, sir," Kurt replied. The two of them stood in the complex's command room, a large metallic room filled with monitors and a central map of the city behind the desk where Nelson sat. A computer sat there as well, along with hard documents in a large file cabinet holding hunter placements and other information.

"I always assumed we'd be using that place to protect innocents, not to shelter a mad hunter." Nelson sighed.

"Shouldn't we at least hope Hunst can recover? He has so much potential—"

"We've lied about that long enough," Nelson said. "When this threat has passed, he will be released."

"But, sir—"

"He has brought down the Elementals once already," Nelson said, cutting off his subordinate. "I can't risk this organization and its secrecy on a loose cannon."

Kurt looked like he might speak but stopped and nodded his agreement.

Nelson sighed and leaned back in the chair. "I had such hope for that boy once. But instead, his anger took over his world after his wife ..."

Kurt said nothing. He simply stood by. Nelson rose and walked over to the map of New York City behind him. As he looked at it, he said, "What do you plan to tell the other Hunters?"

"Why they need to remember mercy, sir."

"Very good," Nelson said. He looked at the map. "Blood, sweat, and tears mark every point on this map. We must make sure that they aren't spent in vain."

"I'll make sure of it," Kurt replied.

Nelson nodded, and then the two men walked out of the room. As the door locked behind them, the vent above it began to shake. Slowly, a black mist drifted down. As it reached the floor, it began to solidify, black-clad legs and a coat appearing from the mist, along with blazing red eyes. Within seconds, Nightstalker had fully formed inside the room.

"Thought they'd never leave," he muttered to himself. He moved over to where the computer was. Opening the search option, the Shadow Knight quickly typed in "sunlight room." The computer hummed for a few seconds, only to come up with, "No file available."

Stalker shook his head, and then went into the documents, also pulling open the drawers and checking every file he could find for information on the sunlight room. But all he found were dossiers on the various hunters and locations of vampire dens.

"Smart man, Nelson," the bat said as he shut the drawer. "I'll bet you're the only one who knows where the place is."

"Then again," Stalker added as he saw the map of the city. What had Nelson said? Blood, sweat, and tears had gone into the map. In other words, plenty of heart.

The bat approached the map and drew his sword. Holding it before the map, he said, "Show me that which is hidden."

The sword sparked, and shadowfire leaped from the hilt. It spread across the map, leaving small pieces of shadowfire across the map. But there were too many spots to examine and no way to determine which one was the room.

"I don't have time for this," Stalker muttered. "There's got to be a better ... Right, there is."

The bat reached into the dark folds of his coat, and with a grimace, pulled out Joe's staff. He held the weapon out in front of him, waving his free hand to remove the shadowfire. Holding out the staff, he said, "Show me where the light burns."

The staff immediately began to shine. Stalker tried to avert his eyes. He could feel his hand starting to burn, even under his gloves. But he held on as a beam of light shot from the staff and attached itself to a spot on the map. The light died away, and Stalker put the staff back into the dark. Moving to the map, he looked at the space where the light glowed. He grabbed a paper and pen from the desk, jotted the coordinates down, and quickly vanished into the shadow, even as the light on the map faded with him.

XXIII

"How did the gremlins get this door anyway?" Forester asked as he made his way down the tunnel with the others.

"It is ... an old story," Nerbino said, wheezing even as Groundquake held him up. "The Architects needed a place to hide ... great power, and they saw ... we were strong enough ... to hold it."

"The story says that we would be utterly destroyed should these doors ever open," Hazari explained. "Rastla gave the king at that time a vision of what would happen."

"He was that scared of what he saw?" Thunderer asked.

"The king was unconscious for six days, and his skin went pure white."

"Ah can't imagine how all this could get any better," Forester said as the group turned the corner into the next part of the tunnel.

"I barred the entrance ... after the last encounter," Nerbino said. The group turned the corner and finally arrived in the large room where the door was kept. As they looked, they saw that the huge pile of stone in which Groundquake had buried the door was still in place.

"Looks good to me," Quake said as he looked over his handiwork.

"Yeah, because stone would never, ever crack," Forester said.

"Hey, you don't think I know my own work?" Quake said. "That thing's as solid as the day I made it."

"It still wouldn't hurt to look," Thunderer said.

"Fine. But I'll do it," the dog growled. Holding out his free hand, he closed his eyes as the rocks began to glow brown. As the dog scanned the stone for any sign of cracks or breakage, his hand glowed as well.

Finally, he withdrew his power, turned to the others, and gave his report. "Solid. Now who deserves an apology from the untrusting squirrel?"

"Fine, it's not the stone," Forester said. "But Ah still think something's wrong here."

"It's sealed away," Thunderer said. "The only way I can figure it to be a problem is if someone could siphon off the power."

"No," Hazari said. "No one like that has been here."

"We should check the stone," the squirrel answered. "Any volunteers?"

Nerbino grunted and, pushing off from Groundquake, shambled over to the stone. Gingerly, he stretched out his hand toward the barrier. Closing his eyes, the gremlin king slammed his hand down.

"Your Majesty …," Hazari gasped.

Nerbino's eyes went wide as he realized his hand was still on the supposedly evil resistant barrier. He pulled himself back and glanced down at his hand. The scales on it were slightly blackened, but he felt no real pain from it.

"This … is much worse than we thought," Thunderer declared. "We need to get Joe here."

Nerbino nodded, though just before nearly falling again. But this time, Forester caught him and helped him up. As he did, he called out, "Call Joe and get him down here, now."

*   *   *

But Joe already knew. The dreams and their meaning would have to wait; the need of the gremlins was far more important. Gathering his coat around him, Joe got up and started toward the door, his mind already working on what could have weakened the light in the stone. The gremlins couldn't have done it, no other demon knew of the doorway, and no being of light would want to release the danger inside. That left just one possibility, and if the Chaos Demons could do something to eliminate light, then their problems were even greater than he had imagined.

As he opened the door to the Nexus, Joe prayed he was wrong. But instead of stairs, he saw black clothes standing before him and heard a voice saying, "Hello, Joe. I need your help."

"That seems to be the order of the day," Joe said. He stepped back, and Nightstalker walked inside. "The others need me in Miami."

"The gremlins need light?"

"Yes. But what's happened with you? I thought my staff would be enough to help you."

"It was. It led me to where Hunst was being kept. But there was a problem when I got there."

"What?"

"First, the hunters are either geniuses or totally insane. Of all the places they could have constructed the sunlight room, I would never have expected ..."

* * *

"A high school," Stalker muttered as he looked out on Petrides High School, a large, multi-windowed school in Staten Island.

The dark night masked the bat as he moved across the front of the school to the entrance. He didn't even bother trying the doors; instead, he simply changed to shadow and slipped through them, reforming on the other side. He took a quick look around the building and then reached into the darkness of his coat and pulled out Joe's staff. Stalker took a breath to prepare himself and then held it up and said, "Show me where the light burns."

The staff glowed instantly. As Stalker fought the pain, it flashed once, and then a wisp of light flew down the nearby hallway. Stalker nodded, put the staff back into the shadow, and followed the light down the hallway. It curved about and then came to a halt. The bat caught up to it and saw that it had stopped right in front of the janitor's closet. He gingerly put out his hand and grasped the knob. When it didn't burn him, Stalker turned it and pulled the door open to see...

A closet full of mops, cleaning supplies, and a basin sink?

Stalker looked a moment and then turned to the light and said, "I'm starting to be glad I got shadow." The wisp responded by disintegrating.

"Great move, Stalker, piss off the help," the bat muttered as he looked about the closet. He searched the tiny room, hoping for any sign that would lead him to the entrance to the sunlight room. But all he saw was bottles of bleach, mop heads, cleaning fluid, a wheeled bucket, and the leaky faucet of the sink.

But if there was one thing that Nightstalker knew, it was illusion. He went to the bottles of bleach first, moving each one to find nothing. He then moved around the mop and bucket and then the cleaning fluid, but still nothing. Finally, Stalker went to the sink. He first twisted the knobs and head and then tried pushing down on them. But none of his attempts made any impact.

Stalker snorted in frustration and actually slapped the leaky faucet head. As the drops fell, Stalker suddenly felt inspiration and looked into the drain as the water fell into it. He could hear it drain away, but as he looked down the drain, the bat could see a small bump sticking out of the side of the drain. Reaching down with his finger, Stalker fiddled with the bump, first trying to push it down and then pushing it in.

That did it. There was a click, and the floor behind the bat pulled away, revealing a set of stairs. Stalker pulled his finger from the drain and then quickly began to walk down the stairs. But he had barely gotten halfway down when he suddenly had to pull up his hands and shield his face; light burst from every corner. Stalker could feel his body burning, but still he pressed on, wrapping himself in his coat as much as he could. But even inside that protection, he could feel his body heating up. The pain grew worse, but still he pressed on. He reached into his own power and threw out a wall of shadow to try to buy some time. But the wall was eaten away by the light in seconds. He tried to gaze out into the light, and through the brightness, he saw the outline of a door. He tried to reach for it, but his hand had already begun to blister and burn. Pulling back at last, Stalker vanished into his own shadow, the only darkness in the room. As the coolness of the dark washed over him and healed his burns, the bat knew that he now had only one option to get inside.

"All that in a high school," Joe said as the bat finished his tale. "One of them must be in charge there. But of all the insane places …"

"It only has students during the day, and nobody would want to attack for fear of exposure."

"Maybe, but I don't like it."

"The bigger problem is how we can get inside," Stalker said. "That light is so bright that I don't even know if a human could make it through without being blinded."

"And the staff won't allow you enough control to use it to diffuse the light," Joe said.

"Then you'll come with me."

"Not yet," Joe said. "I need to help the gremlins first."

"I need to get to Hunst, Joe. If his mind is any indication—"

"The door has lost its light, Stalker," Joe said. "If I don't recharge it, it could release whichever of the Equites behind it."

"The door lost its light?" Stalker asked in disbelief.

"Yes. And it looks like the gremlins have some sort of plague hitting them."

"Go then. I can wait," the bat said.

"Good. Hopefully this won't take long," Joe said. "You can check out the high school again in the meantime. Maybe there's something there that can help you get through."

"Fine," Stalker said. "But wait a second."

The bat reached out into the shadows and pulled out Joe's staff. Handing it back to him, he said, "You're gonna need this more than I do."

Joe nodded, took the staff, and said, "Petrides High School, right?"

"Right."

"I'll be there as soon as I can," Joe said as he vanished in a stream of light, heading right up to the Nexus.

Simultaneously, Stalker vanished back into the shadow once again.

XXIV

"Two more minutes," Sara said, standing outside the pub as she glanced down at her watch. She'd been outside for the last thirteen minutes, shivering in the cold night air as she waited for Mark. Thus far, she was slowly losing the feeling in her feet and rolling her eyes at more than a few looks from the men walking the street. She wore a sleeveless black shirt under her coat, along with a belt with a well-proportioned but not garish circle buckle, a sleek pair of jeans, and the only pair of black heeled boots she owned. Add that to the makeup job, and the unwanted looks were bound to start. But Sara ignored that as she looked down the street once more and started to count down the last thirty seconds.

"I haven't kept you waiting have I?"

"Where did you come from?" Sara said, as Mark had appeared right next to her as if he'd drifted in on the wind.

"I have my ways," Mark said with a smile. He was dressed in a black coat, with khakis and what looked to be leather shoes. "And I got held up at work."

Sara snorted and then said, "Fine, you're here. Can we go inside now?"

"By all means," Mark said, holding open the door as Sara walked inside. He followed her. The hostess gave Sara a wave and then grabbed two menus and quickly led them to a table.

"They seem to like you here," Mark said as they sat down.

"I've been here a few times," Sara said. "Thanks, Pam."

"Clearly," Mark said as the hostess walked off. "Must be good food. Or do you just like the atmosphere?"

"And what does that mean?" Sara snapped. "What, do you think I'm a lush too?"

"I'm sorry, I—"

"Don't. I'm just fucking with you," Sara said with a laugh.

Mark stared at Sara, then grinned and asked, "Do you do that with everyone you bring here?"

"Sometimes," Sara said. "My dad was big on finding authentic Irish pubs. He already knew all the ones back home in Denver, so he really only did it when we took vacations. He wasn't a drinker, he just liked the atmosphere. Of course, Mom thought he just liked beer too much. They argued about that almost as much as they argued about me."

"Oh? Were you a problem child?"

"Oh yeah, I sacrificed children to Satan in my basement."

"Explains a lot."

"Hmph," Sara said as the waitress came by to take their drink order. After she left, Mark asked, "So what were the problems?"

"Mixed religions mostly. I did both for a long time—bat mitzvah and confirmation. But frankly, I just stopped seeing any real difference when I was a teenager. Mom would've flipped out hearing that, though, so I went with being Jewish."

"I'm not sure I've heard of an Irish Jew."

"There are more of us than you think," Sara said as the drinks arrived. "What about you? What's your family like?"

"Pretty big," Mark said. "Lots of brothers and sisters and somewhat distant parents."

"Too bad," Sara said as she took a sip. "Must've been hard growing up."

"My mom did do a lot for us. She always focused on what needed to be done for everyone's good," Mark said, "not that we always listened."

"Oh, so you weren't a golden boy either?"

"Far from it," Mark said. "But none of us were."

"You did all right; said you did bank work didn't you? What do they do?"

"Cooks, doctors, researchers, electricians, the list goes on."

"Impressive," Sara said. "And your mother?"

"She hasn't been on Earth in a long time."

"I'm sorry."

"Don't be," Mark said. "We all just try to live the way she would want."

"I know what that's like," Sara said.

"Oh?"

"My mother and I ... Actually, I don't want to go down that road right now," Sara said. "Why don't we get ready to order?"

"Okay," Mark said as he picked up his menu and started to look it over. "Any suggestions?"

"I'd go for the burger," Sara answered. "It's so good I don't even have to look anymore."

"Hmm ... I think I'll get the pulled pork."

"Oh, you *suck*, you know that?"

"If you want, you can eat steak in front of me on Fridays during Lent."

"If you're Catholic, I'll just make you feel guilty about this. Shouldn't take long."

XXV

"So something is actively working against you and the wolves," Forger said as the knights and Johan convened on the southernmost part of the hill, far from the townsfolk.

"I can't imagine what," Johan said. "Other than the werewolves, there have been no other supernatural creatures in this area."

"That you know of," Sandshifter said. "Windy, what do you think?"

"Me?" the falcon asked in surprise.

"Yes. What would steal wolf cubs and human children in this part of the world?"

"Uh … well, maybe vampires," Windrider said.

"Impossible. Vampires have not been in this land for centuries," Johan said.

"And why couldn't they be here now?" Sandshifter asked.

"Why would they come so far?" Forger replied. "Werewolf and human children wouldn't be useful as new vampires."

"Valkyries!" Windrider said suddenly.

"What?" Sandshifter said.

"The handmaidens of Valhalla, from Norse mythology," Forger said. "Their task was to select the bravest warriors to enter their halls."

"That's Viking legend! What would they be doing in Germany?" Sandshifter asked.

"We have stories of Odin as well," Johan said. "But I can't see what the Valkyries would want with children either."

"Maybe the best thing to do is check areas with otherworldly history," Forger said. "Is there anywhere here like that, Johan?"

"The forest," the mayor answered. "The townsfolk have told stories about beings of magic living there for generations."

"Then we'll go there," Forger said, standing up. "The three of us can examine the woods and see if anything is there. At the very least, we might find some clues."

"Fine," Sandshifter said. "But now I actually wish that—"

The wolf stopped and looked over Johan's shoulder. The others turned and saw Paul standing there behind the mayor.

"Is there something we can help you with?" Johan asked.

"Some of the men are talking, sir," Paul said. "They say since the werewolves are still out there, we should return to the town and arm ourselves."

"The wolves won't be a problem," Johan said. "And I doubt that any of the men are in a mood to go and see their homes burned to a crisp at the moment."

"They would still feel better with some kind of protection from those monsters."

"You get those weapons now, and they'll take it as a violation of our word," Forger said. "They'll be all over you, and we'll never find out who's taking your children."

"I already know who's doing that," Paul sneered.

"The wolves have no reason to lie," Johan said. "Tell the men they are not to leave the hill tonight."

"But if it's safe, then we can go back!"

"Oh, so now you think it's safe?" Sandshifter asked. "Now you trust the wolves' word?"

"I wouldn't trust a word from those filthy beasts," Paul retorted. "But apparently you do ... *sister.*"

"What are you talking about?" Johan said.

"I heard them talking before they set the wolf loose. I heard what he said to her."

"Right. That's why I let them fucking eat you, *gilipollas,*" Sandshifter sneered, moving closer to Paul. "I'm trying to help you, but if you wanna face them on your own, fine by me."

"Sandy, enough," Forger said.

"I'm sure you'd like your family to get me, wouldn't you?" Paul snapped. "What, can't you take me on yourself?"

The wolf didn't reply but let out a growl from under her mask.

Both Johan and Paul started at the sound, and Forger and Windrider move toward Sandshifter. But before they got there, Paul had already regained his composure, and drawing back his fist, he let loose a blow. Sandshifter easily deflected it, but Paul reached over with his free hand and grabbed at her mask. She pulled away instantly, but Paul still found himself with a handful of sand. He looked at it in confusion, and then looked up and gasped, as Sandshifter's exposed wolf face growled at him.

"Oh, crap," Windrider said.

Paul backed away in horror, his hand raising up as he shouted. "Monster! I knew it! All of you are freaks! Stealers of children! Wolves!"

"Shut up, you idiot!" Sandshifter snarled.

"Filthy, stinking, werewolf!"

"Fine then, I'll shut you up myself." The wolf growled as she stretched out her hand. The hand exploded outward, transforming into a sandy mass that covered Paul's mouth. His screams reduced to muffles, he still continued to make noise however.

"Jesus, enough!" Windrider yelled.

"Not yet," Sandshifter sneered.

"Let him go right now," Forger demanded.

But the wolf gave no answer, and Paul kept clawing.

Then Johan spoke. "Sandshifter, I want to believe that you and your friends will find the children for both us humans and the werewolves and destroy whatever has taken them. But if you want me to believe that, you can't let your anger make you harm a foolish but innocent man."

All three watched as Sandshifter stood there quietly. Finally, she sighed and pulled back her arm. The sand followed, pulling away from Paul's face as he fell forward. He took a great few whooping breaths and then looked up with a glare at Sandshifter.

"Don't say a word," Johan said. "I am not in the mood for any more of your foolishness."

"She ... tried to kill me!" Paul snapped.

"She silenced you because you egged her on!" Johan snapped back. "We need their help. Unless *you* want to go looking for your son again? You barely survived the last time."

"His son?" Sandshifter said.

"Yes. The boy was one of the first taken," Johan said. "Paul spent many nights traveling the woods, until he found a pack of wolves, regular ones. He still wanted to search though."

"I ... I," Sandshifter sputtered, but Paul just got up and stomped away.

Johan turned back to the others and asked, "What about you two? I know your intentions, but I prefer open alliances."

Forger and Windrider looked at each other and then nodded. Both of them removed their masks, and Forger's arms emerged from inside her coat.

Johan took a step back at the sight but kept his gaze steady. "What ... what are all of you?"

"We can't tell you that," Forger said. "But I can tell you that we are here to find your children and whatever is responsible for taking them."

"This has been a strange and terrible night," Johan said. "But I suppose that means strange solutions are necessary."

"Thank you," Forger said, tipping her hat, while Windrider grinned and gave the Vulcan salute.

The two knights turned toward the forest, pulling Sandshifter with them. As they moved along, Forger leaned over and whispered, "Joe is going to talk with you about that when we get back."

But the wolf gave no response. She merely kept up with the others as they prepared to enter the forest.

XXVI

THE TWO INTERNS WALKED back into the hospital, carrying the trays of tea between them. The white walls glimmered in the sunlight, patients were wheeled around the linoleum floors, and the loudspeaker blared announcements. Two attendants sat at the large front desk, entering new information into their computers. One of them briefly looked up, saw the two interns, and then waved them over, gesturing for the tea they'd been promised. The interns quickly moved over, and after a few moments, they sorted through the drinks to hand the attendants their tea. One of them quickly took a drink, while the other set it down to finish an entry. As both of them were occupied, the still unopened tea holder suddenly rocked back and forth, popping its lid and spilling out onto the floor. The attendant still entering data felt something hot splash his leg and let out a curse as he saw his spilled tea on the ground. The other attendant saw the spill and quickly moved to get some paper towels from under the desk.

As he did so, the water on the floor began to move, slithering forward across the floor. Even as doctors and patients came into its way, the water deftly moved around them, until it reached a large pillar in the center of the floor. It paused a moment and then began to climb the polished surface, until it reached the map encased behind the glass. It quickly ran over the glass, glancing over every location it had (written in both Japanese and English) until it reached one that said, "Med lab." The water stood there a moment and then quickly slid back down the pillar and reached the floor. It slithered back across the hall, until it reached the central corridor, where it went forward, paused, turned left, and slithered under a door with the silhouette of a woman imprinted on it.

*   *   *

"How long has it been?" Hiro asked.

"Twenty minutes," Firesprite answered as she glanced at the sick people on the cots. "She can't just walk into the lab."

"Yes of course," Hiro said, running his hands though his hair. "But I have an idea."

"What do you mean?"

"Crash'll spend hours in that hospital, trying everything she can think of, looking for answers," the lizard replied. "She'll probably ignore the most basic solution without even trying it."

"You mean the 'healing' you mentioned earlier?" Hiro said.

"Not entirely," Firesprite said as she moved over to the nearest cot. "I think I can reverse the disease, at least for a while. Do you have any matches?"

"What?"

"Matches, lighters, two sticks. Anything that can start a fire."

"Y-Yes."

"Then get them," Firesprite demanded. She spread her hands over the chest of the man lying on the cot. A golden flame spread out from her hands, and she brought them down onto the man's chest. Instantly, he bucked up, but the lizard forced him back down as she fed her healing flame into his body. She felt resistance almost instantly but kept pressing on, forcing the flame to burn the blockage away, slowly but surely, until …

*   *   *

In the surgery wing of the hospital, two doctors stood by the sanitary sinks, scrubbing up. They made a few seconds of small talk and then shut the water off and made their way into the surgery. As the doors shut, the faucets suddenly began to turn, and water flowed into the sink. It gathered there, holding in a puddle despite the drain. It slithered forward, moving over the edge of the basin and then falling onto the floor. It splattered on the tile and then pulled itself together and began to move again on its own, traversing the floor like a snake. The personnel, caught up in their own hustle and bustle, didn't even notice it, as the water took pains to avoid any contact with the people. Finally, it came to a door near the end of the hall. It paused in front of it and then slid under the door, emerging on the other side.

The room was empty, except for diagrams depicting various anatomies; tables of beakers; microscopes; medical samples; and other medical equipment, including small and gigantic machines for data entry, analysis, and taking various samples from patients. The water took it in for a moment and then began to rise up, its liquid form growing more and more detailed as it reached up from the floor. Arms and legs began to develop, along with a body and head, until finally, Wavecrasher stood in the lab, whole once more.

"That was too tight a squeeze," the cat said, rubbing her shoulder as she moved over to one of the large, fax-like machines. Reaching into her coat pocket, Crash withdrew the vial of tainted blood as she turned the blood analyzer on. The machine hummed, and she opened the slot and poured in the tainted blood. Shutting it, she set the machine to scan the blood for various possible problems (even as she wondered how she knew how to do it). Crash finished and stood back, letting the machine do its work as she kept a nervous eye on the door. She knew that she would have an easy escape if it came to it, but she wanted to avoid detection at any cost.

Crash shook her head and breathed in deeply, letting the sterile smell of the room fill her nostrils. It comforted her—another strange holdover from whatever she'd been before. The cat looked around the room, musing on the fact that she might've worked in a place like this once. Hell, she could've worked in *this* place. It wouldn't be anything like the good she could do as a knight, but Crash wondered if …

A *ping* brought the cat out of her musings; she turned to see that the machine had finished its analysis. Crash looked at the screen and felt frustration build up in her gut. All the tests she'd run had come up negative; there was no sign of anything wrong with this blood. Crash sighed and rubbed her eyes, trying to think of something else she could do. But if the machine hadn't found anything wrong with the blood ...

She stopped rubbing. The machine had looked for the normal signs of blood alternation—platelet counts, white blood cells, infection, everything. And if those weren't there, then it meant that whatever was wrong with this blood wasn't physical. It had to be the one thing that would stump any doctor—*magic*.

Pulling open the slot, Wavecrasher removed the blood and grabbed a slide from nearby. Taking a cotton swab, she spread a little blood on the slide and placed it under the microscope. Peering through the lens, she zoomed in on the blood as much as possible. At first, she saw nothing. But as the cat watched, she saw the blood cells bump against each other. As they touched, there was a small burst of green energy and the cells quickly pulled away from each other.

"That's it!" the cat said with glee. It was magic, something that made the blood reject anything it came into contact with, even itself. It was no wonder those people had anemia; there was no way for their bodies to process the blood without causing damage to themselves.

But that didn't mean that there was a cure. Crash wouldn't be able to use the machines in the hospital for anything now; she'd need to study the magic and figure out what to do about reversing it.

Removing the slide, the cat gathered up the blood and poured it back into the vial before placing it back into her coat. Preparing to leave, she closed her eyes to begin the teleport—Just as the door to the med lab swung open.

XXVII

"HAVEN'T YOU ... CALLED him yet?"

"He's already been sent the message," Thunderer said to the group standing around the room.

"He'd better ... hurry," Nerbino wheezed.

"One thought on that. Do you think Joe can heal 'em?" Quake asked.

"It's possible," Thunderer said. "But..." the ram paused, then shook his head.

"Oh, yeah. You nearly blew the place up with thunder," Forester said.

"You did what?" a voice said in concert with a flash of gold. And Joe stood before them.

"See? Told you he was coming," Quake said to Nerbino.

"Your Highness," Joe said, turning to the gremlin. "I see things are as bad as I feared."

"Worse," Nerbino said. "My people's suffering ... will only increase if the door is opened. Seal it first, and then we ... can see what can be done."

"Stand back then," Joe said. He drew his staff and pointed it at the door. The lion's head glowed brightly, filling the room with shades of gold. Joe gathered the power a few minutes more, and then, as it gathered strength, he loosed it at the door. It flew through the air toward the door ...

And then faded away as it drew close.

The knights stared in disbelief. Joe gasped and then looked at his staff.

"Wha ... what just happened?" Thunderer asked. "Joe, did anything happen to—"

"No," Joe said. "I loaned the staff to Stalker for his mission, but it worked fine when he gave it back."

"Apparently not," Forester said. "Ah'm gonna go out on a limb and say he broke it."

"No, I would've known," Joe said as he walked over to the rocky doorway. He stretched out his hand and placed it on the stone. Concentrating, he gathered the light inside him and tried to force it into the stone. He could feel the power grow and travel within him, through his arm, into the very ends of his fingertips. But it would not leave him; it just stopped at his fingers, hovering between his gloved hand and the rock.

"I ... I can't explain it," Joe said as he turned back around. "But somehow, the rock is ... immune to light."

"That's impossible!" Thunderer said. "Isn't it?"

"So, now what do we do?" Groundquake asked.

"The same," Joe said. "You guys have to protect this door and help the gremlins. Hopefully, whatever solves one will be the solution to the other. Nerbino, is there anyone in your kingdom with access to magic?"

"A few," Nerbino answered. "But the amount of magic ... it would take to do something like this ... negate Light God magic ..."

"Ah'm gonna go out on a limb here and suggest that maybe we should round those people up," Forester said. "Unless anyone else has a better idea?"

"Fluffy Tail's right," Groundquake said. "It's the best idea we've got so far."

"But more than half the population is sick," Hazari said. "How could they summon such magic?"

"For all we know, this plague is a result of what they did to the door," Joe answered. "But we can't find out unless we bring them here."

"Two ... are in my court. The rest ... will need to be found," Nerbino said. "But ... I suspect I know ... where they are."

"Good. I'll return to the Obelisk and continue to monitor."

"What? You're ... leaving us?"

"Not by choice, Nerbino. But there are other matters that require my attention—matters as important as this one."

"Um, Joe," Thunderer whispered, moving to the Light Knight's side. "I know that Ralin told you to watch us, but this is really bad here. At the very least, you could help defend the door if need be."

"I hear you," Joe said. "But things are stable for the moment. And besides, I can use the library to find out about magic that could cause resistance to light. Plus," Joe said, biting his lip.

"What?"

"I've been making some discoveries in the library," Joe whispered. "I don't know what it all means yet, but I think it may relate to the Equites. If I keep reading—"

"Joe, I hear you, but are you sure about this? We've got some problems and you don't know for sure—"

"Believe me, its clear-cut. I'll look further into the wall and what might be resistant to the light, but I won't be able to stay."

Thunderer sighed, and said, "All right. I'll explain things to Nerbino, as much as I can."

"Thanks," Joe said. He turned to the Gremlin King, "Nerbino, I promise I will find out what is going on with your people and the door. You've trusted me before; you can do it again."

"I have. And I suppose … I have no choice," Nerbino wheezed. "Work quickly."

"I will. And I will return the second I can help," Joe said. With that, he vanished in a burst of light, leaving the knights and the disappointed gremlins behind.

*　　*　　*

Joe reemerged into the Obelisk, shaking his head briefly at the disorientation and then quickly turned toward the stairs. He knew that Stalker was still waiting for him back at the high school, but he couldn't go just yet. The only things that could resist light involved serious dark magic, and if he could trace it, it might give him an idea as to what was affecting the doorway, or if someone was helping the demons. So, as he headed down to the library, Joe held up his staff and concentrated on Stalker.

"Joe? You're on your way?"

"Not yet. Something came up with the gremlins," Joe said as the door to the library showed itself on his right.

"The gremlins are that big of a problem?"

"They've been hit by a plague. And the door was hit by something that cancelled out my light and made it resistant to me."

"Joe, the only ones who could do that are me, Rastla, or some serious black magic wizards."

"I know. I'm going to the library to check for a counterspell and see if the magic involved will reveal whoever did this. I know that Hunst is important, but—"

"It's all right. Hunst isn't going anywhere."

Joe stopped at that. Turning to the staff directly he said, "Stalker, are you sure?"

"That much dark magic going around is worse than anything Hunst could whip up."

"Are you sure you don't want me to come this time? I know how much this hurt you before."

"I can deal with it. Besides, I can do this easier on my own."

"Alright. Do you want to borrow the staff again?"

"Not right now. But I'll contact you if I do."

"Good hunting then," Joe said as he pushed open the door. Putting the bat's odd behavior on the back burner, Joe headed toward the books, remembering one in particular that Wavecrasher had used on a mission involving a magic trainee being overcome by a tome full of dark magic. It was a massive catalogue of the dark arts, and Joe suspected it would hold the answers this time as well. Heading over to where the tomes on dark magic were kept on the wall, Joe glanced through the titles, only to find the book's spot was empty.

"Of course. She would be rereading that one," Joe muttered as he turned to the massive table that Crash usually presided over. It was filled to the brim with books, stacked on each other in perfect order of their categories. Joe moved the piles quickly, going through linguistics, magical herbs, Russian folklore, and one book about the recipe for authentic Jack Daniels (*Must be Forester's*, Joe thought). But there was no tome of dark magic anywhere.

Sighing, Joe turned back to the door and began to head for the only other place where the book could be—the cat's room. But as Joe was about to leave, a thought popped into his head—perhaps the answers weren't just in the books. Maybe there could be an answer in the dreams he was having.

But Joe quickly shook his head. The dreams must mean something, but thus far, he didn't know what that was. And the gremlins couldn't afford for him to waste time dickering around. So he reached for the door handle and started to pull it open.

But as he did, Joe suddenly felt a wave of dizziness overtake him. He shook his head against it, but the feeling persisted. He held onto the door handle as he felt the room about him beginning to spin. He began to take slow, deep, breaths, but the feeling persisted. Feeling like he was a on a ship caught in a massive clothes dryer, Joe did the only thing he could think of. He let go of the door and gingerly began to make his way toward the nearest chair.

But even as he came closer to the chair, Joe felt the dizziness grow stronger. He could barely put one foot down in front of the other. He tried to press on, as the chair was now within his reach. But as he stretched his hands, the dizziness suddenly shifted into a short, but striking pain within his head. Joe grimaced against it and collapsed onto the floor, his hand still reaching out for the chair.

*   *   *

"Will he be all right?"

"He won't be harmed in that state," Rastla said as she watched Joe's fall. "But I suppose that's little comfort for you, is it?"

"I have accepted Joseph's departure," Ralin answered. "But that does not mean I care for it."

"The High God has need of such a man. And he has promised us a worthy replacement."

"Through your knight," Ralin said. "I admit, sister, I am bothered by the idea of having my representative chosen by a being of Shadow, even one as worthy as Nightstalker."

"You said you voiced your concerns to the High God, and he promised to respect them," Rastla said. "He knows of what we discussed when Joe was chosen. And when it is finished, the Elementals will have a greater force then we could imagine."

"But for what? I know the High God always has a higher purpose, but what would he gain from denying us this information?"

"I don't know. But we have always trusted him before. We shall have to do so now."

"Yes. Yes, we shall. Begin weaving the dream."

"It has already begun."

*   *   *

He awoke to find himself lying not on the stone floor of the Obelisk, but on a bed of dewy grass. Joe slowly pushed himself up, wiped the dew from his face, and looked about. This time, the dream hadn't brought him to a precreation world. Instead, Joe found himself in what looked like the Elysian Fields. All around him were seas of grass, with trees sprouting up out of the green depths. But it was not a forest, just random trees sprouting from the earth. And Joe could see buildings as well. They were large, stocky, and white, built not of metal and brick but of polished stone. The style reminded Joe of ancient Greece, with their large columns that held up the roofs and the intricate designs he could see engraved into the walls, even from here.

Joe moved forward to take a closer look, but as he did, a pair of voices made him turn around. Behind him were two children, a boy and a girl, laughing with each other as they ran toward the buildings. Their clothes were simple—lightly colored tunics, belted at the waist, and sandals upon their feet. Joe opened his mouth to speak to them, but instead they ran through him, not even realizing his presence.

"Dream. Right," Joe muttered to himself as he began to follow the children. It seemed that Crash had been right; these dreams weren't normal but some form of communication—which meant getting through the dream and discovering its meaning was the only option he had right now.

The two children stopped at a great statue at the foot of the building, where a large group of people had gathered. An older man, weathered and bearded, dressed in long, white robes fringed with gold, was standing in front of the group and speaking, occasionally gesturing to the statue. Joe looked up at it, and his eyes widened. The statue was of the five Architects he'd been seeing in the dreams, with Darya, Ruta, Chirron, and Aeris all placed on the side of a large column. And in the center, much larger than the others, was Ralin, his hands held out and up to the heavens. Joe saw nothing of the being, so he turned to the speaker.

"And as we have on each day, we thank you, oh great Architects, for this grand world you have built for us," the speaker said, his voice low and booming as the people watched in silence. "For it is through you that we have the land that feeds us, the rivers that end our thirst, the air that sustains us, and the fire that warms us. And we shall continue to praise you and fulfill our sacred charge from Ralin, most sacred of the Architects, he who has given us illumination in our lives and in our spirits. In his name, we shall continue our great purpose of maintaining this world. In your sacred names, we ask only for the strength to do your will and for you to shine the great light upon all you have made."

The crowd all bowed their heads as the speaker said, "This morning's proverbs are finished. Go now, and be merry as you do the work of Ralin and the Architects."

As Joe watched with confusion and disdain, the people raised their heads and began to disperse. If people had worshipped the Architects in the past, why did no one in his time know of them? Why was there no mention of the being he'd seen? And why was Ralin clearly being presented as the greatest of all of them? Rastla and the others were absent from the statue, and these people didn't seem to mind. They didn't even seem to recognize there was darkness and evil in the world.

Joe came closer to the statue and the speaker, who was moving toward the entrance of the building. But before he reached it, a voice called out, "Prayer-sayer!"

Both Joe and the prayer-sayer turned to see a young, dark-haired woman come up to him. She was barely twenty, her body still young but strong looking. She looked up at the older man with her eyes open and questioning.

"You are still not satisfied, young one?" the prayer-sayer asked, a hint of disapproval in his voice.

"I-I am sorry," the girl said. "I know that I should be, but -"

"Child, we have spoken on this many times," the prayer-sayer said. "Our purpose here is to tend and maintain the world we have been given. Why can you not be happy with that?"

"I know the world is important, master," the girl replied. "But I cannot help feeling ... that there is more—that we can do more than simply till the earth and—"

"Enough!" the prayer-sayer snapped. "You speak against the sacred teachings of Ralin? Of the Architects?"

"No!" the girl said, falling to her knees. "I know what I feel is wrong. I have tried to eliminate it, but I cannot do it alone."

"Very well," the prayer-speaker sniffed. "Return to the temple at sundown. We shall pray for your ... clarification this night."

The girl nodded, stood up, bowed to the prayer-speaker, and turned away. The man went inside, but Joe watched as the girl walked away. He was disgusted by the prayer-Sayer's arrogance, but he was also amazed *by the fact she had allowed herself to be spoken to that way. She might have been younger and perhaps without her powers, but Joe had still recognized her.*

Even buried in her hood, he knew the face of Rastla.

XXVIII

"Why didn't we bring Forester?" Windrider groaned as the trio walked through the massive forest, the moonlight barely shining through the thick cover of branches. "He could've at least given us a path or something."

"He's probably underground with the gremlins," Forger answered.

"Point," the falcon said, as he ducked under another branch. "But I wish we had a better idea of where we were going," Windrider replied as he moved to avoid another tree branch. However, that meant he missed the tree root below his feet; within seconds, he'd tripped over it and fallen to the ground.

"A clear path! All I'd need!" the falcon swore as he started to pull himself up. But before he could, Sandshifter's hand wrapped around the back of his coat and pulled him to his feet. The bird started to say thanks, but the wolf just kept walking without a word.

"She's in a mood again," Windrider muttered.

"Indeed," Forger asked. "She hasn't said anything since we entered the woods. Maybe she feels ... guilty about that thing with Paul back there."

"Sandy?" the falcon asked. "She's probably angry at Paul for provoking her."

"Maybe she's not angry at Paul."

"What?"

"Hey. You guys coming?" Sandshifter called from a distance. "We've got kids to save you know."

"Keep quiet," Forger said as they walked over to the wolf. The spider then asked, "We need more of a path than this. Any ideas?"

"No," Sandshifter said. "I can't even smell anything clearly in this wood."

"Well, we need to figure something out," Windrider said. "Or we'll be walking all night."

"We need something that could attract this being," Forger said.

"Leave that to me," Sandshifter said.

With that, the wolf raised her hand and released a current of sand. As the knights watched, the wolf poured more and more sand out, holding it before her in a cloud. It held a second and then the wolf clenched her fist. The floating sands immediately came together, growing into a mass that then spread out, growing arms and legs and smoothing out until …

"Will that do?" Sandshifter asked, pointing at the sand-child she had made, a perfect model in every way but the flesh.

"Impressive," Forger said. "But can we do anything else to bring it in?"

"I think I can add something," Windrider said. The falcon brought up his hands, and the knights felt the wind moving through the trees. The falcon brought in his index finger slightly, and a whistling noise could be heard. He continued, and as he moved his fingers around like he was adjusting a radio dial, the whistling continued to change pitch and tone. Forger even began to hear something like words forming, and then she heard a child's voice calling out, "Help me, please! I'm lost!"

"*Very* impressive," she said to Windrider.

"Always wanted to try that," the falcon replied.

"Let's hide," Sandshifter said, gesturing toward the sand-child, who began to run about, waving its arms in a panic.

"All right, this should bring it out screaming," Windrider said gleefully.

But two hours later, the falcon had a different mind-set.

"Has anything happened yet?"

"No," Sandshifter growled, still keeping the sand-child moving about in the woods.

"Right, right," the falcon muttered.

"You shouldn't be in a rush to face whatever this is," Forger said. "Something that steals children is likely quite hideous."

"I'll bet it's a boogeyman. Or the Bag Man," Windrider said.

"Another comic book?"

"No, it's a myth about a man who takes away bad children in a bag," the falcon answered. "We're a little far for that story, but it could've migrated and—"

"How about we'll know when we see it?" Sandshifter snapped.

"Jeez, sorry, I'm just trying to—"

"Yeah, well don't! *Trying* never works as well as *doing*!"

Forger and Windrider looked at each, and then the spider said, "You have been acting weird since what happened with Paul back there. What is it about one person that bothers you so much?"

"Yeah, so you snapped at him. Big deal," Windrider said as he silenced the wind blowing through the trees. "I was about one step from hitting him myself."

"Just drop it."

"If you're going to snap at everything and throw this mission into jeopardy, then there's no way I'm going to drop it."

"I said, *drop it!*" the wolf snapped again, raising her fist toward the falcon.

But in that split second, a light suddenly came into focus behind them—small but strong all the same. The three Knights instantly halted their conflict and hid, peering from behind the tree to determine what was out there.

What they saw was a small ball of light, darting across the trees. It moved quickly, spending only a few seconds at each spot, as it came closer and closer to the sand-child.

"Hurry, make it move," Forger whispered. "It'll figure out what's going—"

"I don't think it's that bright," Windrider whispered back as the ball reached the child and began to dance around it, moving everywhere as if to get the child's attention. Finally, it stopped and hovered right in front of the child's face, as if studying it.

"Here's our chance," Forger said. "You two remember the plan?"

The others nodded, and Forger placed two of her hands together. As she did so, Sandshifter glanced at the sand-child, which vibrated and then exploded outward in a burst of sand. Tendrils stretched forth, trying to grab the light, but it bounded away each time, leaving the tendrils empty as it moved farther and farther back. But then, the tendrils fell away as Windrider took a deep breath, sucking all the air toward him in a massive vacuum. The light ball tried to move away, but as the vacuum increased and the trees began to bend toward the group, it finally lost its strength and flew backward.

It was only then that Forger stepped forth, right into the path of the light, opened her hands, and caught the light ball, slamming her hands over it with a *clang*. The vacuum ceased then, and the other two knights joined Forger.

"Do you think we hurt it?" Windrider asked.

"It's a ball of light. What are we gonna do to it?" Sandshifter asked.

"We'll find out in a moment," Forger replied, moving her hands upward. The metal flesh gleamed as the spider slowly welded her fingers and hands together, sealing all but a few holes too small for the light to escape. It was only then that they looked inside and saw what they had captured.

The light had faded away now, showing what, at first glance, seemed to be a teenage girl only four inches tall. Its skin was pure alabaster, and it wore blue boots, short pants, and a shirt, all covered in dew that glistened in the dim light of the moon. Dark hair flowed down its back, where two small, diaphanous wings sprouted. It stood up, its almond-shaped and pupil-less eyes darting around the prison it had been trapped in, and then saw through the hole to where the knights were looking in. It instantly began to scream at them, chittering in a strange language that sounded like squeaks and whistles to the knights.

"Fairies," Sandshifter sneered. "*Great.*"

"Let me talk to her," Windrider said.

"You speak Fae too?"

The falcon gave no answer. He looked into the hole and saw the fairy. Putting his head to its level, he said, "We are kin to the Master of the Woods. We would speak to you in the common tongue."

"Lord, what book did that line of crap—"

"You are kin to Demtia? Master of the Woodlands and its Fae?" a small voice quipped from inside Forger's hand.

"Yes. We are the knights of the Architects," Windrider said.

"Then one of you must control the metals," the voice replied. "Will you release me from this iron prison? I have done you no wrong."

"Not yet," Forger said. "We are investigating thievery in the lands below. Human and werewolf children have gone missing in these woods."

"The Fae would never harm children," said the voice. "We only care for the woods, as Master Demtia told us."

"Then who would?" Sandshifter demanded. "What else resides in these woods?"

"Nothing else," the Fae replied. "Our magic repels all others."

"Sure. I'm sure you just beat your little wings and everything evil runs off."

"Enough," Forger said. "What is your name, little fairy?"

"Avia."

"I'll make you a deal. I will release you if you take us to the fairy glen of these woods and to the fairy queen who leads it."

"No! We cannot bring outsiders to—"

"You are bound to obey the commands of Demtia, his fellow Architects, and those who serve them. I have no wish to poison you with my iron, Avia, but I can do it."

The fairy was quiet then, before whispering, "Fine."

"Wait," Sandshifter said. "Swear on the name of Demtia that you'll take us there and back, and *then* we'll let you go."

"I ... I swear it. On the name of the Master of the Wood."

The falcon nodded then, and Forger undid her hands, withdrawing the iron. Instantly, Avia flew up and hovered between the trio. Then she zipped away, returning to her light ball form as she did, leaving a trail of light for the trio to follow.

XXIX

CRASH FROZE AS THE door swung open and a tech walked in. He was tall and thin, dressed in a white lab coat, and carrying a vial filled with some kind of liquid. He took a second to glance at the vial and then turned toward the scanner. Bu that was when he saw the blue-clad cat woman who stood before it. As the door swung shut behind them, the two figures stared at each other in shock. Crash couldn't think to use the glamour or teleport or even speak; the tech couldn't think to call for help or open the door. As his mind kept emptying in his surprise, the man's hands began to relax, until the vial he was holding slipped and hit the floor. At the sound of breaking glass, the tech started and then began to scream, pointing and yelling in Japanese as he moved to the door.

But as his hands reached for the knob, he suddenly stopped, and his screams became gasps. He pulled his hands up to his face, watching the skin on his fingers start to change. The color faded from pink to brown, and his skin shrank around the bones, growing smaller and tighter until his flesh was simply a latex glove pulled tightly over his body. The tech continued to gasp, the tightening spreading across his body until it reached his face, pulling out every drop of moisture. He grabbed at his throat as he fell to his knees. Barely breathing, he looked up at Crash as his face shrunk in on itself.

The cat didn't respond. She just stood there for another few seconds, until the tech collapsed in a heap. It was only then that the cat let out a sigh of relief. Kneeling next to the tech, she placed her hand on his face, willing the water back into his pores. His skin began to loosen then, as his dried out body accepted what Crash had taken away. With so much water in the body, the chance of doing extreme damage was tremendous; Crash never wanted to do that again. But if he had gotten out and told anyone what he had seen …

The cat pushed the thought out of her mind as she finished rehydrating the tech's body. He would awaken soon enough and think what he'd seen in the lab was a dream. Without Nightstalker here to fully wipe his mind, that would have to be enough. Crash left the man on the floor and concentrated once again on the temple, feeling her body breaking apart.

Moments later, she reformed inside the temple, with Hiro and Firesprite standing next to a man on the cot. The lizard was pulling back from the man, standing back on wobbly legs as golden flame vanished from her hands.

"What are you doing?" Crash asked.

The two started at the sound of her voice.

"Trying to help these people as best I can," Firesprite said.

"Are you insane? You don't know what this magic is!" Crash said.

"Magic? What did you learn?" Hiro asked.

"I saw signs in the blood that prove this is magic based."

"Then we just need a counterspell," Firesprite said.

"Sure. If you don't kill these people by trying to help them!" Crash snapped.

"Hey, can the attitude!" the lizard retorted. "Do they look dead to you?"

The cat looked at the man on the cot; he was still sick, but he was much healthier looking than he'd been before. His skin was a good shade of pink, and he was breathing normally, although he was still unconscious.

"It's like … like you force-fed him the nutrients he needs. It won't last, but … this will buy us some time."

"I figured if I can't fix the disease, I can fix the symptoms," Firesprite explained as Hiro took a wooden match from a box in his pocket, lit it, and handed it to the lizard. She put her hand over the flame, which jumped upward into her palm as her pores absorbed the heat.

She gave a sigh of pleasure and said, "Even then, this won't hold out long enough to do all of them. Now, what counterspells do you have? Or are you gonna tell me you spent all that time in the library and *didn't* learn any?"

"I learned plenty. But they won't do squat unless it's the right one."

"Then what do we do?"

"I need to get back to the library. There should be something about this kind of magic that I can use to devise an antidote."

With that, Wavecrasher prepared to teleport herself again. She closed her eyes, steadied herself for the feeling of breaking apart …

And opened her eyes to see nothing had changed.

"Hey … are you going … or what?"

Startled, the cat shook it off and tried again. She closed her eyes, waited for the feeling …

And again, nothing.

"Crash, are you leaving or not?" Firesprite asked.

"Something's wrong," the cat said. "It won't work."

"What?"

"I-I can't get to the Obelisk. I can't get to the magic we need."

"Then let me try," the lizard said. She closed her eyes, and her body began to burn. But just as the flames spread over her, they snapped off. Firesprite tried again, but the results where the same. Finally, she stopped and looked at Crash in disbelief.

"We are in serious trouble."

"We have to figure out a way back before these people—"

"Not just that," Firesprite said. "It's gonna be dark soon. And *they* are going to show up."

XXX

"So Bob spends ten minutes trying to explain to this guy that we don't have any cookbooks, until I had to finally come over and explain what *Chicken Soup for the Soul* was."

"Wow. Bob doesn't get out much, does he?" Mark said as he bit into his sandwich.

"The store is his life. It's been in his family for years," Sara said. "I don't think he knows what he'd do if it was gone."

"At least he treats you well."

"Yeah. But I.."

"You're not thrilled with it."

"I like working with books and all that, even with the crap I have to deal with. I don't know," Sara sighed. "I guess I figured when I left Colorado, I'd be doing something exciting. But it just hasn't happened."

"I feel like that too," Mark said. "I get a lot done in my job, but sometimes I don't get to do anything else in my life."

"Oh, come on," Sara said. "Look at you. You can't be more then twenty-six, twenty-seven, tops. How long can you have been there?"

"Long enough," Mark said with a small smile.

"So what makes you so unhappy at your job?"

Mark thought a moment and then said, "Just the fact it never ends. I spend so much time looking over other people's lives, and then when I get them in order, I get five more to fix."

"So why don't you quit?"

"And do what?"

"I don't know, something that makes you happy?"

"I'd love to. But I can't."

"Why? What is it you want to do?"

Mark was quiet for a moment and then said, "You know, I really don't know. I just know that my job isn't as satisfying as it used to be."

"You're not alone," Sara said. "But in this economy, all people tell you is, 'Keep trying,' or 'At least you have a job.'"

Mark nodded and then asked, "What about you? What would you want to do?"

Sara was quiet. Then she snorted and said, "I really don't know either. Something with writing or editing. I was always good at that."

"Looking over mistakes and correcting people's lives. I did just tell you it gets old real fast."

"Depends how you look at it. I know people back home who need to be told what they do sucks. But I never got to do that … or a lot of things."

Mark nodded and moved around a French fry. "Is that the problem with your parents?" he asked.

"I … I really am not in the mood to discuss that," Sara said. "And I really don't know you well enough to—"

"Did they try to control things? Do they still try?" Mark asked. "Because if they do, it makes things a lot easier to figure out."

"Well … my mother tried to—is still trying to—set me up with this guy."

"A douchebag?"

"Someone who went on to make money even though he was everything I didn't want. But Mom says I needed someone to take care of me. And even on the other side of the country, she keeps trying. It's why I haven't been home in two years."

Mark was silent as Sara finished her story. As she finished, she looked at him and said, "I haven't said that much about it to anyone."

"Maybe that's enough."

"Enough for what?"

"We're both in our lives because of others," he said. "But I think it takes a lot to still try to get what you can out of a … less than perfect situation."

Sara stared at Mark, then admitted, "I hadn't thought about it that way before."

"I forget too. Maybe we just need other people to say it," Mark said as he brought his glass up. "To screwing with the system, however we can."

Sara nodded and then raised her glass and clinked it to his.

XXXI

"HE'S ... BEEN GONE too long," Nerbino said as his guards helped him back onto his throne. "We ... need to find ... a way to help the people."

"I agree, but I'm not sure what to do," Thunderer said. "My power nearly brought this place down when I healed that girl."

"And I'd probably bury us alive if I tried," Groundquake said.

"What about the Forester?" Hazari asked. "What if he tried?"

"Ah'd imagine the same, which is why Ah'm not gonna try," Forester said.

"Wha— How dare you!" Hazari cried out.

"Listen buddy, Ah'm a plant man in a giant rock and dirt palace. If the vines don't shoot outta me, they're gonna come outta the walls."

"Yeah, whatever excuse you need, fluffy," Quake sneered.

"Oh, like you wouldn't say the same thing!" Forester snapped. "You whined enough just being down here."

"Hey I *know* my powers would cause a cave-in," the dog answered. "You might just make flowers grow on the wall. But you just don't want to risk getting sick yourself."

"What? We're immune to disease, you stupid—"

"And they're sick even with diseased blood to begin with! So no, nothing that might actually get Fluffy's precious fur matted or give him the sniffles, even if others could die."

"You hypocritical asshole!" Forester yelled as Thunderer came between them.

"*Enough*! Look, Forester might be right about what his powers could do underground. And if this really is something that's bad enough to infect gremlins, then maybe we need to check a higher authority."

"The library?" Forester suggested.

"Exactly. We can go back and see what the books say about diseases like this and hopefully come back with a cure."

"Given all our other options, I have to agree," Nerbino said. "Just … hurry back."

Thunderer nodded. He closed his eyes, the others following, willing themselves back to the Obelisk. The air around them began to crackle and then …

"Um, shouldn't you have left by now?" Hazari asked.

The three knights opened their eyes and looked around in shock at their surroundings. They tried again, focusing even harder, but nothing happened. They finally looked at each other in confusion and horror as they realized they were stuck on Earth for the foreseeable future.

*　　*　　*

"I still can't believe I talked about all that with you," Sara said as she and Mark left the pub. "The last time I was on a first date, we spent two hours talking about our jobs and Mel Brooks movies."

"I'm pretty good at making people feel comfortable," Mark said. "But I'm also great at keeping secrets."

"Good. Because I'm great at shooting people from a distance," Sara replied as they walked down the street.

"Did you have a good time?"

"Actually, yes," Sara said after a minute.

"Likewise," Mark said. "I can talk with some people, but finding a pretty girl who understands you? That's rare."

"You're just sucking up now, aren't you?"

"Kinda, yes."

Suddenly, the moment was shattered by the sound of someone screaming. The two of them jumped, and Mark looked at Sara. "Sorry," he said and ran toward the sound.

But he hadn't taken more than a few steps when he heard footsteps following him. He grinned a bit and kept running. The two of them ran down past the pub and down into the alleyway next to it. As the scream sounded again, Mark and Sara turned the corner and came to the back of the pub, where a large dumpster stood. Held to the dumpster by a large hand was one of the waitresses, who was trying to push away from the large man holding her.

"Hey, asshole!" Sara shouted.

The man turned around, seeing the two of them there.

"Why don't you let her go? There's a reason the Internet has porn, you know," Sara sneered.

The man glared at Sara and then shoved the waitress aside and started to lunge toward the newcomers, his gait unsteady but sure.

"Gee, a drunk. What a surprise," Sara said as Mark stepped in front of her.

The man brought up his fist, but Mark caught it, turned around, stuck out his leg, and sent the man to the ground with a thud, as the waitress ran off.

"Look, buddy," he said as the man lay there groaning. "You don't need to be this stupid, drunk or not. So why don't you just— *Ahhh!*"

Mark grabbed his leg in pain as the man scrambled to his feet, the knife glinting in his hand. Giving a nasty, lopsided grin, the man lunged again at Mark, who managed to turn out of the way. The drunk stumbled forward, crashing into a pair of trash cans. But he quickly got back to his feet and charged at Mark again.

This time, Mark sideswiped him but also grabbed his shirt and used the grip to flip the man over onto his back. The drunk hit the pavement with a thud, and lay there, moaning in pain. Mark moved over to the drunk, gingerly kneeling down and grabbing the man's collar.

"What the hell is wrong with you?" he snarled. "Bad enough you have to get lost in a bottle, but going after women? I should just—"

Mark stopped then and grimaced, as the man's fist had crashed into his injured leg. Mark gritted his teeth against the pain, which gave the drunk an opening to slam his fist into Mark's face. Mark went sprawling backward, and the drunk started to get to his feet.

But before he could a loud *clang* filled the air as Sara slammed a trash can lid into his face. The drunk wavered, and Sara followed up that hit with a punch to the drunk's face. That sent him spinning around and collapsing in a heap.

"Bastard," Sara muttered, shaking her hand as she went over to Mark. "You okay?" she asked.

"Depends. Are there teeth lying on the ground?" Mark asked.

"Nope,"

"Then I'm fine. What happened to the asshole?"

"I did," Sara said, helping Mark to his feet. As she did, she saw what the drunk had done to him. A long, diagonal slash ran across Mark's jeans, right in the center of his thigh. The jeans were covered in blood around the cut, and Sara could see the red, angry gash inside.

"How bad did he get me?" Mark asked. "Can I still play the piano?"

"I'm more worried about you walking," Sara said. "Come on. My apartment isn't too far from here. I can patch you up there. Can you walk?"

"I think so," Mark said, gingerly putting weight on his leg. He took a few steps, limping, but still holding himself up.

"Good, let's go then," Sara said, moving close to him, ready to catch him if he fell.

"You know … I really didn't think … I'd get to your apartment," Mark said as they walked.

Sara snorted at that and said, "You better not have planned all this—"

"Oh no … not with … this much pain," Mark said as they left the alley.

Behind them, the drunk lay crumpled on the pavement. Then he slowly began to move. He got to his feet, his gait steady now, all signs of drunkenness gone. He glared out at the two of them as they left, and as he did, his eyes began to glow with a pale light that any one of the knights would have recognized. The glow spread over his body as his human form began to twist and break away. The arms stretched out, the body elongated, and the flesh became hard and crystalline. Within seconds, the drunk was gone, and a Chaos Demon stood in its place. The demon sniffed the air a moment and then gave a grim smile as its body grew transparent and faded away into the night.

XXXII

As the fairy sprinted ahead, the trio of knights trudged through the dark woods. The fairy's glow was a weak light, so occasionally one of the Knights would let out a curse as they stumbled over a root or ran into a tree branch. Avia zipped ahead, unmindful of their cries.

"Do you really think the fairies are involved?" Windrider asked.

"I don't know," Forger replied. "The books say they've always been kind to children."

"Anything can happen. We know that," Sandshifter said. "Why are they so nice to kids anyway?"

"When Demtia created them to watch over his woods, he used a piece of a child's dream to make them, so they're linked to childhood belief and dreaming," Forger said.

Sandshifter snorted at that, just as Avia suddenly called out, "We've arrived!"

The trio came to a halt. Avia floated in front of a huge tree in the center of a grove. The tree was massive and gnarled, its trunk swollen and full of bulges, almost like a patch of tumors had sprouted on it. The branches stretched out in all directions, seeming to reach out for anything that could come close to the tree. But despite all this, the tree looked solid and strong—an iron anchor buried under eons of barnacles.

"This is the fairy glen?" Sandshifter snorted.

"Look closer," Windrider replied as Avia flew into a groove in one of the tumors and laid her hand upon it. The light from her body diminished for a moment as it spread from the little fairy into the tree itself, lighting the bark and revealing complex patterns and drawings of Fae language spread all over it. As the knights watched, the center of the tree began to contract, and then it suddenly opened wide, revealing not a hollowed out piece of wood but what appeared to be a piece of fairy light, glowing within the confines of the tree's trunk.

"Enter, please," Avia said as she flew into the light and vanished.

The knights looked at each other, and Windrider stepped toward the tree. He brought up his hand and stuck it into the light. It vanished into the light, and after a few seconds of no pain, the falcon walked the rest of the way in. Forger followed suit, and after a long sigh, Sandshifter entered as well.

The wolf saw a burst of blue light, took in a smell of bark and sap, and then she walked out into the massive fairy glen. It was a huge series of concentric circles, with the knights at the very bottom. Above them were levels of mossy, wood-like rings, with large holes and lights glowing inside them like windows. Fairies flew all around, their bluish light a strange contrast to the glowing green all around. As the light touched the rings, the knights could see the moss move and grow, infused with the fairy magic.

"I always get weirded out in these places," Sandshifter said. "I can't tell if we shrink or the place gets bigger."

"Some things, even I don't want to think about," Forger said as Avia, still small to the knights, flew up in front of them.

"I went ahead and told the queen's guards you were here," the small fairy said. "She will see you right away."

"Good," Forger said. "What level is the queen at?"

"The top. I've arranged for them to bring you to—"

"No need," Windrider said as he raised up his hands. Forger and Sandshifter exchanged worried looks and then screams as the falcon's winds blew them up past the various rings of the glen. As the winds grew faster and faster, the rings became a blur of green until, finally, they slowed to a halt, floating a moment. Then they were turned upright and gently placed at the topmost ring.

"One of these times ..." Sandshifter breathed as, behind her, Windrider and Avia floated up and landed on the ring, barely ruffled.

"So, everything go smoothly? I made sure the landing went okay," the falcon said.

Sandshifter growled, but Forger said, "The landing has improved. Where's the queen's throne?"

"That way," Avia said, pointing behind the spider.

The two of them turned to see a giant door finely carved with Fae symbols and designs of the forest—curving branches, trees, and plants all adorned it. In the very center of each was the chief Fae symbol—an intricately detailed tree, adorned with a crown around the branches. In front of the door floated two fairies, each one holding a small, glowing spear. One of them glanced at the knights and said, "Welcome, Elementals. The queen will see you now."

With that, the other guard tapped on the door, which swung open. The knights and Avia moved inside, entering a room that looked like the inside of a crystal cave. The walls around them looked like they were formed by rows of stalactites and stalagmites that had been fused together, creating a look like many huge drops of water coming together and solidifying. The purple hue of the 'cascades' were reminiscent of geodes, and as the knights walked by, they could sense warmth coming from them. In the center of the room was a large, circular window that looked down onto every level. And above the window was a massive dais with a small throne, both made from the same crystal substance. Upon the throne sat a larger than average fairy, dressed in dark purple robes, cut to allow her legroom. She wore a small silver crown on her head, resting on a profusion of black hair that framed a slender face with large, pupil-less, purple eyes.

"Queen Miri," Avia said, lowering to the ground and kneeling in front of the queen.

"Welcome, young fairy," the queen said, her voice low and musical. "And welcome to you Elementals."

"Your Highness," Forger said, bowing slightly toward the queen. Windrider and Sandshifter quickly followed suit.

"It is rare that such beings come to see the Fae," Miri said. "What business do you have with us?"

"The disappearance of children from the human village nearby," Forger explained. "We suspect something in your forest is involved."

"Why? Because of the legends the townsfolk tell?" Queen Miri answered with a laugh. "You know Fae would never harm children."

"Even werewolf cubs?" Sandshifter asked. "Something abducted them as well."

"Even a werewolf child would not be harmed," the Queen said. "The only reason the humans sent you here is because of what we've done to keep them away."

"And what would that be?"

"A few strange noises at night and little pranks of the like. We must protect the forest, after all."

"That's all?" Sandshifter asked.

"Yes," the queen answered with a glare. "Unless you need me to repeat myself?"

"Of course not," Forger said quickly. "But we'd like the opportunity to take a closer look at your glen. You are the only ones in the forest who know of the humans and the werewolves. It may be possible that one of your own is doing this out of some misguided effort to protect the forest."

"None would do so without my consent!" the queen snapped, rising out of her throne. But then she paused, rolled her shoulders, and said, "But I cannot allow the fairy name to be dragged through the mud. Avia, guide the knights through the glen. Grant them access to any area the common fairy would be able to use for such a purpose."

"Yes, Highness," Avia said, bowing and nodding her compliance.

The queen nodded back and then turned to the Knights and said, "I will assume that will be sufficient to convince you?"

"Yes, Majesty. Thank you," Forger said as she and the others rose up.

Avia flew in front of the spider, and said, "Please follow me, Metal Knight. I know a room on this level that should be a good starting point."

Forger nodded as the fairy left the room, followed by the trio.

As they walked out, Sandshifter whispered, "I still don't buy it."

"Nor do I. But using logic was what got us this opportunity," Forger whispered. "And logic also says that, until we have some real evidence, everyone is a suspect, regardless of royal standing."

"So where do we start?" the spider asked aloud as the group exited the throne room.

"The most common storage area is on the middle levels," the fairy replied.

"And what do you keep there?"

"Our saps, forest oils, healing bark, almost all of the tools needed to maintain the forest."

"Sounds like a good area to hide something in," Windrider said.

"And way too obvious," Sandshifter snarled. "If someone was going to hide kids, who'd be stupid enough to hide them in a place everyone goes to?"

"Whoever it is could've changed them to something else," Windrider suggested, "like stone or ... or even wood or something—like the Nome King's trinkets in *Return to Oz*."

"And we may have a way to find them," Forger said, pointing at Avia. "The queen did tell her to help us, didn't she?"

"Of course. I would never disobey an order from the queen," Avia said.

"Then you will look for fairy magic that could disguise beings, while we look for other trails."

Avia gave no answer, merely flying down and gesturing for the knights to follow her.

"Hold on, guys," Windrider said, starting to summon the winds again.

But this time, Sandshifter stopped him. "I'll go my own way this time," the wolf said. She held her hand out, and it shot out into a huge, sandy fist, dragging her down toward Avia.

"Not a bad idea," Forger replied. The spider raised her hands and launched a set of chains toward the lower wall. They embedded themselves into the wood, as Forger retracted, pulling herself toward the wall. She landed and then began to climb down, her six hands sticking to the wood with ease.

"Crash a couple time and nobody trusts you anymore," Windrider muttered as he unfurled his wings and pushed the air into them, launching himself upward. He hovered a moment and then carefully began to turn his arms around, slowly lowering himself down along with the others. The foursome pushed their way down almost seven levels, reaching the middle of the glen before Avia finally led them to their destination.

"This is the storage facility," the fairy said once each of the knights had landed on the level. She gestured toward a small, circular door cut into the wood.

"Hope it's ... worth the climb," Forger wheezed, leaning over and pressing her hands onto her knees. Windrider was also breathing heavily.

"You two need to get out more,' Sandshifter said. "Pop the door, wing nut, and let's get to work."

Avia sniffed but did as asked, releasing a small bolt of fairy magic that pushed the door open. She flew inside, and the knights followed, only to stop short in sheer amazement at what they saw.

The room before them was gigantic, a storage warehouse made of wood and stone. It was filled with wooden shelves and holders carved into the stone, all laden with glowing orbs, bags of bark, and various other baubles too numerous to count.

"The Ark must be in here too," Windrider said.

"How in the hell can all this be inside a tree?" Sandshifter asked.

"Magic. Now let's get looking," Forger said, moving over to the closest shelf and looking it over.

"Looking where? For what?" Sandshifter cried out.

"Windy and I will be the ones looking," Forger said. "You will be smelling."

The wolf started at that but then breathed a sigh of relief and began to sniff about the room.

"What is she doing?" Avia asked.

"She's a wolf. High sense of smell," Windrider replied as he reached over and grabbed a glowing bottle.

"Oh, I ... *Don't touch that*!" Avia yelled, which caused the falcon to drop the bottle he was holding. But Avia swiftly flew underneath, caught it, and returned it to the shelf.

"Are you *crazy*?! Do you have any idea what that was?" the fairy screamed at Windrider.

"Uh ... no, not really," the falcon replied.

"Honestly!" Avia snapped. Even Forger stopped looking about. "Here, let me!"

The fairy waved her hands, causing another burst of fairy magic. The room faded away for a second and then suddenly reappeared, but with the knights and fairy in a section far removed from where they had been, standing before a specific shelf.

"Wha— what just happened?" Sandshifter demanded.

"The inventory spell. It takes us to the most recent items that were taken from here," Avia said.

"And you didn't tell us you could do this because?" Forger asked.

"I assumed the Elementals knew how to conduct a search in a room of magic items."

Windrider's eyes narrowed, but Forger said, "Fine then. What are we looking at here?"

Avia turned and examined the shelf, checking each of its levels. At each one, she nodded in approval—until she got to the bottom shelf and suddenly paused.

"Something wrong?" Forger asked.

"This bottle …" the fairy said, lifting up a small, hourglass-shaped container that held green liquid and a faint red aura. "The spell says that this item has been used several times recently."

"What is it?" Forger asked.

"The simplest term is bark regrower," Avia answered. "We use it to repair trees that have been stripped of their bark."

"Which would be useful in a wooden tree," Forger said.

"But who would even want to do that?" Avia asked. "No fairy has touched the sacred glen since Demtia sculpted it from the wood centuries ago."

"Could any other being access this place?" the spider asked.

"No," Avia answered, "not without a fairy to open the door."

"Then we need to start looking for a traitor," Sandshifter said.

"Oh, what a surprise!" Avia snapped. "You already think we are the culprits!"

"One way or another, a fairy is helping out whoever is," the wolf growled.

"How can you be sure it's not a fairy doing this directly?" Forger asked.

"Because I've been doing my job and smelling," Sandshifter replied. "And aside from fairy, I'm getting two other odors—human and werewolf. But too old to be children."

"Then both of them caused this?" Avia asked.

"To restart the old conflict and finally destroy the other side," Forger answered. "Can that spell you cast find out if this stuff has been used anywhere in the glen?"

"Possibly," Avia said.

"Then let's get started."

XXXIII

"Okay, we need to look at this strategically," Wavecrasher said. "Is there any way we can heal these people enough to move them safely?"

"With enough matches and water, sure," Firesprite said. "But even that would take until nightfall."

"Hiro, how long would it take for an ambulance to get these people out?"

"The same time," the monk said.

"We could teleport them away."

"With this many, we'd wipe ourselves out before we finished," the lizard answered.

"Maybe we could command the vamps to leave?"

"If they really are this hungry and pissed, they'll rip the place apart without a second thought. Our only options are either to fight them off or try some sort of counterspell so we can move these people."

"That's not an option," Wavecrasher said. "I have no idea what to use--

"Isn't there something generic?" Firesprite asked. "Like a 'sickness be gone' spell? If I was able to heal them with fire magic—"

"It's not enough for a full recovery. We either need to do it right or—"

"Damn it, if we don't do something, we're all gonna die!" Firesprite snapped. "If you know something that might work, it's worth a try!"

"I don't know if anything I have *will* work!" the cat snapped back. "I can't just try random magic against—"

"Of course, and without your precious books to check, you just give up!" the lizard yelled. "Can't you do *anything* that isn't proven by some goddamn footnote?"

"Not when lives are at stake!"

"Lives are at stake *because* you won't try anything! We're stranded from home, with no access to the books and no idea what to do! If there was a time for trying something, this is *it!*"

"Sure, just try something that might not work and get somebody killed."

"*It's better than trying nothing!!*"

"*Why you—*"

"*Rooooaahhh!!*"

Both knights stopped short then. They looked down at the fox, who was growling at both of them.

"Arguing will not get us anywhere," Hiro said. "I agree with Firesprite—we must at least *try* something. Wavecrasher, is there some kind of spell benign enough to at least attempt?"

"I … well … yes … but our healing is supposed to be more powerful then all of them," Crash said. "And if Sprite had to struggle to heal this much, I don't know what good any of them will do."

"Then we can double it," Firesprite said.

"How?"

"Teach me one of the spells. I can cast one and heal at the same time."

"Absolutely not!" the cat exclaimed. "Do you have any idea how dangerous mixing magic is?"

"As dangerous as allowing vampires to feed on these people?"

"We could kill them or do heaven knows what to them. I can't afford to do that to someone."

"What did you say?"

"I said, we can't afford to do that to someone."

"No you didn't," the lizard said. "You said I."

Crash looked about the room as she muttered, "Well, so what?"

"I should've figured it out," Firesprite said with heat in her voice. "After all, *you* can't dare to take a risk can you?"

"This … this has nothing to do with me!" the cat snapped.

"Then why don't I believe you?" Firesprite snapped back. "You're afraid to let these people die, *and* you're afraid to try anything new to help them because you can't accept being wrong! You're willing to let them die in order to protect your precious ego!"

"Shut up!"

"Is that why you were so obsessed with the stupid glamour? Because it hides the fact that you fail at being one of them? Are you that scared of—"

"*Shut up!*" Wavecrasher screamed as she let loose a huge tendril of water at Firesprite.

But the lizard whipped her hand in front of her, creating a wall of flame that evaporated the water into steam. She opened her mouth to speak again, but before she could get a word out, a thump sounded from the roof above. Everyone went silent and looked out the window, at the darkened skies.

"Hiro, you said they couldn't enter this place right?" Crash asked.

"Yes," the monk replied.

"So what are they doing?"

"Trying to scare us," Firesprite said. "But I'll be damned if I know—"

"*Look out!*" Crash yelled.

With a terrible crashing sound, a huge rock fell through the ceiling, heading right for Firesprite. And it would have reached her, had Crash not sent out another tendril of water, which caught the rock and then froze, suspending it above in a column of ice.

"Thanks,' Firesprite said, glancing up at the frozen missile.

But seconds later, the ice shattered as other boulders tore through the roof. This time, Firesprite had enough time to move aside, and the rocks crashed into the floor.

"They can't get in, so they're trying to get us out!" Crash said.

"Then we shouldn't disappoint," Firesprite said. "Hiro, you and the other monks get these people below ground. We'll deal with the vamps."

Hiro nodded and called for the other monks, the fox running with him as the two knights headed for the door, their argument put aside for the moment.

Pushing open the doors, they sped outside and then whirled around to glance upward. Floating above the temple were about seven figures, each holding a massive rock. As the knights watched, one of them laughed and sent a rock through the roof, relishing the sound of the crash.

"I hate the vamps that figure out how to fly," Crash said.

"Then it's a good thing they still know how to burn," Firesprite replied as two fireballs ignited in her palms. The lizard quickly hurled them toward the vampires, who lit up like candles when the flames touched them. The remaining vamps quickly hurled down their rocks and tried to help their brethren.

Suddenly two streams of water came out of nowhere, spraying down the burning vampires before they could be consumed. It was only then that the vampires looked down to see the two brightly colored figures standing in front of the temple.

"If you wouldn't mind coming down?" Firesprite said, igniting another fireball in her hand.

Their response was immediate; the vampires let out a howl and flew down toward them. But as they came close, Firesprite drew her spear and slammed the weapon into the ground. The spearhead then lit up in a blaze of flame, giving the vampires a perfect look at the beings that stood before them. It was only then that they halted and hovered just above the ground, glaring at the knights with fangs bared.

"You know who we are," Wavecrasher said. "What imbalance has been done to you?"

The vampires glanced at each other and then parted, allowing one to make her way forward. She was tall and dressed in a dark skirt and red jacket, with stiletto heeled boots. Her black and red hair was tied up in a ponytail. Her face was youthful; she appeared to be barely twenty. But it was also hard and angular, and she glared at the knights from behind angry, slanted eyes.

"I am Kimiko, the leader of this clan," she hissed at the knights.

"Then you're not a very smart one," Wavecrasher replied. "There are humans in there suffering from some kind of plague that we can't cure. And it apparently came from vampires."

"Don't lie," Kimiko snapped. "They poisoned us!"

"What are you talking about?"

"Those humans, they are weak? Hungry?"

"Yes."

"So are my clan! This is all that remains of us!" the vampire growled. "We were infected by that same plague after trying to feed on these humans!"

"And what made you come here to feed?" Firesprite asked. "There's a city nearby. Wasn't there enough in Tokyo?"

"City humans are too easy to entrap," Kimiko said, licking her fangs. "And we didn't know."

"Then maybe you should learn to stick to your own territories," Wavecrasher challenged. "Or did you even bother checking with the council here about new hunting grounds?"

Kimiko snarled but gave no reply.

Undaunted, Wavecrasher continued. "And tell me, how was attacking a temple and killing everyone inside going to help?"

"All those who infected us came from this area! They must have a cure!" the vampire hissed.

"They don't," Firesprite said.

"This isn't a plague to wipe out vampires," Wavecrasher said. "But it sounds like we both want a cure."

"But you don't have one."

"Not yet. But we will," Crash said. "And if you want to get help, you will cease the attacks on this place."

"Why should we—"

"Because the Elementals say so," Firesprite answered. "And because you know who we speak for."

Kimiko was quiet and then nodded.

"Good. Then you will tell us what we need to know. Whose idea was it to come here to begin with?"

"One of the sick. He told us about new humans in the area, coming for some kind of sanctuary. We thought it easy to pick on them as they left the temple," the vampire grinned. "And a challenge to feed on the holy."

"You will take us to him. If he knows of this place and convinced you to feed here, he may know something we can use."

Kimiko nodded once more and then gestured to two of the other vampires. The two men came forward and placed a hand on each knight's shoulder. Seconds later, the cat and lizard were airborne; the vampires sped through the skies with the greatest of speeds. Firesprite felt the air rushing past her ears (or the ridges that counted as ears) as the vampires flew them past the dark countryside toward the rapidly approaching lights that could only be Tokyo.

The lizard wondered if this was what Windrider felt when he flew, and as the lights sped past them, she felt herself deposited onto solid ground. The vampires released their grip on her shoulder. She glanced over at Wavecrasher and took a look around at the surroundings. The vampires had brought them to a rooftop in what looked like the red-light district of Tokyo; electric signs, flashing various Japanese characters, were all around them. The buildings they were attached to were well maintained but small, built onto a narrow street littered with motorcycles. Men walked into narrow doorways, while windows displayed posters of women in various poses, all smiling.

"Charming," Wavecrasher said, wrinkling her nose as she shook off her vampire.

"Every city has one," Firesprite replied as she turned to Kimiko.

"We make sure that our clan always has places to stay, no matter where they are in the city."

"Smart. Especially in a country that has a bright red sun on its flag," Firesprite replied. "That sick vampire is here?"

Kimiko nodded and then said, "Stay here. I will make the arrangements for you to enter."

The young vampire turned, heading toward a nearby door. But she had barely taken a few steps when a watery whip snapped out and wrapped around her shoulder. Kimiko stopped, turned, and snarled as Wavecrasher calmly stood there, her arm ending in a tendril of water.

"I know that I'm in a foreign country, but I assume you will take no disrespect if my friend and I go with you?" the cat asked.

"Actually, I would," Kimiko answered. "My clan has rules about outsiders that must be obeyed—"

"And our clan has rules about being given entrance when we ask for it," Wavecrasher replied. "And they don't involve letting someone go and set up a trap for us, so she and her people can go back to destroying a temple."

Kimiko gave no reply, save a twitch of her head. Immediately, the other vampires surrounded Wavecrasher, baring their fangs at the Elemental. But as they did, they heard a cough. They turned to see Firesprite standing there calmly, bouncing a fireball in her hand.

"I happen to agree with our rule," the lizard said. "And I can do worse than splash you, little girl."

Kimiko stared at Firesprite and then gave another twitch. The vampires quickly backed off as their leader spat out, "If you would follow, *honored* Elementals?"

Firesprite nodded, extinguishing the fireball. Crash retracted the water back into her arm, reforming it into flesh as she moved to follow Kimiko and the Fire Knight though the door. The trio moved down a flight of stairs, through the first two floors of the building, and past an open gateway, where a young man was entering a room with a woman in red.

"Do you have a lot of business?" Firesprite asked as they moved past.

"Enough," Kimiko said.

As Wavecrasher watched, the girl exited the room, wiping something red from her mouth.

"We have a good location," Kimiko said as they reached the bottom of the stairs, which ended before a door with a peephole. Kimiko knocked on the door, and the hole opened, revealing a pair of eyes. Kimiko said nothing, only pulled her lips back and showed her fangs. The peephole closed, and the door swung open, revealing a tall, dark-haired man, dressed in a suit and holding a gun. He glanced at Kimiko, and then his eyes widened as he saw the two Elementals. He turned to Kimiko and yelled something in Japanese. The girl replied with an equally venomous answer, which caused the man to grow quiet and move back.

"We may enter," Kimiko said as she walked through the door.

The knights followed, entering a dimly lit concrete room with only a few red lights casting their crimson glow all around. The room held little furniture, save a cot and a cabinet full of vials of dark liquid. Lying on the cot, his body trembling was the thin frame of the infected vampire. He looked to be a man in his late fifties, his face lined and wrinkled as if he had been in the sun too long. He glanced about the room, as if trying to see.

"How long has he been here?" Wavecrasher asked.

"Since he started showing the symptoms," Kimiko said. "The council told us to isolate him."

"He looks like he doesn't know where he is," Crash said.

"The sickness affects his vision and his mind. But he can still converse," Kimiko said as she moved over to the vampire's bedside. Kneeling down, she ran a hand along his face, which turned his attention to her. Kimiko spoke to him in Japanese, after which he replied and weakly nodded.

"He will speak to you," Kimiko said. "I will translate; he was never good at English."

Firesprite nodded and said, "Can you describe the last one you bit before this started?"

Kimiko translated as the vampire spoke. "He was tall," she told them, "light haired, almost too blond. His skin was pale, with no marks. And he was very thin, almost gaunt."

"Was he Japanese?"

"No. He was … not Japanese, but not quite a gaijin—a mix."

"That narrows it down," Crash said. "How did you find him?"

After a moment of quiet Japanese, Kimiko explained.

"Another vampire led him to him. Said he had been trailing the man from the temple for a while. Foreign blood, with a challenge to it."

"What?" Crash said, glaring at Kimiko. "Did you send him out to find a way into the temple?"

"No!" the girl snarled. "He told us he found the man on his own. But it did lead us to the temple."

"Tell him to describe this other vampire," Firesprite said.

Kimiko spoke to the vampire but then grew puzzled. "He cannot. He says the man was just average, nothing truly defining. Except …"

"What?"

"He said the other never drank around him. And once he thought saw his … his skin move. And his eyes … his eyes flashed?"

Kimiko looked at the knights in confusion; she saw the color drain from their faces. She was about to ask them what was wrong, but then the sick vampire coughed and spoke again, though his voice faltered more then once.

Kimiko listened carefully and then said, "He also says … he heard the vampire talking about … looking for something… a…"

But the vampire on the cot coughed loudly and then weakly whispered a single word, a word so quiet the Knights couldn't hear it.

Kimiko leaned in.

Firesprite asked, "What is it? What was he looking for?"

Kimiko pulled back, looking even more confused, and spoke the translated word to them.

Firesprite had little reaction, but for her companion, the effect was like a bomb hitting a mountain. Wavecrasher's eyes grew wide and frantic; she grabbed her friend and yelled, "We have to get back there! We have to get back there *now!*"

"What is it?" Kimiko asked.

"Crash, what the hell is going on?" Firesprite demanded.

But the Water Knight barely seemed to hear. She pulled herself and Firesprite to their feet and pushed their way past the guard and through the door. Then Crash stuck her head back and said, "Gather every sick vampire you have together. And move them to the biggest space available and far away from the city."

"*What*? What the hell is going on?" Kimiko demanded.

"Just do it! Or else this plague is going to get a million times worse!" Crash said.

Kimiko would've said more, but the cat grabbed Firesprite and evaporated away in a slightly larger cloud than usual, leaving Kimiko and the other vampires alone in the room.

XXXIV

Joe watched Rastla walk away from the prayer-sayer and then quickly ran after the Architect, even as his mind tried to wrap around what he had just seen. No one ever spoke to the Architect of Shadow that way, not even Ralin. But that priest had just shamed and humbled her. It made no sense. And if Rastla was here, why was she dressed as a mortal?

The questions buzzed in Joe's head as he followed Rastla to her destination. It was a house of a kind, a large, circular hut that resembled a huge boulder. It stood to what would've been a little more than half the size of Joe's old house, with a great flat roof, a chimney, and four windows all around it. A man stood outside, dressed in the same simple robes as the rest of the townsfolk. His body was strong and tan, and he was sharpening a scythe, the rock ringing against the metal and throwing sparks. Rastla gave a cough, and the man looked up, revealing a proud face with high cheekbones, covered with long, black hair. Dark blue eyes gleamed out as he smiled at Rastla.

"You're back early," the man said, his voice gentle and low. "I would've thought the Prayer-sayer would go on for a while longer today."

"I-I was late for it, Father," Rastla replied nervously as Joe watched in the background. "I missed the sermon."

Rastla's father shrugged and said, "Well, the main point is to give thanks to the One. And we do plenty of that here with the farm."

"I ... I tried to speak with him ... about my thoughts of late," Rastla said.

It was only then that her father stopped sharpening, put down his scythe, and gazed up at his daughter. "And what did he say?"

"He ... Father, he was angry with me!" Rastla cried out. "He said I am an ungrateful child and that I am a disgrace to the One. He hates me and everything I try to speak of."

"I'm not surprised," her father said as he walked over to his daughter. "No one in our village has ever had thoughts of something beyond the Presence and our care of the earth. Even I have never heard of it."

"Does that mean I'm wrong, Father? That my unhappiness is because I really am an ungrateful child?"

"If you were, you wouldn't be trying to understand it," her father answered. "I do believe that there is a reason for this."

"What?"

"That I don't know. But whatever we are comes from the One and the Architects. If they made you feel this way, then they have a plan for you."

"Do you think I'm meant to lead us to something else? That there's a reason I feel such unhappiness in the village?"

"You very well may be. But I do believe that, whatever these feelings are, they will lead you to something incredible."

"I hope you are right, Father," Rastla sighed. "I just feel so … empty doing all of this. Even if the earth needs caring, don't we deserve something as caretakers?"

"Perhaps you will find it," her father answered.

Rastla smiled a little at that and leaned against her father's strong frame.

"Thank you, Father. You always know what to say to help me."

"I simply speak the truth," her father replied. "Now come; we still have work in the fields. You get the animals ready, and I will prep the harness."

Rastla nodded and walked to the left of the house as her father stuck his scythe in the ground and walked to the right, toward a nearby shed. Joe was tempted to follow Rastla's father; he liked the man, and he was genuinely curious about the father of Shadow. But he knew that his answers were likely to be with the man's daughter, so he turned and followed her.

Rastla had traveled to a large fenced-in area, where several oxen were grazing. A young boy stood at the gate, watching the oxen with a large crook in his hand.

A shepherd of oxen? Well, why not? There doesn't seem to be a lot of violence around here, Joe thought as Rastla approached the boy.

"Greetings, Haven," she said to the boy, who turned and greeted her with a smile.

"Good morning, Rastla," Haven replied. "Did the prayer-sayer have a good sermon today?"

"Oh, the usual. Love the earth, walk the path of the Architects, Ralin is king," Rastla replied with a wry grin as she walked to the gate and began to open the lock.

"It would make more sense if he just wrote it down and read from it each day," Haven said, pushing open the gate.

"Careful, Haven," Rastla warned, "even if he repeats himself, the prayer-sayer is wise. We should listen to his words."

"And he should write them down," Haven answered with a laugh. "At the very least, he would not speak himself hoarse each day. Now, which oxen does your father need today?"

"The fields have been hard and rocky of late. We would need Arabi today."

Haven nodded and moved toward a large ox near the back of the area. He reached out with his crook, gently hooking the animal and giving it a light tug toward him. As Joe watched, the animal obediently rose up and moved toward Haven, lightly flicking its tail back and forth.

"If Arabi can't plow your rocky fields, nobody can," Haven said as the great animal plodded through the open gate to Rastla's waiting hand. She stroked the ox's head gently, as Haven continued.

"I wish we could use him at my father's land. Whatever rocks you have, we have a thousand fold."

"I'm sure Father would be happy to loan him to you," Rastla said as she led Arabi back to her father's field.

"I hope so. My father is breaking his back to keep the fields fertile, and help from this big one would save him much pain," Haven said, tapping the ox with his staff. But as he did so, the crook slipped from his grasp, accidentally striking Arabi in the eye. The animal reared its head in pain, and Haven backed away in surprise. Rastla tried to calm the creature, reaching out with her hands, but Arabi whipped his head back and forth and ran from the girl, still whipping his head in pain.

"Haven! Look what you did!" Rastla said, pointing at the injured animal.

"It wasn't my fault! He ... he moved!

"To where you dropped it!" Rastla said back. "How many times has Father told you to be more careful with—"

But Rastla said no more, as the sound of thundering hoofbeats suddenly filled the air. Both Rastla and Haven turned around to see Arabi charging them, snorting wildly as he continued to shake his head. They gasped and then quickly dove out of the animal's way, rolling to the side as he ran about.

"He's gone mad!" Haven cried out. "We've got to get away from here until he calms down!"

"And just leave him here?" Rastla said back. "What if he hurts himself? Or someone else?"

"No one else comes here!" Haven said. "And we wouldn't be able to stop him without hurting him!"

Rastla glared at Haven and then grabbed a rock from nearby and stood out in the open. Haven screamed at her to stop, but she stood her ground, even calling out to Arabi. The ox turned at the sound of his name and began to charge at Rastla. But the girl stood still, still holding the rock in her hand. As Joe watched, she suddenly hurled the rock forward. It flew straight and true, moving through the air and striking Arabi right between the horns. He bellowed in agony but fell to his knees in pain, and Rastla stepped forward and gently caressed the ox's now bleeding head. Haven approached and gaped in disbelief.

"Rastla! You ... you hurt him!"

"And I'm the second one to do that today," Rastla said, glaring at the boy.

"But ... but that was an accident! You actually hurt him! The Prayer-sayer said we should never harm any of the Architect's creations on purpose!"

"No, he says whenever possible. And Arabi will be fine."

"But ... it's not right!"

"Arabi won't die from his injury. And now he won't hurt himself or others, which he would have had we left him here."

"You don't know that!"

"And neither do you. We'll just take him back to my father and say there was an accident."

Haven was silent at that, so Rastla said, "Or would you rather I tell him that it was his shepherd boy who caused his best oxen to be injured? Or that he wanted to leave it alone rather than do his duty to restrain it?"

Haven was quiet a moment longer but then finally nodded and picked up his crook. Rastla gently wiped the blood from Arabi's head as Haven gave the animal a light tug toward the field. Arabi slowly rose and followed his masters, who walked the path back in silence, neither looking at the other.

XXXV

"JESUS, WE'VE GOT TO do something," Thunderer said as he paced about the room

"No shit," Groundquake snapped. "This makes no sense! What the hell could block us from the Obelisk?"

"That's the least of our problems," Thunderer added. "Nerbino, your healers, do they have anything we can use against the plague?" the ram asked.

"Not much," the gremlin king answered. "A plant from the surface, and it is not ... strong enough to cure this."

"Great. Just great," Quake spat.

"Wait," Forester said. "A plant? And it can heal you?"

"Yes ... it is an ancient ... salve of my kind."

"Then maybe Ah could enhance it, make it stronger."

"Good, but not enough. If we are going ... to save my people, then the question is the same as it was before—*what* is this plague? Because knowing *that* ... is the only way to find a cure."

"Then where do we look? At this point, the only thing we have is a door that we can't open or the end of the world starts." Quake said as Thunderer continued to pace.

"Then you should travel through the earth ... find some of the other supernaturals," Nerbino said. "With your authority, you could ... get someone from light or dark to work with our healers."

"That is a good idea, sire," Hazari said. "But even then, it is possible that Groundquake could spread the plague, having been exposed to it."

"Yeah and— Wait, you *don't* want me to infect the outside world?" Groundquake asked.

"Of course not," Hazari said.

"We do have some respect … for living beings, Earth Knight," Nerbino said.

"Either way, these sound like our best options," Thunderer said. "Forester and I should go with the healers and see what we can do."

"What about the door, sire?" Hazari asked.

"Even if the magic is gone … it still remains sealed … by the blood magic," Nerbino said. "For the moment, it isn't a concern."

"As far as I can tell, it's a *major* concern," the dog argued. "It's the only clue we have to go with, and I need to look it over again."

Nerbino grunted, "Fine. You can take a much closer look … while the healers are only keeping the disease at bay right now."

"I'll speak with them. Maybe I can find something out," Thunderer said.

"I'll help the Earth Knight then," Hazari said. "He may need a second set of eyes."

*   *   *

"Do you see anything?" Hazari asked some time later as Groundquake continued to examine the door.

"I'll tell you when I figure out what's wrong with it," the dog answered.

"Then perhaps we are wasting our time," the gremlin said. "We don't even know if the plague and the door are linked."

"Your people get sick, the light leaves the door at the same time, and you tell me that's *not* a link?" Quake snapped.

"Well … I … I guess …"

The dog just muttered something and kept examining the door. He ran his hands over the tracings in the door and looked for any sort of cracks or alterations. But no matter where he searched, he found nothing that looked like even a tiny fissure. Sighing, the dog finally put his hands on his head and leaned back onto the door.

"I hope to God the others are having better luck than I am," he said.

But Thunderer and Forester were not. They had moved to the alcoves where the gremlin healers were working on the few patients they could treat. And despite everything, the chief healer was unwilling to allow anyone to tamper with the only healing agent the gremlins had.

"Sir, I know how this sounds, but I truly believe that my friend can help you," Thunderer said. "His power has been shown to strengthen plant life, and—"

"Bah!" the healer, a tall, thin gremlin, snapped, his teeth clicking shut as he spoke. "You don't think we've tried herbs? If you want real healing, why don't you whip out that magic you Elementals have?"

"Our powers are too dangerous to use here," Thunderer said. "But if there's some way we can work together to stop it, then everyone wins."

"Against this?" the healer retorted. "Has it occurred to you that gremlins normally *carry* diseases in our blood?"

"I ..."

"Exactly. The best I can do right now, the best *anyone* can do, is to try to ease the pain until someone finds a permanent cure—or until someone comes here who *isn't* afraid to use their all-powerful healing magic."

Thunderer started to say something and then paused and said, "Can you at least show us what you are using to help them?"

The healer snorted but said, "Fine. Follow me."

The two knights watched as the healer reached into a nearby ceramic bowl and pulled out what looked like a small yellow flower.

"This is the healing agent?" Thunderer asked.

"Very good," the healer snapped. "We call it—"

"The canna lily. It's native to this area of Florida."

"How did you—"

"Forest Knight."

"Well, do you think there's anything you can do with it?" Thunderer asked.

"It's a plant. When can Ah not do something with it?"

"Let him try," Thunderer said to the healer.

The gremlin grumbled, but he still handed the herb to Forester. The squirrel took it carefully and balanced it on his open palm. He then placed his other hand over it. A green light began to emanate from his enclosed hands, growing stronger with each second. Even the healer's crusty expression softened a bit in amazement at the show of power.

Finally, the light stopped, and the squirrel pulled his hand away. The flower lay in his hand, now glowing with a green aura.

"You … have enhanced it?" the healer asked.

"Very good. Any other questions?" Forester said.

The healer snarled, but Thunderer stepped in. "Let's just try it. For the sake of the patients?" the ram asked.

The healer bared his teeth but nodded and held his hand out for the flower. But Forester pulled his hands back.

"Ah can keep enhancing the flowers' potency if Ah hold onto it."

The healer's eyes narrowed, but he said, "Fine. Try it on this one."

The healer gestured to a particularly ill gremlin, lying on a slab—her body covered in sores, her skin pasty white. Her head twitched on occasion as she moaned in pain.

"She'll do," the squirrel said. He reached out his hand to place the flower on the woman, but before he could, Thunderer grabbed his arm.

"Are you sure about this?" Thunderer asked.

"Didn't you want a cure?"

"Yes … but you saw what happened when I did it. And besides, you're putting a lot of yourself into this by enhancing the flower."

"Which is why it'll work. Besides, Ah've got a better reason for doing this."

"Saving the gremlins?"

"And," Forester whispered, "shutting this guy the hell up."

The squirrel put his hand, still holding the glowing flower, onto the gremlin's chest. He closed his eyes, placing his other hand over the flower as he began the healing process. The light began to glow brighter, and the gremlin's shuddering increased. The healer moved forward, but Thunderer held him back. As Forester held the flower down, the shuddering became a spasm, the gremlin held down on the slab only by the knight's hand. And still he pressed; the flower under his hand began to sprout, its blossoms pushing outward, grander and brighter than any flower before, the red and yellow a brilliant contrast to the green.

Thunderer looked about, waiting for the vines to begin sprouting through the slab, but all the plant growth seemed to be confined to the flower.

Finally, there was a final scream from the gremlin, and a brilliant flash of green blinded everyone in the room.

The light started to fade, and Thunderer, rubbing his eyes, moved forward, holding out his hand as he called for Forester. Slowly, his vision began to clear, and he could make out the shape on the slab. The ram saw a form rise up from the slab; and as his vision cleared, he saw it was the female gremlin, her body cleansed of the sickness. Thunderer turned to Forester to congratulate him, but the words died on his lips. The Forest Knight was slumped over the slab, his body barely moving, save for his breathing.

Thunderer ran to his friend, and gently turned him over. Forester stared blankly up at him; the sores that had covered the gremlin were now erupting on the side of his face.

∗   ∗   ∗

"Did you hear that?" Groundquake asked.

"Hear what?" Hazari replied.

"Something like … glass breaking or something. I dunno. I got a weird feeling about it all of a sudden."

"Perhaps you have been studying this door too lon— lon—"

"What?" Quake asked, looking over at Hazari. But the gremlin was transfixed, staring at the door in horror.

The dog quickly turned back around to face it and gaped as well. A crack had suddenly appeared in the door, and as the dog watched, it began to spread, flowing down the door like water carving stone itself. And with the crack widening, Quake could hear something through the door—a sound like metal clanking about and the cries of an animal, an animal caged for far too long and ready to escape.

XXXVI

"OKAY, JUST A FEW more steps," Sara said as she helped Mark through her apartment building. One by one, she helped him up the stairs, though he still stumbled on a step and let out a hiss.

"Crybaby. Here we are," Sara said as they came to her doorway. Reaching into her pocket with her free hand, Sara pulled out her key and slid it into the lock. The door popped open, and she half-dragged, half-carried Mark over to the couch, finally laying him down on it.

"Jesus, you're heavy," Sara said, arching her back.

"I think anyone would seem that way after five blocks," Mark replied, rubbing his leg.

"Hang on," Sara said. She went into the bathroom and opened the medicine cabinet. Inside were a couple bottles of Advil, tampons, hydrogen peroxide, a tin of Band-Aids, cotton balls, and a roll of gauze. Sara grabbed the pills, gauze, and cotton and returned to the couch, where Mark was rubbing his leg and looking around.

"Not a bad place," he said. "I like the character."

"You're sweet. But a bad liar," Sara said as she pulled off a length of gauze and then soaked a cotton ball in peroxide. Wrapping the gauze around her free hand, she turned back to Mark and placed her hand on the bloody rip in his jeans.

"This is gonna sting," she said as she opened the rip wide enough to see the wound from the knife. But when Sara saw it, her eyes widened in surprise.

"The guy freaking stabbed you!" she said, looking at the cut, only four inches long, in Mark's leg. The wound was long, but not deep; the bleeding was already down to a light trickle, despite the exertion of getting here.

"He was drunk," Mark suggested. "He could've missed or not made a deep enough cut."

"I-I guess," Sara said as she applied the cotton to the wound. The blood became awash in white foam as the peroxide cleaned out the infection. Sara moved her hand to steady Mark's leg, but found it too surprisingly still. She looked up to see Mark calmly sitting there, his face neutral and calm.

"This ... doesn't hurt?"

"Not enough to bother me."

Sara murmured a reply and then removed the peroxide foam, held more cotton against the leg, and began to fix some cotton and gauze around the wound. Again, Mark stayed still until she had finished and then gingerly flexed the leg a bit.

"Feel better?"

"Much. You do good work."

"I had plenty of experience on my ex."

"He got stabbed a lot?"

Sara snorted and then said, "No, he was just the sort of idiot who would talk until someone beat him up and then wonder why."

"Is that why you broke up?"

"Among other reasons," Sara said. "But I'm tired of talking about me. I dragged your wounded ass all the way to my apartment. I wanna hear something about you now."

Mark swallowed, but then gave a grin. "Okay. Like what?"

"I don't know; something. You aren't going anywhere for a while, so we should try to talk about something."

"Well, I've been teaching myself guitar."

"See, there's something," Sara said. "Wasn't hard, was it?"

"Ha, ha," Mark said. "But I've been trying to learn for about three months now."

"And you have a problem already?"

"Seems like every song has about three chords too many," he answered with a sigh. "I dunno. I can't seem to keep up with it."

"Well, you know, they do make songs with *just* three chords," Sara said.

"I have heard of the Ramones."

"I've heard better," she said. She turned and rummaged through a nearby pile of CDs, pulling out a green and white album.

"And that is?"

"The Pogues. Lemme guess, you've never heard of them?"

"Uh … no."

"So uncultured," Sara muttered, putting the CD in the stereo and selecting a track. Pressing play, she stood back.

Mark was bombarded with the wheeze of an accordion; a shrill whistle; and, after a moment, the most slurred, unintelligible vocals he had ever heard, with the pounding and jingling of guitars, banjos, and drums underneath.

"What the hell happened to this guy?" he asked as Sara sat back down.

"Bad teeth, alcohol, the usual," Sara said. "But he had some great songs."

"Lemme guess, your dad introduced you to these guys too?"

"Yeah, he was a big fan," Sara said. "He'd play them whenever he was working around the house. I just bought my own copies when I left."

"I can't imagine why," Mark said as the first song ended and the trill of piano keys suddenly filled the room.

"Oh, this is the perfect song for you," Sara said. "It only has three chords, and it's just gorgeous."

"It's certainly different," Mark said. The voice from the previous song had come on, still mumbling but singing slower, and almost intelligibly. In fact, as Mark listened more, he began to make out the words.

I've been loving you a long time
Down all the years, down all the days
And I've cried for all your troubles

Smiled at your funny little ways

"This was always one of my favorites," Sara said, leaning back on the couch.

"I like it," Mark said as the lyrics spun on, painting the picture of the last of a group of friends, their love guiding them through life as the music swelled behind them.

Sara listened with the expression of someone wrapping themselves in an old, familiar blanket. But Mark looked as if he'd been punched in the face. He listened to each declaration of love as if he was hearing the concept for the very first time, his mouth open, his brow furrowed as if he needed to analyze every single word. He only stopped when Sara leaned further back, closed her eyes, and draped her arms out, brushing his shoulder. He stiffened at the touch as the last few lyrics of the song played out.

Still there's a light I hold before me
You're the measure of my dreams

Mark sat there, first looking ahead at the stereo and then turning back toward Sara as the song entered its crescendo. With the music soaring about him, Mark looked over at Sara. Sara glanced at him. He tipped his head toward the stereo and smiled. She grinned and lay back on the sofa, closing her eyes as she listened. Mark looked at her and then lay back himself, though he kept his eyes on her as the music filled the air.

XXXVII

Time didn't move properly in the dream. Before, Rastla's father had just starting tilling the earth. But now, Joe stood before a fully tilled area as Rastla helped her father lead a harnessed Arabi in from the fields.

"The old ox did well today," Rastla's father said. "The fields are ripe for planting."

"I'm happy enough he didn't go wild again," Rastla said.

"As am I. You did well to try to restrain him."

"But this wound," Rastla said, tracing the outline on the ox's forehead. "It will leave a scar."

"Better a scar on Arabi then something worse for the people here," Rastla's father replied. "Haven acted cowardly in wanting to leave him."

"And he was so worried that I struck Arabi," Rastla said.

"Even the most loyal creature can be dangerous. Haven is young; he will learn this ..." Rastla's father trailed off then, causing the young Architect and Joe to turn.

A group of men were walking down the path to their home, led by the Prayer-sayer himself. Rastla and her father quickly bowed as the procession reached them.

"We welcome you to our humble home, oh, wise ones," Rastla's father said. "How may we serve you and further your good name?"

The prayer-sayer sniffed and said, "You may start by answering questions for us, Harabi—questions concerning your daughter."

"Has she done something wrong?" Harabi asked.

"She has shared troubling thoughts with me. And there is talk she has committed acts of violence against an innocent animal."

"Haven," Rastla whispered.

"She has spoken to me of what happened," Harabi said. "She was retrieving this ox with my shepherd boy, and it was spooked. Rastla acted to calm the beast and prevent it from causing injury to herself and the boy."

"And is that the result?" the prayer-sayer asked, pointing to the injury on the ox's head.

"Yes," Harabi replied. "But I would think it is a far smaller price to pay than—"

"Apparently, your daughter has not been listening to the most basic of my teachings—that all creatures are to be given respect and kindness, never violence." The prayer-sayer sneered.

"Wise one, an animal is not a man. I have farmed for many years, and I can tell you that a firm hand is often needed."

"Except with your daughter, it seems."

"I beg pardon?"

"Do you know what your child has been speaking of?"

"Yes. We have discussed it together. In fact, I suggested that she should see you and gain your insight."

The procession gasped, and one of the followers cried out, "You dare send such a heathen to the prayer-sayer?"

"I have a whole village to guide," the prayer-sayer said. "I cannot be expected to waste my time with foolish notions that you, as this girl's father, should have expunged in her."

"Don't blame my father!" Rastla cried out. "He trusted your wisdom to—"

"Enough!" the prayer-sayer said. "I have had enough of this. You two are hereby banned from the village until you have atoned for these impure thoughts."

Harabi gasped, and grabbing the prayer-sayer's robes, he pleaded, "Please, I must trade my crops for—"

"Away from the master!" one of the acolytes said, grabbing Harabi and pushing him back. The farmer stumbled backward, accidentally landing on Arabi. The ox let out a roar of surprise and then began to snort and stamp as everyone backed away.

"Fear not!" said the prayer-sayer. Gesturing to the ox, the old man said, "In the name of holy Ralin, I give you eternal peace—"

"Look out!" cried one of the Acolytes as the ox charged the prayer-sayer.

The entire procession ran off, save the prayer-sayer, who stood there, paralyzed with fright. The old man would have been gored, had he not suddenly been pulled down by something. The ox ran past him, stampeding off into the farmland.

Slowly, the prayer-sayer opened his eyes and looked about. Realizing he was unharmed, he started to give thanks, until he noticed an arm over him. He looked over to see Harabi draped over him, moaning in pain. The prayer-sayer looked down and saw the mangled pieces of meat that had once been the farmer's legs.

"Father!" Rastla screamed, running to her father's side.

"We ... we ... Acolytes!" the Prayer-Speaker yelled. "We must return to the temple and help this man!"

The acolytes quickly came out of hiding and came to their master. First, they lifted Harabi off him. Though they were being careful, the man screamed in pain. Another helped the prayer-sayer up as Rastla moved past him and went to her father. The prayer-sayer glared as she walked by him, but she still followed the procession back to the temple, as did Joe, pulled along by the same force keeping him in the dream.

* * *

The music swelled to its climax and then faded; silence filled the room.

"That ... was a good song," Mark said after a moment.

"Right," Sara said, opening her eyes and looking over.

"So ... I'm sorry I didn't show you a better time tonight."

"It could've been worse," Sara said as a new song began to play in the background. "Besides, I haven't had many nights out."

"I have you beat."

"Really?'

"I honestly can't remember another time out like this. Oh God, that was too much, wasn't it?"

"Yes. But honest at least. You want some coffee?"

Mark nodded, and Sara got up from the couch, heading for the kitchen. As she turned on the coffeemaker and loaded the coffee, she glanced back into the living room. Mark was sitting quietly on the couch, listening to the music.

Wonder how long it's been for him, Sara wondered. *He's not that bad looking … Oh Lord.*

Sara shook her head. She barely knew anything about Mark. Granted, he didn't sound like a nut job, and tonight had been decent, even a little fun. But so what? What else did he do? Where did he live? What was he really like? Did he have blood slides in his air conditioner?

For God's sake, Sara, that *was just a stupid TV show,* Sara thought, as the sounds of Shane McGowan and Kristy MacColl filled the room. But as the coffee finished perking, and she drew two cups, she realized something else—she wanted to find out, because Sara hadn't been curious about a man like that in a long time.

Taking the mugs, she walked back into the room, ready to start some real conversation. But when she got there, she stopped dead in her tracks. Mark was off the couch, listening as "Fairytale of New York" came to a close. He stood at the door, looking at Sara sadly.

"Mark?" Sara asked putting down the coffee and moving to his side. Taking his hand, she asked, "What is it? What's wrong?"

Looking directly at her, he said, "I'm sorry."

"What?"

"I …" he said, looking away. "I can't be here."

"Mark, what are you talking about?"

"I know how this will end. And I can't … not to you … not to anyone."

He pulled away, opening the door the door. Before Sara could respond, he was already through, the door closing behind him. Sara grabbed the knob and swung the door open. But all she saw was an empty hallway.

XXXVIII

FIRESPRITE COUGHED AND WHEEZED, her lungs slow to take in air after the unfamiliar teleport. Turning to see Crash, who was already moving to speak with Hiro, she managed to hack out, "What ... in the hell ... is wrong with you?"

"It's worse than I could've imagined," Crash said to Hiro, not even noticing Firesprite.

The lizard let out a particularly loud cough, bringing the cat's focus back to her.

"What did the vampires tell you?" Hiro asked.

"They say the plague came from humans," Firesprite said. "They've got sick people of their own they're dealing with."

"How can vampires have any kind of sickness?"

"Because this is way bigger than humans, vampires, maybe even us," Wavecrasher said.

"What in the hell are we dealing with?" Firesprite yelled.

Wavecrasher turned and looked at the Fire Knight in disbelief. "Are you telling me you haven't figured it out?"

"A blind man could see this is some kind of Chaos Demon, but clearly you think it's something else because of what a dying vampire said!"

Crash snorted in frustration and said, "Think! We're sent here to check on something that's locked away in a door that no one from good or evil is supposed to open. We get here to find people and vampires suffering from a disease that makes them starve to death. And now we find out the cause of this was a vampire that was looking for a horse."

Firesprite stared in confusion, and then slowly but surely, a light began to brighten in her eyes. Her face slowly twisted in abject horror.

She looked at the cat and said, "You mean … they're real? We were sent here to safeguard *that*?"

"Four of them, with a name like Equites? Why not?"

"Oh, my God," Firesprite whispered. She stumbled backward on legs that had suddenly turned to Jell-O.

Hiro caught her and helped her to a chair and then looked at Crash and said, "What is this evil we face?"

"There's no time to tell you, Hiro," Crash said. "We need you to take us down there."

"To the door?" Hiro gasped. "But it is sealed tight—"

But before Hiro could finish, the sounds of barking echoed through the temple. The monk and two knights quickly followed the sound as it echoed throughout the temple. As they approached the center, it began to grow louder, until they found themselves in front of a large statue of Buddha. Hiro reached behind the left ear and pressed a small button. After a loud click, and then part of the wall swung aside, revealing a stairway.

"Sealed tight, huh?" Firesprite said as she lit a fireball over her hand and headed down, the others following. They ran down the stairs, until they came to the source of the barking—the fox, growling and snarling at the door. The door was within a gigantic cave, with walls that had been carved with long, twisting arcane symbols that carved around like spiked, tattooed snakes embedded in the walls. At the sound of their approach, it turned to them, briefly made eye contact, and then continued barking.

"She has never come down here before," Hiro said.

"I think I can see why she's here now," Firesprite said, pointing at the door.

Hiro looked and gasped. Huge cracks were spreading through the door; as they watched, a new one began to form on the right side. The cracks gleamed with a strange, pale light, and the sounds of something moving around behind the door could be heard.

"How … How can this be happening?" Hiro asked.

"Because of what's happening out there," Crash said. "We have to stop this."

"How?"

"The disease is causing this. We have to cure it."

"We don't have time for that," Firesprite said. "We only have one option."

"What do you mean?"

"If we can't cure the sick people, we have to get rid of them."

"What? What are you talking about?" Crash asked.

"You know well enough," Firesprite answered. "If they aren't around to be sick anymore, then our problem is subdued, if not solved."

"You can't be serious!" Hiro cried out, the fox standing next to him. "You would condemn them to death to save us?"

"No, I'd do it to save the whole damn world," the lizard snapped. "This won't stop here, and we both know it, Crash! The vamps are already sick, and we don't do something—"

"But the people!"

"Do you think I *like* having to suggest this?" Firesprite snapped. "But it's not the first time we've done something like this, and it won't be the last!"

"*We* never did anything like this!" the cat yelled back. "And I, *we* aren't going to start now! There must be another way!"

"What are you babbling about? Don't you remember that crowd of possessed rioters that would've ripped their own town to shreds?"

"I was finding the way to free them!"

"The soldiers stuck reliving their old battles and killing people? Did we or did we not put them in the grave?"

"I was getting people to safety!"

Firesprite stared in shock.

"You never actually had to do this yourself?" the lizard asked

"No, I've killed plenty."

"But never innocents?" Hiro asked.

The cat tried to answer, but Firesprite jumped in. "Of course not! You were always doing something else! What, you figured you could do what Joe couldn't?"

"*No!*" Crash yelled. "That was never it!"

"Then what? What's making you hold back?"

Crash didn't answer but instead turned her back to the lizard, growling and running her hands over her face as she began to pace.

"Jesus Christ, I hope Joe never acted like this when we didn't see him," Firesprite said.

"Stop comparing me to him! I'm not like Joe!"

"Really? Then why are you doing this? 'Cause it sure seems like it to me! Or are you afraid that the last thing they might see before you die is your furry face—"

"*Shut up!*" the cat screamed, shooting a stream of water at Firesprite. But the lizard quickly threw up a small square of fire that evaporated the water.

"I'm done talking about this with you. Not with somebody who wants to torch people," the cat sneered.

"Oh, no you're not," the lizard said. "What is this, Crash? You were always the one telling us to take the monsters down, no matter what."

"Wavecrasher, if we talk, we might be able to find a solution," Hiro said. "At the very least, it may lead to something less radical than what Firesprite is proposing."

"What is it?" Firesprite pressed as the cat gritted her teeth. "Why are you suddenly horrified by the job we do? Why do you always want to take the easy way out?"

"I … I …" the cat sputtered and then whispered something.

"Say again?" Firesprite asked.

"I can't be what they see."

"What?"

"Joe isn't my problem. Hell, I *envy* Joe," the cat said. "Joe can at least walk down the street. Joe can just put on some clothes and go to a city and sit down in a park."

"And you can't," Hiro said.

"Crash," Firesprite said. "Is that what all this is about? Is that why you've been so intent on things like the glamour?"

The cat took a breath and said, "Yes."

"But why do you blanch every time you have to do … this, with innocents? It hurts all of us, but we do it. And you've always been so focused on the mission, no matter what."

"I focus on the mission for the same reason I need to know everything, for the same reason I can't do this now—because if I make a mistake, because if I fail or let things fail, then people could die because of my mistake. And then I'd be …"

"A monster?" Hiro asked

The cat looked up as Firesprite asked, "That's it, right?"

Crash looked back down and wiped her eyes, saying in a husky voice, "I know it's stupid and selfish, but it's how I feel every time I look at my hands or in the mirror. But knowing I can do some good—"

"Why didn't you ever tell us about it?" the lizard asked. "Didn't you think we could relate?"

"Oh, yeah like I could really go to Sandy about it," the cat snapped. "Everybody else came to terms with it, even Forger. And she's probably the worst of us."

"And how do you know?" Firesprite asked. "Didn't you ever ask someone how they felt about it? Ask me how I felt about it?"

"What?" the cat asked.

"Yeah, mate," Firesprite said. "There are days I hate this too—when I get up and look at the scaly face in the mirror and wish I was still dead. Or did you think you were the only one stuck in a weird body, tormented by a name you can't remember?"

The cat stared at her fiery friend and then asked, "How … how do you deal with it?"

"I remind myself that I can't do anything about it," Firesprite said, "that having a malformed life with some measure of purpose is better than no life at all. And I accept that feeling sorry for myself isn't something I can waste my time doing, not with all I have to do."

"Grant me the power to change what I can and to accept what I cannot and the wisdom to know the difference," Hiro said.

Both knights turned to the monk, who shrugged and replied, "Wisdom is wisdom."

Crash wiped her eyes and then said, "But Sprite, I still can't let you do this to these people."

"Then you need to think of an alternative," the lizard replied. "Believe me, I'm open to suggestion."

"Perhaps you need to tell me what is going on here," Hiro said.

The two knights looked at each other and then Crash said, "We think the Chaos Demons are spreading this sickness around. And we think it's related to the door."

"How?"

"It's the thing behind it," Firesprite said. "It's feeding off this sickness, this hunger. And the more people suffer, the stronger it gets, until—"

"I understand," Hiro said. "What is behind that door? And how can we hope to stop it?"

"We need to eliminate the sickness," Firesprite answered. "If we do that, it should stop the H—"

But that was as far as the lizard got. Shrill barking filled the air as the fox ran up the stairs, jumped toward the door, and began to angrily scratch at it.

"What the hell's gotten into her?" Crash asked as she and the others followed her back up. Pulling the fox back, she opened the door and glanced outside. But when she did, she gasped in horror and whipped around to the others.

"Why, why did we trust them to do something right?" she spat out.

"Who? What are you— Oh God, they didn't. Please tell me they didn't," Firesprite said, running over to the door and looking out and then letting out a loud, "*Shit*!!"

"Now what?" Hiro muttered. He joined the knights, and looking out, he saw a group of figures on the land outside, some of them supporting each other as they waited, as if unable to actually enter the—

"They came here?!" Hiro exclaimed as the knights pushed past the doors and ran over to one figure that stood in front of the others.

"What in the hell are you doing?" Crash asked as they approached the figure. "We told you to—"

"You told me to get them out of the city," Kimiko answered. "But none of our safe houses are open—the unaffected are terrified of the plague."

"But it's holy! You can't even enter!" Firesprite snapped.

"That is what I told the Eldeus! But they said the great Elementals would *surely* be wise enough to make preparations for us to come here."

"God, I hate our reputation," Crash muttered.

"You didn't do anything? Then how are we standing here?" Kimiko asked.

"Something must have upset the balance of the temple," Hiro said. "Or perhaps because they came here for help."

"It doesn't matter. You have to get them out of here—all of them! Right now!" Firesprite said.

"And take them where? I told you, we have no hiding places left," Kimiko snapped. "Besides, if you can take care of the humans in there, you can help us here."

"Oh yeah, until the sun comes up in two hours!"

"We can bury ourselves, you idio—"

Boom.

Everyone jumped at the sound, and all the arguments stopped. Slowly, everyone turned to the temple as the sound emanated again.

Boom.

"What is that?" Kimiko asked, the anger gone from her voice now.

"What we wanted to keep you away from," Crash said. "God help us, it's trying to break out."

"Can we still get them out?" Firesprite asked. "Would that—"

"I don't know anymore," the cat asked. "They're not even in the temple, and it's getting stronger. We may need to fortify the door—"

"*What are you talking about*?!" Kimiko screamed, grabbing Crash's coat.

"Fine. This disease isn't a disease. It's famine," the cat said.

"What?"

"Everyone is affected, vampire and human; their bodies can't process nutrients they'd get from eating," Crash said. "They're starving to death."

"But ... what could be doing this?"

"You said that the sick vampire met another that was looking for a horse?" Firesprite asked. "A horse is the symbol of what's a group called the Equites."

"Latin?" Kimiko asked.

"Yeah. Pity we didn't figure it out before now," Crash said. "See, there's four of these things out in the world. Translated, Equites means ... horsemen."

Boom.

XXXIX

THE HIGH SCHOOL STOOD empty as the two hunters watched it in the glow of the moon. Hidden within the trees, one lit a cigarette, casually tossing the match aside.

"You really shouldn't do that," the other advised.

"Burning the place down would be more interesting than guard duty," the smoker replied.

"We joined the hunters to protect the world from danger," the other replied. "Don't you think that protecting one of our own would help us do that?"

"The way I see it, they should just let Hunst out when they've got a serious vamp to kill. He gets his bloodlust filled, and a vamp dies. Everybody wins."

"You know they wouldn't allow that. Besides, at least we get to test the sunlight room this way."

"Eh, still seems like a stupid idea to me," the smoker said. "I mean, we can't run somebody through a high school every time there's trouble. And the power source—"

"At least we have the option," the other said. "And lower your voice."

"Good idea. Someone like me might hear you two idiots."

Both hunters started, their heads swiveling about, trying to see who had spoken. But instead, they felt a pair of hands grab their collars and pull them upward through the tree. They crashed through branches and leaves, before coming face-to-face with a pair of gleaming red eyes.

"What the hell!"

"I can send you two there if you don't help me."

"W-What do you want?" the smoker stammered.

"I've been watching your little operation here. And since I don't seem to have a way past that light show in there, you're going to tell me how it works."

"We don't know," the second hunter said. "We were just sent to guard it during the night."

"I heard 'power source,'" the blackness whispered. "Tell me where it is and how to shut it off."

"Why should we?" the smoker managed to get out.

The voice was quiet, and then suddenly the two hunters found themselves being pushed forward but held upright in a strong, black grasp. They were pushed out beyond the reach of the branches, right over the asphalt parking lot. They looked at the height for a moment and then screamed as they were turned over, putting their heads directly over the black asphalt.

"You're going to tell me because I don't think you'll be much good to the hunters with serious brain damage … *if* you live. Now where is it?"

"It's hidden in the school!" the smoker blurted out.

"Good. Now be more direct."

"The art room. It's inside the kiln, next to the power switch. They made the switch double as the emergency cutoff, so there was less chance of someone tampering with it."

"Very good," the voice said as the hunters were slowly brought back to the tree. They breathed a sigh of relief when they touched the solid branches again, even as the voice whispered, "Now, don't worry about getting in trouble, boys. You won't have seen a thing."

The hunters turned at that, but then they saw nothing but blackness wrapping around their heads. They felt a sense of coldness drifting into their minds and then nothing.

And as the blackness faded away, they looked back at the school with apathy, as if nothing had happened. They didn't even notice as the blackness drifted along the ground and through an open window, pulling itself onto the floor of the school like a fog in a horror movie.

The blackness began to pull together, rising up from the floor into a pillar of mist, growing more and more solid, until Nightstalker stood inside the school once again.

The bat glanced about the hallways, looking at the doors around him. Unfortunately, all of them were labeled with numbers, not titles. He moved to the closest door and peered in. It was fuzzy, but he managed to make out the shape of beakers and unlit Bunsen burners. But if the lab was here, then it was unlikely that the art room was nearby. He needed to find a map of the school or get into the mind of someone who knew where the art room was. But at 1:00 a.m., it was dammed unlikely to find anyone in the facility around to—

Suddenly, the bat heard the sounds of wheels rolling down the hallway. He whirled around just in time to see a janitor pushing his mop and bucket down toward him. Stalker dissipated back into the shadows as the janitor moved down the hall, humming a song to himself as he did. From within the shadows, the bat rolled his eyes as the janitor made his way down. But as the bat watched, the janitor suddenly stopped, paused, and took a piece of paper out of his shirt pocket. Looking at it, he muttered, "Christ! Another damn mess there. Can't they learn not to give those kids paints anymore?"

The janitor then turned to the left, resuming his humming/singing as he walked. But this time, the shadows moved toward him. As they got closer, they merged into the janitor's own elongated shadow, moving with him as he headed toward the art room. The janitor pushed his mop through the hallways, taking time to clean a few areas here and there, all the while still humming, until he reached a room with a large double door. Pausing a moment, the janitor reached for his keys, and after a few minutes of fumbling, he found the correct one and unlocked the door.

Walking inside, the janitor beheld a large room with posters of student art projects—posters, clay sculptures, and even a few statues lying around. There were six large wooden tables as well, stationed right in front of the teacher's desk, which sat away from the massive kiln. The tables showed marks of heavy use—nicks, paints drips, and spots of clay. But what truly drew the janitor's attention was the rainbow—a vomit of colors that lay dumped on the floor between the tables.

"Better get the good shit," the janitor said, leaning over his bucket and pulling out bottles of various chemicals.

As he did, part of his shadow broke off and moved toward the large kiln. Keeping close to the darkness, the living shadow moved up the teacher's desk, pausing as it turned in the direction of the kiln. There were three large levers on the side of the kiln. One was marked "On/Off," one other clearly stated "Emergency Open," and one said "Lock/Unlock." The shadow stood still and then reached forward, wrapped a black tendril around the emergency lever, and pulled it down. There was a clank, as the door to the kiln unlocked and swung open.

The janitor heard the noise and turned toward it. But he had barely taken two steps when he felt something cold wrap around his ankles. The janitor stumbled and then fell to the floor, hitting it face-first. He groaned a moment, and then lay still upon the paint-covered floor.

The shadow unwrapped itself from his ankles and moved over to his head. It began to rise up, once again taking the form of Nightstalker. The bat knelt down and checked the janitor. His head was bruised, but his breathing was regular.

"Sorry, old man," Stalker said as he got up. He paused, only to bend back down and take the janitor's keys.

"This time, I think I'll just open the door myself," the bat said. He left the room and turned in the direction of the janitor's closet.

XL

"WHAT IN THE HELL is this?" Groundquake said as he stared in shock at the crack in the door. For a moment, he started to reach out his hand to touch it, but before he could, another crack burst through, slicing its way down the door.

"You have to do something! Can't you heal it?" Hazari cried out.

"I just handle rock, remember?" Groundquake snapped. "This door's got a hell of a lot more running through it than that right now."

Hazari bit his lip and started to speak, only to stop as the dog's hammer began to glow with a sliver light. Quake quickly pulled it from its holster and then said, "Thunderer, we've got a serious problem here."

"We've got a more serious one up here," the ram's voice said through the magic. "Forester's sick."

"Nothing new there."

"No, he's got the plague."

"What?" Quake cried out as Hazari gasped.

"I don't know what happened. He was trying to heal this gremlin using this flower the gremlins have. It worked, but it's like the plague transferred back into him."

"So give him his ax. Let that do its mojo."

"I've already tried. It's not working. I need you to get back up here now. Come to the gremlin healing chambers."

"That's not such a great idea," Quake said. "The door's starting to crack. And it sounds like something big and pissed off is moving around in there."

"But it was … Wait, when did this start?"

"A couple minutes ago, why?"

"Forester got sick a couple minutes ago."

Quake was silent then, his eyes first widening in shock and then narrowing. Turning to Hazari, he said, "I'm going to check on this. Forester might be an annoying shit, but I'm not about to let him die."

"But what about the door?" the gremlin asked.

Quake thought a moment and then grabbed his left hand and pulled off his middle finger. Hazari gasped as the finger turned to earth. The dog then tossed the finger to the gremlin and said, "If something happens, smash that."

"S-Smash it?"

"I'll feel it. Figured it out this one time I left an arm behind."

Hazari stared at the finger in wonder. Then Quake suddenly turned into earth and broke away, returning to the ground he championed.

*　　*　　*

And then reappearing in the healing chambers, Quake's body regrew out of the earth itself. The dog stayed frozen in stone a moment and then his body returned to flesh and blood. He gazed out at the sight before him. Forester was lying on top of a stone slab, his coat and shirt removed so the doctors could work on him. His fur was matted with sweat, and boils had burst all over his chest. His hand gripped his ax, but the weapon was only faintly glowing.

Quake quickly moved to the head of the slab, where he gazed in horror at the squirrel's face. The boils had crept over the left side of his face, distorting and twisting the flesh and fur there. In some spots, the fur had fallen out; in others, the skin underneath was bloated and lumpy. Two boils had grown over the side of his lips; as Quake watched him breathe, he realized the two were connected, creating a fleshy rope connecting the lips.

"Sweet Christ," the dog whispered as Thunderer came up to stand by him.

"The healers are saying that this is the worst case they've seen," the ram said. "It's like he not only absorbed it, he sped it up too."

"And the ax?"

"Just seems to be keeping him alive," the ram answered.

"Then we need to give it a boost," Quake answered, taking hold of his hammer. The weapon glowed with brown light, which passed into the dog's hand. Reaching over, he placed his hand over the handle of the ax and, with a breath, released the energy into the axe. For a moment, the green and brown mixed together, glowing brightly. Then suddenly, the brown vanished, and the green dimmed.

"I tried that already," Thunderer said. "God, why did I let him do it?" the ram cried out. "He was just doing it to piss off that doctor. Stupid!"

The ram would've kept going, but Quake grabbed his friend and gave him a hard slap across the face. "That's not gonna help him!" the dog said as Thunderer breathed in deeply from shock. "You wanna cry about this, you do it later. Right now, you figure out something we can do to keep him from dying."

Thunderer took a final breath and then said, "I-I did have one idea."

"Great. What?"

"He needs a direct transfusion of forest energy. And there's nothing here that can help him with that."

"So what, we take him to a forest?"

"No, I don't want to risk him losing grip on the ax. We need to get him a direct dose."

"And who has... Wait, you don't mean ..."

"Yes."

"Are you nuts?" Quake yelled. "We can't even get back home, and you think we can call one of the Architects here? They can't even leave their plane of existence anyway."

"Forester is one of us. Don't you think they would try to save him?"

"Then where is Demtia? Don't you think he'd be here doing that if you were right?"

"Isn't it possible they just don't know what's going on? They do watch the whole planet."

Quake stammered and then bit his tongue as Thunderer said, "What I do know is that, if we do nothing, Forester may die. We need to try, for him if for no other reason."

Quake began to speak, but then one of the healers said, "Actually, we may have a solution."

*   *   *

"Brother, please, you must let me help him!" Demtia pleaded as the Architects watched over the scene from their plane of existence.

"I understand your anguish, Demtia, but leaving your post empty is a tremendous risk," Ralin said, "even for a matter such as this."

"But my knight is dying!" the green-clad Architect begged. "Surely you would not let everything we have built together be destroyed."

"You know as well as we do that the knights cannot die," Rastla whispered.

"And you think that is an excuse?" Demtia demanded. "If it was Nightstalker, would you be so calm, so uncaring?"

"She would be held to the same restrictions we all are," Darya said.

"Demtia, has it occurred to you that this could all be contrived?" Zeuia asked. "The Equites being threatened, this confusion with the hunters, and now, something to draw one of us from this realm and into danger."

Demtia bit his lip and replied, "Yes ... but still ..."

"Zueia, you are correct in your assessment, but it does not solve the problem at hand," Ralin said. "We need the knights at full strength if this becomes what we fear it to be. Demtia, if every other avenue is exhausted, you will go and save Forester. But not until then."

*   *   *

"Calm down, Rastla. I'm sure that everything is fine," Haven said as the girl slung a rope over her shoulder.

"You wouldn't say that if it was your father!" Rastla said as Joe watched her. The future Architect had been in great stress since her father had been taken to the temple of the prayer-sayer. Rastla had attempted to see him after the first day, but she had been denied entrance then and every day since. She was told that her father's injuries were severe and slow to heal. But Joe's work had proven to him that even the most holy of men would lie to suit their interest. Besides, if the prayer-sayer had the power of Ralin as he claimed, then he should be able to heal the man. Rastla had every right to investigate.

"But to go out now—" Haven insisted.

"Haven, there is nothing else you can say to change my mind," Rastla said. "I don't care if you are afraid of the prayer-sayer. I am going to see my father."

"Please, Rastla, you are going against everything we have ever been taught. I beg you, don't do this."

"Did it ever occur to you that we were taught those things for other reasons?" Rastla asked as she grabbed her father's scythe. "That the prayer-sayer doesn't want us to see what he does?"

"Rastla!"

But the young girl gave no reply. She simply walked through the door of her home and ran toward the direction of the temple. Joe followed her, wondering just what it was the young Architect had in mind and why it was so important he needed to see her plan unfold.

Rastla traversed over the village quickly; she was young and fit, and no one was around to stop her (as everyone was in the fields). She jumped over every rock and turn without even a glance, reaching the temple quickly.

Rastla slowed her approach, avoiding the front of the building and making her way to the back. Joe watched as she crept under the windows, until she finally reached one that was directly underneath a rooftop statue of Ralin, his arms outstretched to the masses. Joe saw her plan immediately; she undid the rope and began to twirl it. She then hurled it upward, wrapping the end around one of Ralin's arms. She gave a few tugs and then hoisted herself up and began to climb, with Joe following right behind. Just *before she reached the window, Rastla paused and cocked her ear, listening for the sound of people above. After a few seconds, she was satisfied, and pulled herself into the temple. She quickly got to her feet and started to look about, but suddenly she heard footsteps coming from the side of the corridor. Rastla frantically looked around for cover and then saw a huge vase standing in the corner. Without thought, she jumped inside, while Joe just stood and watched from the comfort of his invisibility.*

He could hear the voice of the prayer-sayer. "And that is why we must continue to remind the people of how much we are given by the great Ralin and how we must continue to obey the teachings he gives me," the prayer-sayer said as he walked the hallway, surrounded by his acolytes.

"You are right, Great One," said one of the acolytes. "But does not Ralin say we should encourage the happiness of others?"

"Of course."

"Then … Great One, his daughter misses her father very much. Since her mother left our village, they have grown close. And he asks to see her constantly."

The prayer-sayer stopped and looked at the young acolyte. Speaking gently, he said, "You are young, and I know your heart is in the right place. To see his daughter again would please him. But soon, her questions and lack of understanding would cloud that over, because he himself does not see how foolish such talk is. Under our care, he will come to this realization, and he will correct his daughter. This will make both of them happy."

"You are wise, Master," the acolyte replied, bowing.

"You will learn. As will this man. When the light of Ralin flows through him, as it does me, he will understand, and his daughter will no longer be a deterrent to the happiness of this village."

The acolytes nodded, and they all walked away, the prayer-sayer continuing to preach. But Joe had stopped listening. To think that a follower of Ralin, in a time and place where the Architect was known, would talk of such blindness and propaganda. But as Joe thought on it, he wondered something else—why had Ralin not corrected the unbalance himself? This early on in the world, with no darkness to counteract him, surely Ralin could work his influence on the man.

But Joe had no time to muse on this, as he heard the sound of Rastla exiting the vase. He turned toward the young girl, only to back away from what he saw. Rastla's face was twisted into a mask of rage, with enough potency to reduce a man to ashes. Her clenched teeth were bared, and she glared in the direction of the prayer-sayer, breathing in and out rapidly. She brought her clenched hands up and suddenly whirled around and punched the wall. She didn't dent it, and as Joe watched, he saw blood trickle down from her fist. But Rastla didn't flinch; instead she turned and continued on down the hallway, not even noticing the blood on her hand.

XLI

"CAN YOU SENSE ANYTHING?" Forger asked Avia, who sat cross-legged in her palm.

"Too much," Avia said, her almond-shaped eyes closed in concentration. "There are strains of magic flowing all over this glen."

Sandshifter asked, "Does fairy magic differ from fairy to fairy?"

"You mean like an individual scent or something?" Windrider suggested.

"The magic is always the same for each fairy," Avia replied. "But … every spell does feel different."

"And what did this feel like?"

Avia crinkled her nose, as if she was detecting a scent herself.

"Almost a teleportation spell. But there was something else—a tinge on the edges that is unlike what I've felt before."

"Can you track it?" Forger asked.

"I will try. But it was very faint."

"Try anyway," the spider said. "Good thinking, Sandy."

The wolf nodded and watched intently as Avia increased her concentration, scanning outward for any sign of the magic. Suddenly, her eyes snapped open, and she cried out, "There!"

"Where? Where is it?" Forger asked.

"I-I … it's gone," the fairy said. "Whatever it was, it has faded away. But I know what level it was at."

"Show us," Sandshifter said.

Avia nodded and flew from Forger's hand into the air and up beyond the level. Windrider raised his hands, and the trio rose up on the currents of air, floating about gently as they followed the fairy up through the levels of the glen. They rose higher and higher, the levels flying by and the ceiling coming closer until Avia finally came to a halt.

Windrider carried them over onto firm ground, where the fairy was looking about in confusion.

"Avia? What's wrong?" Forger asked. The level they were at was bare of any activity. No fairies bustled about; no doors or windows shone. The level was simply solid wood and hard earth, save for one thing—a small door that stood before them, emblazoned with the sigil of the queen and a single lock below that.

"This is the queen's private storage level," the fairy answered.

"Really? Wow, I'll bet there's all sorts of cool stuff in there," Windrider said.

"Let's find out," Sandshifter said as she stepped forward and pushed on the door. But the lock only rattled as she tugged, harder and harder.

"The door is always locked. Only the queen holds the key," Avia said.

"Not a problem," Forger said, stepping to the door and raising her hand. Extending her finger, Forger pressed it into the lock, the flesh changing into pliable metal as she did so. She waited a moment for the metal to assume the shape of the keyhole and then turned her hand. But instead of a click, she felt something hold her finger, and then the spider screamed as energy flew from the lock into her body. She convulsed for a moment and then collapsed onto the ground. The others rushed to her aid.

"What the hell was that?" Sandshifter snapped.

"The security. I-I didn't know what it was, just that magic protects the door," Avia said.

"Man, that was a pretty cool way to do it," Windrider said, gazing at the lock even as he helped Forger up.

"Glad ... you approve," the spider muttered.

"Oh. Uh, sorry."

"So ... how else can we get in there?" Windrider asked.

"We could ask the queen to open the door," Avia said.

"I have a better idea," Sandshifter said. Before anyone could ask what it was, the wolf's body melted away into a pile of sand. The pile then began to move, spreading out toward the door. As the others watched, a tendril snaked up out of the pile toward the keyhole. It pushed itself through the hole, dragging more and more of its body into the door. After a few moments, everything had been sent through. Then there was a click and the door swung open, revealing Sandshifter standing there.

"You coming?" she asked.

"We should not enter like this," Avia said. "The queen..."

"I have a feeling the queen knows more than she is telling us," Sandshifter said. "Now come on."

"Of course *you* would," the fairy grumbled.

The wolf turned then, as the others expected another rant. But instead, she said, "Blind loyalty never works out, little fairy. You want to serve your queen, don't put her on a pedestal. Make her accountable. That's something the humans did get right."

Avia glared at the wolf, but said nothing, as the Knights walked forward. She followed as the group entered the huge room, and Windrider said to the spider, "You know how you said this could lead us to something? I think you might've been wrong."

"As much as I hate to admit it, I think you may be right," Forger said, as the knights and their fairy guide looked around the vast, empty room that surrounded them.

"What is this? Some part of the tree that didn't get used?" Windrider asked.

"The queen would not have barricaded it with magic if there wasn't something here," Avia said as she flew about.

"What about a glamour that covers a room instead of a person," Forger said.

"You know of such magic?" Avia asked.

"We use glamours to move about with humans," the spider answered. "But I doubt it's the same kind of magic that—"

"Why not?" Windrider interjected. "Didn't Crash get it from some book written in German?"

"I don't … No, she might have," Forger said. "And if that's the case…"

The spider quickly knelt down and touched the ground. Whispering, she spoke the words that undid the glamour the knights used. The others watched in anticipation, and sure enough, the walls around them began to shimmer as the magic was stripped away, revealing …

"Uh, shouldn't something have happened?" Windrider asked as he looked at walls that had not altered in anyway.

"I don't understand," Avia said. "There was clearly a glamour in place, but what was it hiding?"

No one replied, but Sandshifter walked over to the walls and leaned in close. Placing her face very near the wall, she breathed in deeply, taking in the smell of the earth and wood. Finding nothing, she continued to move over the wall, taking inventory of each inch of it. Suddenly, she stopped, and took a second, deeper breath. Pulling back from the wall, she growled and then began to dig, pulling away at the soil and vines.

"What is she doing?" Avia asked.

"What wolves do—track," Forger said. "C'mon."

The spider moved over and began to dig along with the wolf, using her extra arms to add more width to the hole. Windrider and Avia looked at each other in confusion, but after a moment, they too began to dig, though the tiny fairy couldn't do much, pulling away clumps of dirt the size of fingernails.

At first, it seemed like nothing but soil was there. But then, Sandy's claws brushed against something hard and solid under the dirt.

"I knew it," the wolf said. "There *is* something here."

"Something big, from the feel of it," Forger said, spreading out her arms to gauge the width. "It'll take forever to dig it out."

"Man, I wish Quake was here," Windrider said.

"We can do fine without him," Sandshifter said. She lifted up her hand and pointed it at the wall. Her hand transformed into sand and grew out toward the wall, stretching into a long tendril. It reached the wall and then pushed into it, the grains of sand moving through the cracks in the soil. Sandshifter gritted her teeth and put more and more of herself into the tendril, allowing it to spread out through the entire wall. Finally, she stopped, and grabbing her other arm, the wolf pulled back with all her strength. The wall shuddered but didn't break. Sandshifter prepared to pull again, but then Windrider wrapped his arms around the wolf's abdomen.

"Excuse me?" Sandy snapped.

"Just trying to give some extra pull," the falcon said.

The wolf sighed, but said, "Fine."

Forger sent a length of chain into the tendril, spreading it out through the wall. The three knights glanced at each other and then, with a heave, pulled at the wall with all their combined strength. The dirt heaved and shifted and then finally exploded in a burst of soil and rock. The knights backed away quickly but not before seeing what their efforts had unearthed.

"God, what is that?" Sandshifter coughed out as the dust around them settled.

"I ... have no idea," Forger said, looking at the object before them. It resembled nothing so much as a giant walnut, easily fifteen feet long and five feet high. The base was square, allowing it to balance on the floor, but the top ended in a raised, circular section that along, with it's weathered, dry-looking, brown skin, gave it its nutlike appearance.

"So the queen makes the walnuts for all of Germany?" Windrider asked.

"I have no idea," the fairy answered. "No fairy magic I know of would make something like this."

"Then let's stop talking about it and take a closer look," Sandshifter said, moving over to the nut. Once again, she began to sniff, this time around the lip of the two halves. But she had barely sniffed for half a second when she stopped and then frantically began to jam her staff into the lip, trying to pop it open.

"I was hoping I was wrong," Forger muttered as she moved over and pulled the wolf away.

The spider held out two hands, the fingers already growing long, thin, sharp, and metallic. When her blade fingers were ready, Forger jammed them into the lip, slicing through the connecting section, and with a heave, she pulled upward. The lip began to crack further down, and Sandshifter and Windrider helped pull.

Finally, they flipped the lid over, and looked inside the nut.

Inside lay six sleeping children, all aged between six and nine. Gingerly, Forger reached out and touched one of the stems wrapped around their bodies. Each ended in a flower that pressed against one of the children's mouths. The stem jiggled, and a small burst of yellow gas leaked out of its flower.

"It's ... some sort of pollen tranquilizer," the spider said.

"No, duh," Sandshifter said. "This some sort of fairy magic too?"

"It ... we use something like this to calm wild animals," Avia said in horror. "But I've never see anyone imprisoned like this. Those poor humans."

"Not just them," Sandshifter said. "I smell werewolf in there too. Some of them are cubs."

"What?" Windrider said. "But doing that would reignite the war between the humans and wolves."

"Which is exactly what I was hoping for," said a voice behind them.

XLII

"HORSEMAN?" KIMIKO SNORTED. "YOU'RE telling us that this is being caused by a demonic cowboy?"

"That, we could deal with," Crash said. "We're talking about one of the destroyers of the world."

"You truly think this is being caused by one of the Four Horseman?" Hiro asked.

"Like the old story the *gaijin* tell?" Kimiko asked. "And then this must be…"

"Famine," Firesprite finished. "Designed to destroy the world through starvation. And I'd say it's doing a bang-up job."

"Then what do we do about it?" Kimiko demanded. "I can gather the healthy vampires and have them take the sick ones back—"

"I don't think that'll make a difference," Crash said. "If it's already strong enough to start banging like this, then it's taken what it needs from them already."

"Then what do we do?" Hiro asked. "The other monks have either left or grown sick themselves. We are all that is left."

"We do the only thing we can, mate. We get down there and fortify that door," Firesprite said.

"After all this, you still want to kill those people?" Hiro said in disbelief. "Wavecrasher already stated that—"

"No, Hiro," the lizard replied. "I'm saying we go down to where that door is and we do everything we can to force that thing back."

"You're serious?" Kimiko asked. "You believe that a vampire, two opposing Elementals, and a monk can do anything against something designed to end the world?"

"I think we have to try," Firesprite said. "If we don't, that thing is just going to break out anyway. If we can keep it from fully emerging, we might be able to weaken it enough to force it back. Besides, do you have any better ideas?"

Kimiko glared but stayed silent.

Hiro however, asked, "Do you really think it is possible to hold a horseman off with what we have here?"

"I have no idea," Crash said. "But we don't have a choice. Hiro, grab anything you can use as a weapon and show us how to get in the door."

"I will gather the other vampires to come with us," Kimiko said as she turned to where the sick vampires had been dropped off. But the healthy vampires were no more; they had fallen into a pile with the sick ones, their bodies already showing the signs of the famine.

"Okay, I guess it's just the four of us then," Firesprite said. "Let's just hope that's enough."

*   *   *

Stalker stood before the door to the sunlight room once more. He stuck the janitor's keys into the lock, opened the door, and then stepped inside. For a second, he shut his eyes, still expecting that burst of light. But instead, he looked upon a dim corridor, lit only by a small light from the door at the end.

"Much better," the bat said as he ventured down the hallway, moving silently toward the hunter behind the door. He heard no sound from the other end as he grew closer.

Stalker transformed into shadow, slipped under the door, and reformed inside the cell. He walked over to Hunst, who was slumbering on a table and once more placed his hands upon his temples. The bat closed his eyes and quickly found the heartspeech. Again, it was muffled and layered, but without fear of discovery, the bat pushed through the layers. He went in, and he found his presence slowing, the force of his probe growing weaker as he dug deep into Hunst's slumbering mind.

*   *   *

"I suppose this will do," Hiro said as he picked up a wooden walking staff from the wall. "One of the older monks uses this on his daily excursions."

"What happened to him?" Firesprite asks.

"He lies on a cot upstairs," the monk replied.

"Already I feel better about this," Kimiko muttered.

No one replied, however, as Hiro led them back to the statue of Buddha. He hit the switch, and the wall swung aside. The foursome glanced down, trying to see what they were up against.

Boom.

"That … is very angry" Hiro said, gripping his staff.

"I don't suppose that the other monks had some sort of plan for this?" Kimiko asked.

"If they did, we'd be using it," Hiro said as he began to down the stairs.

The Elementals quickly flanked him, Firesprite summoning a flame to light their way, while Kimiko followed behind. The door behind them began to swing shut, but not before something managed to slip past.

*   *   *

Something was wrong.

Normally, when he entered a mind, he could feel his own essence behind him, a trail that would allow him to keep in control as he walked through the foreign mind. But now, he felt like an anchor was attached to his foot, dragging him deeper and deeper into the muck of Hunst's mind. Even so, he managed to look at the images that flashed before him as he was pulled along. At first, he saw things he recognized—Hunst's children, the slaughter of vampires, the man's training and induction as a hunter. But as he went deeper and deeper, he saw other things—two great armies, one of men and angels, the other of demons and men, battling one another. He saw the sky cracking open, fire lacing across the edges. He saw what appeared to be a man, clad in robes that looked to be made of the stars and all the colors of the elements. And then suddenly, the anchor around his leg was dropped. The bat hung in place before something he never expected to find.

It was a massive sword, far more elegant and beautiful than any the bat had seen before. The hilt and guard were pure white, more so than even the purest ivory. The blade was long and wide, looking as though it could slice through a redwood with a single blow. A white fire laced up and down the blade's length glowing in the darkness of Hunst's mind. Gingerly, Stalker reached out his hand to touch it.

*　　*　　*

"How deep does this all go?" Kimiko asked as the group made their way down the stairway.

"Not deep enough to keep this thing and its hunger away," Crash answered.

"It could still be worse," Firesprite said from the front.

"How?" the vampire asked.

"This could be the Death door."

Kimiko started to say something on *that*, but before she could, Hiro came to a halt and said, "We've arrived."

The others stopped and stared at what lay before them. In front of them stood a sight that was familiar to the knights but totally new for Kimiko and Hiro—cracks and fissure had spread across the door's body, cutting across the symbols and giving small windows of something flashing behind them. As the group watched, the door shuddered again—another blow had struck it from the other side.

"This ... this really is what you said, isn't it?" Kimiko asked.

"Now you believe us?" Crash asked.

"Yes. Because I already feel hungry."

"I can feel it too," Hiro said. "Its power must be leaking through the holes."

"We could actually use Quake right now," Crash said.

"We'll improvise," Firesprite said. "Maybe I can fuse them back together."

The lizard stepped forward and held out her hands, splaying out each finger as far apart as possible. She closed her eyes, and her fingertips began to glow, slowly igniting into eight flames flowing from her fingers. Firesprite opened her eyes, and the flames shot toward the door, stretching and growing into huge tendrils of fire. They slammed into the holes, heating the stone as the others watched, still not noticing what had slipped in behind them.

But they did a second later, when a tendril wrapped around Kimiko's leg and threw her against the wall. Crash and Hiro turned around to see the tendril, which ended in something clothed in glowing scales.

"Oh, just what we don't fucking need," Crash said as she watched the tendril retract into the body of a male vampire, which strolled out of the shadows, his eyes shining with silvery light.

"We must thank you for your help," the Chaos Demon laughed as Firesprite cut the flames (which had done nothing to heal the door cracks) and turned to face the monster. "We could never have gotten this many sick here on our own—at least not this quickly."

"You are responsible for this!" Hiro cried out. "How? The door was sealed!"

"Did you really think we couldn't overcome a lock?" The demon laughed. "True, we spent many years trying to break down the doors, but then we realized it was far easier to sneak underneath one and simply take a little energy back with us to spread."

"And it wouldn't affect you in the slightest while you turned people into carriers," Crash sneered.

"Of course," the demon sneered. "Do you have any idea how much chaos famine causes?"

"How did you even find this place?" Firesprite demanded. "You only had the gremlin door."

"We've been searching for the Equites for millennia," the demon snarled. "The plague door was the first, but it allowed us to finally study the energy their captives put off. It wasn't a perfect map, but it led us here."

"And how the hell did you learn about that door?"

"Oh, the builders never told you? How surprising," the demon laughed. "Weapons of such power only they can ever know of them. Weapons they caused to be created. Weapons that destroyed their balance enough that we were allowed to remerge! And you still in the dark!"

"Well, it's not gonna happen this time," Crash said, drawing her trident. She glanced at Firesprite, who drew her spear, though not before exchanging a look of confusion with her friend. Hiro gripped his staff as behind the demon, Kimiko rose up, hissed, and bared her fangs. The demon took a moment to survey all of them and then simply shook its head and laughed.

"We would so like to destroy you. But we no longer need to. Enjoy oblivion."

With that, the demon faded away, its body vanishing into the air. The group stopped their advance, as another *boom* suddenly shook the cave. They turned and saw that the cracks on the door were spreading rapidly.

Crash brought up her hands, perhaps ready to freeze the door shut, when the stone exploded outward in a burst of strange, pale light. Firesprite threw up a wall of flame to melt the rocks, but even through the fire and the strange light, the group could hear the sounds of hooves clopping forward and the image of something coming out of the doorway. Finally, the fragments of the door stopped raining, and the lizard dropped the firewall, allowing the group to see the horseman.

The horse that slowly came forward was a thing out of a graveyard. Its body was thin and emaciated, its bones peeking out under an almost transparent layer of skin. In some spots, the bone was actually poking out of tears in the skin. But if the horse looked like it had been dead for a decade, the rider looked like he had been dead for centuries. Famine was a slumped over corpse that had been robbed of everything but skin and skeleton. Bone gleamed out from patches all over its body, each one visible through the papery skin. Its body was naked save for a tattered and filthy cloak and hood. In one boney hand, it held a wooden stick, topped with a scale and two weighted ends. The hooded head remained slumped down and then slowly brought itself up, revealing a thin, hollow-eyed skull that hissed as it looked over at the small group assembled to stop it.

*   *   *

Stalker's fingers glanced over the handle of the sword, but then he drew them back as the white light increased a thousandfold. The bat threw up his hands and tried to pull his coat around him as the light began to burn his body and push his mind away …

Stalker gasped a second later; he was hurled back into his body. It felt as though he had been thrown into cold water, and he struggled to draw breath into his lungs as the pain of the burns began to hit. Meanwhile, Hunst's body began to glow with that same white light. The bat saw it and tried to pull back, but suddenly, the light retreated as a large, white orb lifted itself out of Hunst's body. It hung there for a moment, and then Stalker heard a voice within his mind.

I return. And I will have vengeance on all they have made.

With that, the orb shot upward and passed through the ceiling of the room, leaving Stalker alone. And as the bat glanced at Hunst, at how his body had stopped breathing, he realized he was truly alone.

XLIII

"I CAN'T SAY I'M surprised," Sandshifter said as the foursome turned and saw Queen Miri and her personal guard fluttering behind them, their hands glowing with magic.

"You really should have waited for me to help your search," Miri said. "Then you would've gotten out of here alive."

"Your Highness, please!" Avia said, flying in front of the knights. "Why are you doing this? You've always preached protecting the forest and nurturing life."

"And I am, little one," Miri said. "I am protecting everything within this realm and this wood, just as Master Demtia demands of us."

"Perhaps you could explain that to us then," Forger said.

"You know nothing of the master's word," Miri sneered. "He charged us to protect his woods, but not even he understands the dangers this forest faces. When the humans and the werewolves were at war, ripping and clawing at each other, where did their battles take place? Here. And the trees took every blow and shot and scratch they threw at each other. I tried to hold them in control for years, but eventually, I came to a realization—that sometimes, to nurture healthy life, weeds must be cut out."

"I get it," Windrider said. "It's like when Batgirl used the Matches Malone plan—you're setting them off and letting them destroy each other."

"Exactly," Miri said. "And with the advances the humans have made, the battle will be quick, with minimal damage to these woods. And when they are gone, no one will ever threaten the forest again."

"And you thought we wouldn't come to stop this?" Sandshifter growled.

"Oh, once my master sees the safety of the wood, he will understand," Miri said. "I have nothing to fear from the Elementals."

"You think?" Forger said as her fingers began to lengthen, growing into sharp, pointed spikes of iron. Without a word, the spider swiftly reared back and pressed her hand forward, the spikes shooting off like missiles.

But the fairies let loose with their magic; it streamed forward in a green and purple stream, hitting the spikes with a spark of energy. The spikes held in the air for a moment and then fell to the ground with a clatter as the knights stared in disbelief.

"You see? Even now, Demtia rewards our efforts," Miri said. "Soon, my people will be in full control of this forest. And from there, we will reach out to others of our kind and form a true army to protect the forests of the world."

Miri stopped then and glanced at Avia. "Child, I know you see the truth of the words I say. I am willing to forgive your transgression, if you swear your allegiance to me once more."

"You ... You are my queen," Avia said. "And I've always followed you. But... I can't serve a queen that would resort to kidnapping and bloodshed to protect the woods. You... you have disgraced the crown!"

Miri's eyes narrowed, and her magic flared up. She pointed a finger at Avia. "*Traitor*! I cast you down with the forest-destroying monsters that will tear themselves apart for their evil!"

Boom.

"What was that?" Forger asked, looking past the queen to the outside of the room.

"Never mind that. What's happening to her?" Sandshifter asked, pointing at the queen.

Miri's magic had continued to spread over her as she ranted her threats against the outside world. It was now covering her entire body and glowing fiercely. The same magic had also covered the other fairies, and as the knights watched, it began to change color, from brown and green to a dark crimson. And as it changed, the noise came once more, this time twice as loud.

Boooomm!

"Uh, guys, I think we might need to find some cover," Windrider said as the magic surrounding the fairies began to shimmer and crackle around them.

"But the queen—" Avia said.

"Trust me, I've seen *Ghostbusters 2* enough times to know what this means," Windrider said. He grabbed the fairy and leaped behind the pod containing the sleeping children. Forger and Sandshifter looked at each other and then followed suit (Sandy taking time to cover the pod with a protective layer of sand) as Miri, her rage-filled rantings at their peak, screamed, *"And I will drink their blood from my goblet!!"*

Booooommmm!!

A blast of crimson energy shot over the room, coating everything as if in a lens of blood. It only lasted a second, and it was quickly replaced by the sounds of screaming. The knights and Avia glanced up, but the queen and her soldiers had vanished. Moving quickly, they raced out of the room to the ledge of the level, where they glanced down at what had caused the screaming.

The cause stood in the wreckage of a great stone door, on a low level near the ground. A figure straddled a huge horse, clad in spiked armor all over its body. The rider himself was a gigantic man; even in the stirrups, his feet nearly touched the ground. His body was covered in crimson, spiked armor, so bright it seemed to be made of blood. He carried a massive sword, but strapped to his back were more weapons—maces, morning stars, blades, and even guns and automatic weapons. He wore a horned helmet, also covered in spikes but with inlets carved into it so that it looked like blood was raining down its face. Even the eyes were covered by the armor, but it was still able to turn to the knights and point its sword at them, as the fairies of the glen flew about in fear of the intruder.

"*That's* one of the Equites?!" Windrider spat.

"Yes," Forger answered. "And I might be out on a limb here, but I think this one is War."

"What?" the falcon asked.

"Equites, equestrian, horses," Forger said as the fairies continued to scream and panic, flying about in a haze of small, glowing bodies.

"So what do we do about it?" Sandshifter snapped.

"For the moment, I'd say we get the kids the hell out of here and make sure their parents don't go to war," Forger said. "Then we try to make sure that thing stays down here."

"I can get the kids out," Avia said. "But what about the other fairies?"

"I can deal with that," Windrider answered. "All I need is—"

But a massive ax cut off the falcon's words, slashing just past his face and embedding itself in the wall. Everyone turned back to the floor, where War had turned to face them, brandishing its sword and morning star.

"Avia, do whatever you have to do to get the kids out of here," Forger said, drawing her mace. "Windy, Sandshifter, and I will buy you time."

The young fairy nodded and moved off. Forger and Sandshifter looked down at War, even as Sandshifter whispered, "You know it might be powerful enough to kill us."

"When has that ever stopped you?" the spider asked.

"Good point," the wolf replied as she drew her staff.

And the three knights leaped off their level and landed with a thud in front of War, their weapons bared. The horseman held out his sword but made no move to attack. Instead, he held up his morning star. His horse let out a strong, piercing whinny. The knights grabbed their ears in pain as a group of small, red lights winked into view before them. The whinny stopped, and they watched as the lights suddenly took on very familiar physical forms. Hovering before them were the queen and her foot soldiers. But their fairy garb had been replaced with leather and spiked armor, their weapons small axes and swords. They glared at the knights with burning red eyes, and the queen bared her razor sharp teeth at them.

"You know how I said before I wished I could smash these guys?" Sandshifter said.

"Yep," Forger said. "Go for it."

XLIV

"Has his condition improved?" Hazari asked as he entered the sickroom where Forester lay.

"No," Thunderer said. "The ax is still managing to keep him alive, but it's not strong enough to cure him."

"I still can't believe that the power of an Elemental cannot halt this disease," the gremlin said.

"I still believe it can," Thunderer said, rubbing the space between his horns. "I ... I just wish I knew how."

Hazari looked down at the ground for a moment and then said, "Why don't you go speak with the king and your brother?"

"No, I need to—"

"You said it yourself; the ax will keep him alive," Hazari said. "And you can't help him by just sitting here. Believe me, I have learned that lesson well."

Thunderer sighed and then nodded. "I suppose you're right. Maybe I could figure out how to get a signal out."

"Exactly. And if you want, I will sit here with your brother while you are gone."

"I would appreciate that," Thunderer said as he got up and walked out of the sickroom.

Hazari watched him go, and then turned to Forester.

*   *   *

"Are you telling me ... that you can't simply go up there and find someone who can contact the architects for you?" Nerbino asked.

"Oh yeah, there are plenty of people who can rip through dimensions and talk to the gods," Groundquake snapped. "Nobody just *talks* to the Architects, no matter how much magic they have."

"Except you of course. When your magic actually works!" Nerbino snapped back.

Groundquake snarled at the king, but the sound of thunder caused both to stop as Thunderer teleported into the room.

"What happened? Did Fluffy Tail wake up?" Groundquake asked.

"No," Thunderer said. "I came to see if you two had made any progress."

"You can see how that's going," Nerbino answered. "Whatever's going on here clearly ... requires greater power then you two have. But apparently talking to the Architects is akin to talking to God."

"It's actually pretty close," Thunderer concurred. "The whole reason we were made is because they can't leave their plane of existence."

"Eh, one of them could leave for a few minutes," Groundquake said. "But it ain't like it matters. I've tried to call 'em for an hour, and I'm getting squat. It's like something's blocking the signal."

"Then maybe we can find someone to boost it—some sort of mystical power amplifier," the ram suggested. "Hell, we've seen enough to know things like that actually exist."

"I know a few demons that might have ... access to such a device," Nerbino said. "It would take some work to loosen their grip, but I think it could be done if we—"

Boooooommm!

The throne room shook as the explosion echoed all around the palace. The knights were thrown to the ground; Nerbino was hurled back into his throne, only to spring forward a moment later as the shaking subsided.

"What in the name of the first gremlin is going on now?" he snarled as one of the guards suddenly ran into the room.

"Highness, I saw the explosion start! It came from the hospital!"

"What?! We're under attack?" Nerbino spat out as the knights slowly got to their feet.

"No, sir, it wasn't from outside. The explosion came from inside the hospital."

"Dear God, the sick! And Forester!" Thunderer exclaimed.

"Did you see anything about the explosion that could give a clue?" Nerbino said.

"No … wait, there was one thing. I thought I saw something in the west wing, some sort of flash of light. I couldn't tell though; it hurt just to look at it."

"That's the wing that Forester was in," Thunderer said. "And a flash of painful light … Oh God."

"We gotta get to that door!" Groundquake said, grabbing Nerbino's arm.

As the guard watched, the king and the Earth Knight crumbled away into the ground, while Thunderer vanished with a thunder crack.

*　　*　　*

A second later, the trio remerged in front of the door. Nerbino stumbled forward, falling on his knees and vomiting as his body reformed.

"Could you warn me next time?" he moaned as Quake and Thunderer finished reforming.

But neither answered; instead they stared ahead at Hazari, whose body glistened in scales and who held the body of Forester slumped across his shoulders.

"We were wondering when you would figure it out," the Chaos Demon sneered as the two knights drew their weapons.

"And I've been wondering how long you losers were gonna keep trying this," Quake said back.

"One thing that doesn't change about us is that we always keep planning," the demon said.

"Not enough to know that taking one of our friends was a bad idea," Thunderer said.

"Your friend is the perfect tool," the demon sneered. "An immortal infected with a sickness. It is the perfect incubator for that which will finally destroy this world."

With that, a thud sounded on the door as a huge new crack spread over it, while the others began to widen.

"And it begins." The demon laughed. "So by all means, fight me, knights. The longer we stay here, the longer your friend's sickness will— Ummphh!"

A burst of demonfire shot into the demon, knocking it backward and causing Forester to tumble to the ground. Nerbino slowly got to his feet, wiping his mouth as he did.

"I never liked him … anyway," the king sneered as Thunderer moved to retrieve Forester.

But a huge, glistening tendril shot forward, knocking him back as the demon leaped forward, shedding its gremlin shell and becoming something akin to a huge, tendrilled amoeba. More tendrils reached out for the others, but they deftly avoided them, launching both rock and more demonfire at the creature, who merely shrugged them off.

"We have to get him out of here before that thing opens up!" Thunderer said, lacing the creature's body with electricity.

The demon let out a howl of pain, backing away from the others as Groundquake brought up his hands and cupped the palms together. There was a rumble, and then two hollow, half globes of earth snapped up on either side of the demon. They snapped together, trapping the amoeba inside as Nerbino picked up Forester's body.

"Even if we get him out of here … that thing is still coming," the Gremlin king said. "I don't understand how this is even possible—my father always told me it required our blood to open."

"Maybe it just takes sickness, like the disease in your blood," Thunderer said. "C'mon, you get him out of here. We'll deal with the doors."

"Fine, but how?" Nerbino asked as both knights ran toward the opening doors. As he watched, the knights threw themselves at either side of the door, pushing at them with all their strength, their weapons glowing as they were pumped with power. Nerbino snorted in disbelief but then realized that they were at least holding the door from opening any further.

"Whatever works," the gremlin said as he turned toward the stairs.

But he had barely made it a few feet before the sphere holding the demon exploded and a new, winged, gargoyle-esque figure rose from the ashes and charged the Gremlin king. Nerbino let loose with bursts of demonfire, but the demon avoided each burst and swooped over Nerbino, knocking him down and grabbing the prone body of Forester. Nerbino attempted to knock the creature off course, but it let loose with pale fire of its own that sent Nerbino spinning into the air, slamming him into the wall.

It then turned back to the door. Groundquake managed to turn and sneer at the demon as it flew toward them. The dog glanced at the earth, and a series of pillars rose up to block the path of the demon. But the creature deftly avoided each pillar as it rose up and managed to soar up in into the open doors. Slinging Forester over its body, the demon let loose with a pale fire blast at each knight, knocking them from the door before they could react. As they both slammed against the stone walls, the demon's hands began to melt, running into streams of fleshy goo. The demon waited a moment and then hurled the thick goo at the knights. As it flew toward them, it grew in the air, until the two knights found themselves pinned to the wall by something as big as a tarp and as heavy as iron.

"A worthy attempt, but we are not letting you stop us this time," the demon said, dropping Forester's body down in front of the door.

Instantly, it began to open again, this time even faster than before. Thunderer and Groundquake watched in horror, listening to the sounds of horse hooves and the demon's laughter.

But a second later, the demon's laughter changed to a grunt of annoyance. Groundquake looked and saw that a small vine had erupted from the earth and wrapped itself around the demon's leg. It moved to swat the vine away, but then another shot out and grabbed its arm. It snorted in anger as more vines began to erupt from the ground, holding the demon's body back even as they wrapped around it. The Chaos Demon snarled and cursed and spit out pale fire, but none of it made a difference, as the vines continued to grow around it, thickening and hardening, until the demon was trapped in a living prison of wood and vines.

"Fluffy Tail! Come on, if you did all that you must be able to hear me," Quake yelled.

"He did not," a voice said.

As both knights turned toward the sound, a green light spread over the cavern. A figure slowly emerged from it, a crown of leaves upon its head. It waved its hands at the two knights, and vines grew above their heads, leaking oil that dissolved their prison with each touch.

As they finally freed themselves, the light faded, and Demtia stood over the prone body of his knight, shaking his head in sadness, even as the sound of the hooves grew louder and louder.

XLV

"So what happened?" Tina asked as Sara put on her name tag and walked out of the break room.

"I'm not in the mood to talk," Sara answered as they walked along.

"C'mon, you can tell me, Sara."

"Tina, when have we ever talked about my love life?"

"Well, never, so—"

"So let's not break a long-standing record, shall we?"

"Oh, don't be like that!" Tina said. Sara tried to walk away, only to have Tina pull her back. "I'm not asking for all the details, I just wanna know if you like him or not."

"Again I ask, when did you ever become privy to that?" Sara said, pulling her arm away.

"Please, no one ever talks about this with me—"

"Maybe it's because you can't shut the hell up about it!" Sara finally snapped. "Or maybe because you get all your ideas about relationships from some stupid book about vampires who watch women while they sleep and think it's romantic!"

Tina backed away, her face trembling as she looked at Sara.

Sara kept her angry scowl for a second later and then sighed and said, "Tina I'm sorry. I … just don't want to talk about it."

"Was it that bad?"

"No, it was actually pretty good for a while. Then …"

"What?"

"I thought we were having a good moment, and then … then he ran out."

"What?" Tina asked.

"Apparently I got a commit-a-phobe."

"Sara, I'm so sorry," Tina said, putting her hand on her friend's shoulder.

"It's not like I knew him long term or anything. I've just never had anyone run from me for no good reason."

"Maybe's there's something you don't know?" Tina asked.

"You think? I could almost deal with it all if I just knew what was going on in his head."

"He sounds like a hard guy to understa— Oh!"

"What now?" Sara sighed as she turned, expecting to see Bob standing there. But instead, another man stood there, dressed in the same clothes he'd been in the night before. There was one major difference from the previous night though—his face was dirty, with more than a few cuts lining it. His cheeks were dotted with burn marks, like he'd been over a fire. Still, Sara recognized him instantly.

"What are you doing here?" she asked.

"Sara, I ..."

"You know what, I don't care."

"Sara, I know last night was ... bad."

"Really?"

"Can I at least have a chance to explain myself? That's all I want. And if you don't accept what I have to say, I'll never bother you again."

Sara glared at Mark for a few minutes and said, "Back of the store. You have five minutes."

*　　*　　*

Thunderer said in disbelief "Demtia? How did ..."

"Ralin promised me a chance to help if the situation grew dire enough," the Architect of Forest said as he knelt before the stricken body of his knight. "And I can see that it has."

"Any chance the rest of you are coming?" Groundquake asked as he glanced at the open door where the figure of the horseman came closer.

"No, but if you can delay the horseman, I believe I can stop this," Demtia said. "He comes because he senses an immortal filled with plague. But if I remove that plague, he will sense the time is not yet right, and he should willingly walk back through the door."

"*Should*?" the dog barked.

"We don't have a better plan. I say we use it," Thunderer said. Standing before the door, he unleashed a pair of thunderbolts directly at the horseman's steed. They struck the creature head-on, causing it to stumble and forcing the horseman to pause as it shook off the effects.

"Now, Quake!" the ram yelled.

Groundquake quickly followed the order, bringing up his hands and then swiftly bringing them down. As he did, the ceiling above the doorway began to tremble and crack, until huge chunks of rock fell in front of the door, barricading it.

"That's not gonna hold him long, Demtia," Nerbino said. "If you can help, do it now before this attack on my people grows worse."

But Demtia was already at work. Holding one hand on Forester's ax and another on his chest, the Architect was slowly bringing life back into his knight. Green light flowed from the Architect, causing both ax and knight to glow. As the others watched, the boils and lesions on Forester's face began to fade, the fur slowly reclaiming the damaged flesh. Demtia's brow furrowed as he doubled his efforts, adding more power to the healing. The light flowed everywhere as the healing continued, spreading even to Nerbino, who watched his boils vanish under the green light. And as they listened, the sounds of the horseman behind the doorway lessened.

"It's working. We may get out of this yet!" Thunderer said.

"Please don't say that," Groundquake said.

"But we— *Gahh*!!!"

"I told y— *Shit*!!" Groundquake cried out as he, Thunderer, and Nerbino felt long tendrils wrap around their bodies and lift them off the ground.

Demtia turned toward them, only to scream in pain as another tendril slid across his forehead and then directly into the flesh, circulating through his very face.

"You didn't think we would go away that easily, did you?" the Chaos Demon once called Hazari sneered as it rose up from where Demtia had hurled it. "We were around before you builders, and we will be here afterward."

"You ... cannot ... do this ... to me ..."

"Everything and nothing is possible to us," the demon snarled as the green light began to fade. "Now, you have done enough healing. It is time for you to go back home, as soon as we find the— Ah."

There was a clicking noise, and then Demtia screamed, even as his body and that of the demon began to glow in green light. The knights and Nerbino struggled to free themselves, but suddenly, Demtia, the demon, and its tendrils vanished. The group fell to the stone floor. Forester lay there, his body now healing on its own, albeit slowly.

"Did it work?" Thunderer asked.

"*Who gives a shit*?!" Groundquake yelled. "That thing just hitched a ride to all the other Architects!"

"Obviously!" Nerbino snarled. "But since we can't deal with that right now, why don't we worry about the monster that might be emerging from that door, unless your friend heals in time?"

"Demtia healed him most of the way," Thunderer said, walking over to the squirrel. "Maybe now we can give him a jump start."

But just then, the rock pile burst apart, and the sound of hooves could be heard. The group turned and saw the last of the three earthly Equites emerge. The horse's flesh was covered in boils and sores, its hair matted and disheveled. The rider was of strong build, but leaking, pus-filled sores covered its naked body in armor of infected flesh. It carried a rust-covered sword, which it pointed at the prone Forest Knight, even as his body finished healing.

"The Architect felt safe leaving *this* one on Earth?" Groundquake sputtered.

"So that's what's been infecting my people," Nerbino said, his voice a mix of defiance and fear. "How do we kill it?"

"I ... I wish I knew," Thunderer said. "Maybe we—"

"Unngghh," said a voice behind them.

They turned to see Forester slowly getting to his feet, the signs of the plague completely vanished from his face. He shook off the dizziness and then saw the open door and the sickly figure that had emerged from it.

"What the hell is that!?" he yelled, even as he picked up his ax and brandished at the horseman.

"That would be the source of the plague," Thunderer said. "We're currently trying to figure out how to fight it."

"Huh. You think. Ah'm gonna pay it back!"

With that, Forester raised his ax and charged the pale horseman. Plague watched him without a word or movement, even as the others screamed for Forester to stop. But the squirrel would have none of it. He leapt upward, his ax glowing with all the power of the wood. But before he could bring it down, Plague suddenly flipped his rusty sword and swung it upward, right at the squirrel. A cry of pain rang out, along with a sudden stream of blood, and then both knight and weapon fell to the ground, with Forester clutching the side of his face.

"Fluffy! *Bastard*!" Groundquake screamed. He swung his hammer about and hurled it at the horseman. Thunderer and Nerbino followed suit, sending lighting and demonfire at the pale one.

But the horseman deflected the hammer with his sword, and the impact of the energy only burst some of the pustules upon his body, causing a filthy residue to fall to the ground and begin to bubble away.

"Oh, that's disgusting," Groundquake muttered.

"Dear Christ ... Nobody attack him!" Thunderer said. "That's how he spreads the plague!"

"Then what the hell are we supposed to do?" Nerbino snapped. "Just hope he leaves and takes his plague with him?"

But as the Gremlin king spoke those words, the horseman held up his rusty sword. It glowed with a sickly light, and then suddenly, the horseman and his mount vanished.

"Well … I guess a request from the Gremlin king is hard to ignore," Nerbino said.

Quake turned to argue, but a moan of pain caught everyone's attention. The trio ran to the fallen Forester, who was still clutching his face, awash in blood.

"Jesus Christ, that thing made him sick all over again!" Quake cried out. "And we don't have an Architect to wait for this time."

"Let's see what it did to him first," Thunderer said, He turned his friend over and gingerly peeled his hand away from his face. What he saw made him cringe back in shock. The fur was matted with blood, and in a few spots, it was burned or showed malformed flesh, almost like when he'd been sick. But the worst was Forester's right eye. The sword had left a long, vertical slash from eyelid to eyelid. The eye itself had turned yellow and now gazed outward blankly, as if nothing was before it.

"Thunderer," Forester whispered. "Something's wrong. Why … can't … I see everything?"

"The … the horseman," the ram said. "He … blinded you."

"What?! But why … isn't it healing?"

"You couldn't heal the plague. I don't think you can heal this either."

Forester stared at the ram through his good eye and then closed both and screamed to the ceiling. Or he did until Nerbino slapped him.

"Be thankful you still have one eye," the Gremlin king snapped. "You might still have both if you had listened and not foolishly charged Plague. Now if you want to avenge it, get up and help us find the horseman."

Forester glared at the gremlin and then slowly got to his feet, Thunderer helping him up while Quake took his ax. He was handing it back to Forester when, suddenly, a host of fresh moaning and screaming came from above the stairway.

"The horseman! He has gone after my people!" Nerbino cried out.

"But how do we even attack him?" Quake asked. "Every blow we release just unleashes more plague."

"Then we need to contain him," Thunderer said, "lock him up until we figure out how to get him back inside."

"And what about the demon hitching a ride on Demtia?"

"*What*?!" Forester yelled.

"We can't get to the Architects' plane anyway. This is what we can deal with now, so let's deal with it," Thunderer said. "You up for this, Forester?"

"More than ready for round two," the Forest Knight said, brandishing his ax.

"Then let's go."

XLVI

"So what now?" Firesprite asked, glancing at Wavecrasher.

"What?"

"You're the one who has plans for everything!"

"For demons and angels! Not this!" the cat snapped.

"Fine then," the lizard muttered. Walking forward, Firesprite held her spear aloft, the head bursting into flame as she spoke to the horseman.

"Hear me, Famine! I am Firesprite, Knight of Fire, emissary of Darya, Architect of Flame! Your time has not yet come! Return to the door and—"

Famine jerked the reins and the horse whinnied and then charged. Firesprite unleashed the flames onto the creature, but Famine outstretched its hand and the flames dissipated.

The lizard was shocked but still had enough sense to dodge when the horseman reached out for her.

The others quickly moved into position, Wavecrasher holding her trident, Kimiko baring her fangs, and Hiro holding his staff while trying to look as intimidating as possible. The horseman took no notice and continued to charge, reaching out for them with its clawed hands. Kimiko was the first to attack. She leaped at the demonic rider, her fangs poised and sharp. But the horseman came to a halt and reached up and caught her by the throat in midair. Kimiko struggled and pulled, but the horseman's grip was strong. And as the vampire struggled, her face began to pull in on itself, the skin tightening over the newly outlined bone. Her eyes rolled back in her head, as even the moisture from them began to evaporate. Her struggles lessened, and her body began to grow limp.

Suddenly, a blast of water struck the horseman, knocking it off its steed. Kimiko's body fell to the ground as the horseman was pushed back by the impact of the water.

"Grab her!" Crash yelled, holding the trident steady. Firesprite quickly ran in, grabbed the vampire, and brought her over to the monk.

"What did that thing do to her?" Hiro asked. "She looks like a raisin."

"The same thing it did to the people up there," Firesprite said.

Kimiko weakly cried out.

"She needs help," Hiro said as he rolled up his sleeve. Before the lizard could stop him, the monk pressed his forearm to the vampire's fangs. Instinctively, she bit down and began to suck as the blood leaked from his arm. Hiro grimaced in pain but held steady, and Kimiko's body slowly began to regenerate.

"Mate, you don't have enough blood to—"

"Then ... help me," Hiro managed to get out.

Firesprite was puzzled but then understood. She placed her hand on the man's shoulder. A red light flickered under her hand, and Hiro's face relaxed, even as Kimiko continued to drink.

Meanwhile, Crash continued to push Famine backward with the water. But the horseman was managing to slowly pull itself to its feet. Crash increased the pressure, putting enough force to push Famine against the stone wall, cracking it. For a second, the cat thought she had the upper hand. Then she heard a whinny to her side. She turned, bringing one hand around as she tried to create a second stream. But it was already too late. Despite its sickly build, the horse rammed into her; the cat flew into the wall. She fell to the ground and shook her head.

But then a thin and spindly hand wrapped around her throat and lifted her up, tightening its grip as the face of Famine was brought close. The sickly face stared blankly. In its free hand, a pair of scales appeared, the weights layered with spikes and the body held on a short staff. Famine swung the scales, and the spikes whirled about faster and faster as it drew back, ready to slam them into the cat's head.

But just as Famine moved to bring its hand forward, it stopped and let out a grunt. Crash managed to look down and see the nameless fox biting into the horseman's leg. Famine seemed more annoyed than in pain and made a move to bring the scales down on the creature. The distraction, though, allowed Crash just enough time to bring her hand up and blast the creature with another water stream. The horseman was knocked back, and the cat fell to the ground, free of the horseman's grip. The fox watched the horseman lie against the wall and then went over to Crash, nudging the cat and growling.

"Coming," Crash managed to get out as she slowly got to her feet, taking in air as best she could. While Famine was still slowly moving, the cat moved over to her allies, still feeding Kimiko with Hiro's blood.

"What ... happened?" Crash wheezed.

"The black rider over there," Firesprite said, her healing hands still keeping Hiro upright. "He just held her and this happened."

"Then I guess ... he just wanted me dead," Crash said as Kimiko, her face finally restored, finally pulled away from Hiro. Wiping the blood from her mouth, she spoke two words. *"Domo arigato."*

"Dōita shimashite," Hiro said as Firesprite's power healed his arm. Turning to the cat, he said, "You may be the only one who can restrain it, Wavecrasher. Kimiko and I are vulnerable to its touch, and it is denying flame's air to burn."

"Famine in all sense of the word," the cat muttered. "But all the water can do is restrain it. Beyond that—"

"That may be all we need for right now," Hiro said. "I think if it could've been destroyed, it would've been. Instead, it was locked away."

"By some sort of ancient magic," Kimiko said. "What do you think we're going to do? Freeze it?"

Hiro started to answer, but another loud whinny cut the air. The four turned to see Famine remounted on its horse. It glanced at them for a moment and then held its scale/mace up. The scales began to glow in the dark, and then, noises echoed down the stairways behind the group—noises that sounded like shrieks and screams of pain and then ones of terror and even greater pain.

"What in God's name did it do now?" Firesprite asked.

Famine's response was to lower its weapon and tug at the reins. The horse whinnied in response and then reared back and began to gallop. The four scattered out of its way as Famine drove its mount into the wall … and vanished.

"What in the *hell* is going on here?" Kimiko snapped.

"We need to get upstairs for that," Crash said as she ran for the stairs, the fox trailing at her heels.

The others quickly followed, racing up the stairs with all the speed they could muster. They reached the top and flung the door open, only to instantly wish they had left it sealed.

The people and vampires that Famine had affected were still there. And they were off their cots and walking about. But they were not well. Their bodies were little more than skeletons covered with the thinnest coat of flesh. They looked like corpses that had been left out to bake in the hot summer sun. A few reached out with bony hands, searching because their eyes had been dried out and made useless. As they shuffled along, they moaned and cried out, as if the very act of movement or breathing hurt them.

"Zombies. It made goddamn zombies," Firesprite said as she looked out onto the horrific scene before them.

"No," Kimiko whispered as a fanged creature shuffled past her. As it passed, it stopped, sniffed the air, and then turned toward the group, its thin face stretching further as it bared its fangs.

"Kenzu, no," Kimiko said as the emaciated vampire hissed at them.

Suddenly, it leaped forward, bony claws stretched out for their necks. But instead of flesh, it hit a wall of fire, and with a scream of pain, dissolved into a pile of dust.

"Okay, fire still works on these guys," Firesprite said as Kimiko stared in horror at the pile on the ground.

"Good. Because I think we're going to need a lot of it," Crash said as the other zombies turned in their direction, each one baring its teeth at the smell of those still living.

*   *   *

"Is this explanation going to start soon or what?" Sara said as Mark stood there, running his hand through his hair, trying to come up with something.

"Uh ... well, God, I never thought I'd have to do this," Mark muttered.

"Apologize?"

Mark sighed and said, "Do you remember what I said about my work?"

"Yes. Checks and balances."

"Well ... it takes more time than I said, and I have to make a lot of commitments because of it. I haven't had anything like a relationship, except for—"

"And being with me brought you to tears? Is that it?"

"*No!*" Mark exclaimed as the doorbell shook and three men entered the bookstore. "I just didn't know if I could balance a relationship with my work."

"Jesus, Mark, if your job means this much, why did you even waste time with me?"

"I ... it's just ... I didn't waste time with you. But I ... I wish I could say more."

"No shit," Sara said.

Just then, Tina moved over to the trio of men who had entered the store.

"I just didn't want to leave things that way."

"Look, if you're done already, just spit it out."

Mark sighed and started to speak, but a nearby shriek caused both of them to stop. It had come from Tina, who was backing away from the trio of men in horror. They simply glared back at her, their eyes glowing with an odd, pale light.

"What in the hell?" Sara swore.

Mark suddenly moved in front of her. "Get out," he said. "Now."

"What?"

"They're here for me."

"What are they? And how do you— *Jesus Christ*!!!"

As the men took a step forward, their bodies began to ripple and change. Their clothes shimmered and then sank back into their translucent skin as they stretched up and out, like taffy being pulled in all directions. People in the store began to scream and panic. As the 'men' grew, their bodies twisted, growing long arms; strange, glowing scales; and a series of long, clawed arms that looked ready to slice through steel. Finally, they stopped, their bodies long and sinuous, topped by diamond-shaped heads.

They ignored the masses of people running in all directions and focused directly on Mark. (Bob briefly left his office to check the commotion but then swiftly went back in and locked the door.) Sara just stared in disbelief as Tina let out another scream of horror.

That proved to be a mistake. The creatures suddenly turned their attention to her, and with a grin, the one closest to her grabbed her and held her aloft. It gently ran its clawed hands though her hair and then glanced at Mark, almost as if daring him. But Mark's only response was a dark glare of his own. Then he started to run forward, toward one of the book displays. He used it as a stepping stone, first jumping on top and then pushing himself off and right up onto the creature's arm. He ran along it as easily as if it were a stone path and then grabbed the fist holding Tina. As he touched the strange flesh, smoke suddenly began to rise off it. The creature howled in pain and dropped Tina. Mark tried to swing down and catch her, but she slipped through his grasp. Luckily, Sara was there to catch the girl, albeit with a *thud*.

"Sara! What's going on?!"

"Get off me first," Sara wheezed as she pushed Tina off. Sara got to her feet and then helped Tina, who was still watching as Mark dodged between the monsters, to her feet.

"Whoa. Does he ... Does he know what he's doing?"

"Apparently. But no way is he going to do it alone," Sara said as she grabbed a heavy cart loaded with books and sent it spinning toward the creatures. It hit the nearest one in the back of the leg, forcing it down to one knee, which allowed Mark to grab a metal rod from one of the broken displays and drive it directly into the creature's eye. It roared in pain, and Mark yelled at Sara, "*Go!* Get out of here!"

"What about you?" she yelled back.

"I can handle these things. And I owe you one! Now *move!*"

This time, Sara didn't bother arguing; she just grabbed Tina and ran for the back door. But as she got to the door, it suddenly blew apart in a burst of brick and wood as another creature pushed its way through.

"Dear God, how many of these things are there?" Sara swore. She quickly looked around for anything she could use as a weapon, even as the creature advanced on her and Tina.

Behind her, Mark saw the new creature and tried to move to help them, but the others blocked his way. He reached out to touch them, but one of them threw the previously used book cart at him, knocking him to the ground.

Sara and Tina continued to back up as the creature advanced. Nothing around them was of any use (unless the creature could be beaten to death with a used encyclopedia). But Sara had still managed to quickly get a plan together, and she whispered it to Tina.

"I know it's scary, but it's also really big and really slow. I think we can get to the back door."

"Are you crazy? It'll kill us!"

"If we just stand here, it'll do that anyway. Just follow my lead— one, two, *now!!*"

Sara took off, dragging Tina along with her as she raced toward the monster. It roared and slashed at them, but Sara ducked and weaved and rolled under each blow, just narrowly avoiding each one. And with each dodge, the door grew ever closer, until …

"Sara!"

"Shit!" Sara muttered as she felt Tina's hand slip through hers. Skidding back, she grabbed Tina's shirt and hurled her through the door.

Sara had started to go for it herself when a sudden jolt and sharp pain suddenly coursed through her. Gingerly, her hands moved to her stomach, where a trio of blood-stained claws emerged. From a distance, she could hear Mark screaming as the claws retracted and she fell to her knees. Blood oozed from her mouth as Sara collapsed to the floor. Somehow she managed to look up and see the monster backing away from Mark. But as the world grew dimmer, Sara saw something strange. *Why are his eyes on fire?* It was her last thought before blackness overtook her.

XLVII

Joe watched as Rastla stalked the hallways, anger and resentment frozen on her face. She still managed to move quietly, but her method was now to open each new door, glance inside, shut it, and growl in disappointment. Joe floated back behind her, waiting for one door to reopen and a flight of monks to come out and find them. But she seemed noiseless and invisible. As the future Architect shut another door and growled, Joe briefly wondered if, even now, Rasta had some vestige of her future power. But this time, Joe heard not only frustration and anger but also sadness. She came to a halt, leaning up against the wall, her body shaking as she let out a small moan. Joe's heart ached for her and he reached out, forgetting his own invisibility.

But as his hand reached her shoulder, another moan echoed forth, this time from behind a nearby door. Rastla's head snapped up, and she ran for the door, flinging it open in her eagerness. Joe quickly moved in, only to gape at what he saw inside.

Rastla's father was laid out on a wooden frame, his limbs tied to it at the wrists and ankles—not that the binding was necessary; the jutting angles of his legs made it obvious they were broken. His chest was sunken in and misshapen; Joe surmised that multiple ribs had to be broken. Blood covered his lips, and his head rolled back and forth in pain. Rastla went to her father, stroking his head and using the hem of her shirt to clean the blood off him. Joe however, simply stared. This man had been in constant pain from broken limbs and ribs for days. What in the name of all the Architects was keeping him alive? It sure as hell wasn't any kind of treatment.

Rastla didn't seem to find it odd. She began to undo her father's bindings. As he gave a new yelp of pain each time she moved him, Joe almost told her to stop, until the sound of a slamming door caused both of them to stop. Rastla's angry look returned as the prayer-sayer stood in the doorway.

"I believed I sensed a disturbance earlier," the old man said. "And now, Ralin has led me to it."

"What have you done to him?" Rastla cried out, pointing at her father's broken body. "You said you were going to help him."

"Your father grew worse after our attempts," the prayer-sayer said calmly. "We left him here to prevent further harm and wait for the Light to heal him."

"Lies!" Rastla yelled. "You couldn't help him and you left him in here so no one would see your failure!"

"How dare you!" the prayer-sayer yelled. "I am the voice of Ralin and the Light on this world. If your father has not been healed, it is through his own failures, not mine!"

"You are no one's voice but your own," Rastla sneered. "If this is what happens to those who preach of the Light, then I am done with it! I will have no more of a Light that gives no answers and is used by foolish men for their own power!"

"Betrayer!" the prayer-sayer screamed, throwing down his staff of office and lunging for Rastla.

The girl tried to move away, but the old man wrapped his hands around her throat and began to squeeze.

"You are not worthy of the Light," he sneered as Rastla gasped, her eyes rolling back in her head. "You will be cast out!"

But as he spoke, Rastla's hands, waving about in desperation, managed to close around the handle of the stone jug the monks used to give her father water. She gripped it tightly, and then with all her strength, brought it done upon the prayer-sayer's head. It connected with a crack, shattering over his skull and forcing him to release his hold. He staggered back, holding his head as blood dripped down his skull. But Rastla, still holding a piece of the jug, was not finished. She charged the monk and slammed the piece of stone into his face, knocking him onto his back. He lay there, holding his face and writhing in pain, even as Rastla straddled him and, holding the stone over his head, brought it down onto his face again and again and again. Blood spurted out from between the sayer's closed fingers, and pieces of flesh and bone oozed down the side of his face. But Rastla was unrelenting, bringing the broken jug down again and again, not noticing the blackness that was starting to radiate from it, until finally, the moans of pain stopped.

She sat there, the stone shard over her head for one final blow, breathing in and out rapidly from the exertion. She stared at the body, as if expecting it to make one final gasp for breath. But the shattered body simply lay there, and as Joe watched, the anger and rage slowly left Rastla's face, to be replaced with utter confusion. Placing the rock down, she leaned in and looked at the prayer-sayer. She gingerly poked his ruined face, unmindful of the blood and broken bone that covered it. She looked at his cracked forehead and peered in, as if to see the brains inside. Joe was horrified, but as Rastla looked at the blood on her hands and then at the blood that was covering the prayer-sayer's body, he realized a simple and horrifying truth about the situation.

No one here has ever died before.

As Joe tried to wrap his mind around this, the body of the prayer-sayer suddenly twitched. Both Joe and Rastla stared in shock as the body began to twitch and shake violently, first throwing Rastla off and then shaking about as though electrified fire ants were running about his nerve endings. Rastla backed away in horror. The body's mouth opened wide, and an inky blackness began to pour out of it. It hovered in the air for a moment and then shot out toward Rastla. She screamed in terror. Joe moved in front of her to block it. But the blackness shot through his incorporeal form and right onto Rastla, covering her body like ink. She continued to scream as it poured all over her, a liquid wetsuit that covered every inch of her. Joe could only watch as it encased her entire body and then suddenly held it rigid, pulling her up and holding her in the air like a child holding a Barbie doll It hovered there a moment and then suddenly, erupted in flames—the black-blue flames of shadowfire.

The flames burned brightly for a moment and then suddenly went out. Rastla fell back to the floor, landing on her feet. The blackness that had surrounded her was gone. Instead, she was clothed in the black hooded robes Joe knew. She stood there silently and then slowly raised her head.

Joe looked in the hood and stumbled backward. Overlapping Rastla's face was the image of a skull, ghostly and translucent. As Joe watched, the skull faded away, revealing Rastla's face with black eyes and a dark smile. She glanced at the body of the prayer-sayer and then extended a finger to it. The shadowfire shot forth, consuming the body in mere seconds.

As Rastla walked to the body of her father, Joe realized what he had been brought here to see. This was not only a death, but a birth—the birth of darkness, which was born with the first murder, darkness, which for all its names and subterfuges, was simply death.

XLVIII

"Your Highness, please stop," Windrider said to the transformed fairies, who hovered and snarled before them. "Remember the vows you have taken!"

"I don't think that's gonna work," Sandshifter said as the war-infected fairies snarled in reply.

"*Get down!*" Forger yelled, just as the fairies screamed and charged them, their weapons drawn.

The spider came forward and quickly launched a series of iron spikes at them. Most of the fairies dodged the spikes, but a few of the weapon managed to find themselves a home in their chests. Even that didn't slow the tiny army down. The fairies swarmed the group, slashing and biting and clawing at them.

"It's like—*ow*—being attacked by—*Gah*—metal-tipped bees!" Sandshifter screamed, throwing her staff and sand all around.

"Let me ... uhh ... try something. *Hold on!*" Windrider yelled, holding his staff aloft. There was a sudden boom, and then a huge blast of wind shot out, blowing the infected fairies to the far walls of the glen.

"Now let's get the head," Sandshifter growled, leaping off the ledge toward War. As she fell, her body began to change, disintegrating into a huge sand cloud that fell onto War.

The horseman looked at his speckled body in confusion for a moment. Then, as the sand gathered around him and his horse, forming a huge sand dune, the confusion turned to annoyance. A sandstorm built around the pair. It whirled about, gathering speed and power with each passing second—that is, until War's armored hand popped out of its sandy prison, holding the now-glowing morning star. It swung the weapon about a bit, and then suddenly delivered a vicious swing to its front. The sands immediately stopped swirling and dissipated around the horseman as Sandy's body instantly reformed and flew into the wall.

"Oh, we're in trouble," Windrider said.

Forger leaped off the balcony. The falcon followed, creating an air pocket to cushion their fall. They landed in front of War, who turned its mount to them. Forger held up her mace, her other arms already transforming into various weapons, while Windy held up his staff. War glanced at them both, though he looked longer at Forger, even tipping his helmet to her, to Windrider's surprise.

"What the—"

"He likes weapons," the spider answered. "Let's see how much he likes them when I use them."

With that, the spider raised her mace, stretching forth her bladed hands and ready to slash. But just before the blades could touch him, Windrider suddenly screamed, "*No!*" and knocked them aside.

"What are you doing?" Forger demanded.

"The fairies! Remember, he got control of them because the queen was angry at the villagers and the wolves."

"Right, so … Oh, God, it feeds on violence!"

"Exactly!"

"Then we need a plan B," Forger said. "If we can at least restrain him—"

But there was no time for that, as a howl erupted behind them and Sandshifter leaped over them, her sandy hands already stretching out for War. The horseman drew his sword and sliced through them, but the wolf took no notice, as they regrew in seconds and she hit War with a thud.

The horseman fell off his mount with a crunch of armor, and Sandshifter held him down. She grabbed his morning star, and began to pound him with it. As the others watched in horror, a red mist grew around Sandshifter's head, and she let out a howl of triumph. They quickly ran over and pulled her off, even though she struggled and screamed as they did so.

"Damn it, get a hold of yourself!" Forger snapped, grabbing the wolf's wrist and forcing her to drop the weapon, while Windrider grabbed her other arm.

But suddenly, both knights were knocked back by a burst of sand. They skidded back as Sandshifter snarled at them and started to advance, her hands growing into long, sandy talons.

"Even we can be infected," Forger whispered in horror.

"Sandy, no!" Windrider yelled as the wolf advanced, the mist settling around her head. "You can't do this! You're not going to let some medieval reject control you!"

"Listen to him," Forger added. "Think about Paul. If you give into this thing, you're just the monster he thought you were."

Sandshifter took one more step and then stopped. She shook her head back and forth. The mist stayed with her, though some of it was starting to vanish. The wolf grabbed her head, trying to grab some of the mist as well, and then screamed, *"No! No more," she howled. "I am not a monster. Get out of me!"*

With that, the mist evaporated, and Sandshifter fell to her knees. The others moved to catch her. The wolf panted as Forger asked, "Are you all right?"

"Not ... like that," the wolf panted.

"I believe you," Windrider said.

Forger started to speak, but then the sound of crunching metal could be heard. They all turned, saw War pick up his morning star, and reached out to stop him.

But it was already too late. War raised his morning star, and a rumble sounded through the glen. The un-possessed fairies turned toward the exits and made to flee. But even as they did, the very walls collapsed around them.

The knights glanced at each other and then at War, who suddenly vanished in a haze of red light. With their enemy gone, the two knights grabbed Sandshifter and were about to teleport out, when suddenly a huge chunk of the ceiling fell toward them...

And then they were outside in the forest.

"What in the hell?" Windrider said, glancing about.

"I think our savior is right there," Forger said, pointing to the pod of children and the very tired looking fairy resting upon it.

"I … could sense the glen … collapsing," Avia said, breathing hard. "The others—"

"Were leaving when you saved us," Forger said. "But War got away."

"We … cannot let them … succeed." Avia said, still catching her breath. "The village—"

"Um, guys?" Windrider said, glancing into the distance. "I think we might be a little late."

Avia and Forger turned in the direction falcon was looking, only to gape in horror. For in the direction of the village, a pillar of smoke and flame was steadily rising.

XLIX

WALKING OVER TO HER father, Rastla knelt at his head, brushed back his hair, and whispered, "Father."

"R-Rastla?" her father wheezed, slowly opening his eyes. But upon seeing his black-clad daughter, he started crying out, "What has happened to you?"

"Something wonderful Father," Rastla answered. "I finally have the answers to my questions. Look!"

With that, Rastla held out her hand, and the shadowfire blazed forth. Her father stared in wonder and then said, "But what of the prayer-sayer?"

"He will not trouble us," Rastla said.

"He spoke of keeping me here until my body's pain cleansed me. He ... Gahhhh!!"

"Father, do not speak! I will help you!"

"No!" he said, grasping her hand. "My body is too wracked with pain to move. I understand now that the prayer-sayer and men like him have fallen from the path of Ralin. And perhaps if the path of a god can lead one down such a twisting road, it is not worth following. I ask you, daughter of mine, give our people a new path. Use your power to show them our lives belong to us, not to men and gods who allow such evil."

Rastla looked at her father and nodded. "I will do as you ask, Father. I will show the world the error of its ways. And I will set you upon a new path, free of pain."

Rastla placed her hand over her father's eyes, and a black mist surrounded it. At first, her father shuddered in fear. But slowly, he relaxed, his breathing going slower and slower, until finally, it stopped. Rastla removed her hand, revealing her father's face with a calm, peaceful expression, as if he had gone to sleep. Rastla kissed her father's brow, and said, "I shall carry you with me, Father. And I will make your words come true."

With that, Rastla turned and walked to the door. Joe doubted she would have any trouble getting out—the monks no longer had any power to stop her. He moved to follow but then heard a rustling. He turned, to see the prayer-sayer's body twitch as a ghostly mist poured from his eyes and mouth. As Joe watched, the mist took on a familiar shine, a glow he recognized all too well. And that was when he realized another terrible truth—that darkness, for all its necessity in the world, had been born from chaos.

Joe backed away from the body and then made for the door. He passed through it, only to come to a halt. Standing before him was the cloaked figure. The figure looked at him and then behind him to the doorway. Turning his gaze again to Joe, the figure spoke. "From the light comes dark. And from dark comes light. Never ending, until the force that binds."

Joe tried to ask what that meant, but suddenly the figure's eyes were upon him and then …

Joe's eyes snapped open, and he found himself back in the library. He rubbed his eyes and then began to massage his temples as his mind tried to make sense of what he'd seen. Had all this been about Rastla's origins? But why? The whole experience had left him with a headache, and he felt like boulders were moving around in his head.

Boom.

Yes, giant boulders crashing around and crushing his gray matter.

Booom!!

The table shook then, and Joe realized that that noise wasn't just in his head. He jumped out of the chair, grabbed his staff, and headed out the door. The sounds grew louder. Joe reached for the door, but as his hand gripped the handle, the framework groaned and then shattered, throwing Joe back as an all-too-familiar pale glow filled the air. Stunned, Joe still managed to get to his feet and hold out his staff as a pair of Chaos Demons forced their way into the library.

Joe didn't waste time asking how the creatures had entered the Obelisk. He simply unleashed a barrage of light at the two monsters, causing screams of pain and fury as he forced them back into the stairway. Once they were outside, Joe sped up, his body moving in a golden blur. He shot out of the room, across the stairs, up the wall, and over the monsters, delivering another blast that sent them further up the stairway. Thinking with as much speed as he was moving, Joe quickly focused on the door to the Nexus; he released another blast that sent the demons scurrying and running up for the closest doorway. Once they were inside, he could force them through the Nexus somewhere else, until he figured out how they'd gotten in here.

Joe heard the click of the door opening ahead, and he knew the bait had been taken. Zooming ahead, he ran into the door of the Nexus, only to come screeching to a halt. The two demons were still there, looking beaten and worn. But standing about them were a dozen more demons, each one in a more hideous form than the others.

But that wasn't what had stopped Joe in his tracks. What had stopped him was the sight of the Architects, looking beaten and bloody, their bodies limp, held in the ten arms of a horrific octopi-demon.

"Ralin! Release them! This instant!" Joe cried out, holding out his still glowing staff. "You saw what I did to your friends; don't make me do it to you!"

"You have no power here," a voice said in reply.

Joe looked about, but none of the demons had spoken; they were, instead, glancing at the ceiling. Joe looked up to see a strange, glowing orb of energy. Without a second's hesitation, he fired a beam of light, but the orb merely absorbed it with no ill effects.

"You do not listen well," the voice said. "A common failing of the mortals. But all will be rectified soon."

"I am a Knight of the Elements. I command you to release the Architects!" Joe yelled.

"If you serve them, then I will offer you a boon," the orb said. "Once, they served me. You may do so now, man of Light."

"Who are you?" Joe demanded.

"One that finally has the chance to undo all the mistakes that have occurred in this failed experiment of existence."

"With the Chaos Demons?" Joe snapped.

"They'll have their place in the world I shall create—as shall those I once called brother, before your masters drove me from the world for your precious balance."

"Then I already know they did the right thing," Joe said.

"I see you are not worthy of my reign."

With that, the closest demon roared and let out a burst of pale fire. Joe quickly threw up a shield of light to hide behind. As the flames slammed into it, Joe frantically thought about what to do.

If I can call the others ... No, they'd be coming right into the room; it'd be a massive firefight. And if this thing can capture the Architects ...

Joe ...

Wha— Ralin?

You must ... leave us. Find the knights. Bring them here.

But I can't leave you here!

There is nothing you ... can do against this creature. The knights ... can stop his plan. The Equites ... he will try to bring ... them here. You ... you must stop him.

But what about you?

We were weakened ... by the attack, Demtia more than the rest. But we will survive. You must ... obey me ... my knight. Or the world ... will not survive.

Joe tried to think of something else to say, but at the moment, the pale fire cracked his shield into golden mist. Joe hung on for a moment, and then as the demons began to advance, Joe gritted his teeth and sent out a final burst of light to drive the demons back. Then he zipped ahead, past the monsters to the steps of the Nexus itself. He screeched to a halt and placed his hand on the crystal, willing it to take him to the place that would allow him to solve all this. His body glowed pure gold, and he vanished into the spire.

The demons screamed in anger, but the orb suddenly echoed over above them. "He cannot stop our efforts, and now he cannot return. Prepare the Architects for the next step. After that, this world will finally be as it should be."

L

"THERE'RE TOO MANY OF them!" Kimiko yelled out as she slashed at a zombie. She managed to cut across its face and stun it, before the vampire quickly reached out and snapped its neck.

"Tell me something I don't know!" Firesprite panted as she let loose with another burst of flame. The fire spread out, setting at least five zombies ablaze, but the lizard still fell to her knees, holding her spear as she gasped for breath.

"Sprite!" Crash yelled as she sent out a waterspout to knock away some nearby zombies. She started to run for her fallen comrade, only to be pulled back by a rampant pair of zombie hands. She could smell rancid breath as the creature brought its mouth closer, ready to chomp on her shoulder. But suddenly, it backed off and unleashed a howl of pain; there was a crunching noise, and the zombie fell over. Crash whirled around to see the fox sitting there, holding a broken zombie foot in its mouth.

"Thanks," Crash said as she turned back to Firesprite. Sending out more waterspouts to push the zombies back further, the cat raced over to her friend, who was slowly getting back to her feet.

"Hey ... are we winning?" Sprite asked as she was helped to her feet. Glancing down at the fox, she then said, "Okay, we should be winning."

"There are just too many here," Crash said. "And you can't keep expending yourself like this."

"What do you want me to do?" the lizard snapped. "Let them take this place?"

"This place won't matter if Famine gets out there with no one to challenge it," Crash said back. "We need reinforcements to escape here."

"But we can't contact anyone!" Firesprite said.

"No, but we can still teleport," the cat answered. "And even when we couldn't get to the Architects, I could sense them up there, just out of reach. If we focus on the closest knight—"

"Fine, but we can't go alone."

The cat nodded and yelled out, "Kimiko! Hiro! The temple is lost! We have to retreat!"

Hiro, who had managed to knock off quite a few zombies with his staff, regarded the announcement with regret, but he still started to clear a path toward the knights. Kimiko, not arguing for once, leaped above the zombies attacking her and landed on their shoulders, using them as stepping stones to reach the knights. She paused only once, to grab Hiro's robe and hurl him over to where the knights were. She then landed next to the cat, lizard, monk, and fox.

"If you have a retreat plan, I'd love to hear it!" the vampire snarled.

"We just need a few minutes," the cat said as the zombies around them grew closer.

"I've got … an idea," Firesprite said. "Everyone … behind me."

"Are you sure you can do this?" Hiro asked.

"Not like … it matters," Firesprite said as she held out her free hand. A fireball gathered in her palm, and when it was large enough, she clasped both hands together and then pulled them back, causing the flames to spread all around them in a ring of fire. Unfortunately, this also caused her to fall back once again.

This time, though, Crash caught her as she yelled out, "Everybody, get close!"

"Can you transport all of us?" Hiro asked as everyone moved in tightly.

"Like she said, not like it matters!" Crash said, holding her trident and reaching out for the closest knight to them. Within seconds, she found the familiar energy and concentrated on reaching it. Her body began to evaporate, and the others slowly followed. The cat gritted her teeth at the strain of pulling everyone through, but eventually, everyone vanished as the zombies howled into the flames.

And miles away, in another location, the air began to bubble and then to liquefy. Water poured from nowhere, slowly forming into shapes that then morphed back into flesh and blood.

"Well ... that sucked," Crash muttered as the group shook off the effect of the mass teleport.

"Where on earth did you send— *Gahhh*!" Kimiko cried as she looked around, only to accidentally move into a beam of sunlight. Her right arm and shoulder burst into flame, and she quickly pulled back. Hiro ran over and beat out the fire with his robes.

"We must be on the other side of the world," the monk said.

"Wherever ... that is," Firesprite said as she took a look around. Wherever they were looked like it had seen major action. All around them were scorched walls, broken shelves and books, and sheaves and sheaves of charred pages. The walls were covered in a strange, translucent goo, and most of the walls had burn marks and holes that let in the outside sunlight.

"And you sensed one of the others in this?" Firesprite asked.

"I thought I—" Crash began but then stopped as a sound filled the air—the sound of a man weeping.

The two knights looked at each other and then quickly moved toward it. They followed it to the back of the store, where they found a man knelt over by the exit. He knelt there, barely moving and cradling a body in his arms. The two Knights glanced at each other and then slowly moved near the man, who took no notice of them. He simply held the girl in his arms, weeping, and once the knights saw her, they saw why. The woman had no stomach, only a huge, gaping hole in between her waist and chest. Crash put a hand to her mouth and then slowly knelt down and whispered to the man, "Sir, what happened here? What happened to her?"

But the man only sat there weeping, his long, black hair hiding his face.

Crash quickly went silent, got up, and walked over to Firesprite.

"This must have something to do with the Equites," Firesprite said. "This place looks like a war zone. Do you think—"

"I don't think War did this," 'Crash said. "Look at that goo on the walls. Look how it's glowing and tell me you don't recognize it."

Sprite looked at the walls, sighed, and said, "I was hoping that I'd be wrong. But that stuff is Chaos Demon, isn't it?"

"Right. God, how many of them had to be here to do all this?" the cat asked.

"Four," said a voice behind them.

The knights turned toward the man, who spoke again. "I don't really know what I did, but I'm guessing I smeared them around after they got here. It's funny, I couldn't kill them, but man, could I hurt them."

"You ... you did all this?" Firesprite asked.

"Yes ... because of this."

"I'm sorry," Firesprite said as she put a hand on the man's shoulder. But as she stood over him, she looked down at the woman in his arms, and her eyes widened.

"It's her," the lizard said.

"Who?" Crash asked.

"The woman from the other night in Hoboken—the one we couldn't figure out."

"What?" Crash said as she came to take a look. She saw the red hair and the green eyes and let out a moan. "God, it *is* her. Is that what caused all this?"

"I couldn't forget her," the man said, ignoring the others. "I knew I should have, but I couldn't. I thought, I'll do it just this once. One time with her, and then I can go back and forget. But even that was too much. And now ... now look what I've done, Crash. Just look at her!"

This time, Crash knelt down and looked at his face. She brushed back the hair and gently turned his face to hers. She looked into his black eyes and whispered, "I thought Joe would be the one to break someday. Not you."

"Surprise," the man whispered back, as he then spoke a few words, and to Firesprite's shock, the glamour fell away, revealing the teary eyed form of Nightstalker.

"What the hell is this?!" Firesprite yelled, her voice loud to enough to draw Kimiko and Hiro's attention. "Are you telling me we were out there fighting the Four Horsemen while you were here chasing some woman around?!"

The bat held her gaze and then looked at the floor and said, "I did my job. I monitored Hunst like I was supposed to. But there were more than a few gaps in between when I could do something. So when I could, I came over here."

"For what?!" the lizard yelled. "What in the hell made this girl so special? Maybe if you hadn't been so obsessed, you could've noticed that we're cut off from the Architects and a famine-carrying horseman is riding the Earth."

"I … wait, what? Cut off? And horseman?"

"We haven't been able to contact the Architects or return to the Obelisk," Crash explained. "And Equites is the Latin word for horsemen—the Apocalyptic kind."

Stalker took a deep breath and wiped his eyes. He gently placed the girl's body down and rose to speak with the others. It was then he also noticed Kimiko, Hiro, and the fox.

"Who are they?" he asked.

"We are from the door holding Famine in Japan," Hiro said.

"They put themselves in serious danger to help us," Firesprite said. "And we need all the help we can get."

"Agreed," Stalker said. "The first thing we need to do is figure out who released the horsemen."

"Oh, that would be our chaos-loving friends," Firesprite said.

"So then we need to worry about what horseman could be released here."

"Why does that matter?" Kimiko asked.

"Because I say it does," the bat said. "And because we know there's a door in Miami and a door in Japan. There's probably a horsemen for each major continent, or one that can spread down to what's left."

"So we could have either War or Plague or Death to deal with," Hiro said.

"No, I think we would've noticed Death," Crash said. "There'd be bodies every— Oh God, I'm sorry, Stalker."

"Don't bother," the bat said. "I should've known I was crazy to try this," he added as he turned to take a last look at the body. "I should've known—"

"What?" the lizard asked as she glanced over. But when she did, she let out a gasp. The girl's body had disappeared; even the bloodstains on the floor were gone. Instead, what lay in the space was a familiar object—Joe's staff.

"Isn't that …?" Hiro asked as Crash and Firesprite went to the staff. Picking it up, Firesprite looked at the weapon and nodded.

"What the hell does this mean?" Kimiko asked. "Is the Light Knight gone?"

"I don't know," Crash said. "But I don't like it."

"Where did she go?" Stalker whispered.

"Stalker, I—"

"*Where is her goddamn body?!*"

At the sounds of the bat's scream, the staff suddenly began to glow. Surprised, Firesprite dropped it, and the staff glowed brighter and brighter. Everyone shielded their eyes, and Hiro blocked the light from Kimiko with his body. But one being wasn't affected. The fox, glaring right at the glowing weapon, slowly made her way to it. Standing right over the weapon, she bent down and sniffed it. Suddenly, the light enveloped her, surrounding her in an aura of light. It rose the fox up into the air and then halted. The animal floated there, as its body suddenly began a strange transformation, one that Joe would've known very well. Its body lengthened and grew, the paws stretching out into fingers, the hind legs straightening out, the lupine face slowly drawing back into itself as a mass of hair grew from it. Energy surrounded the new form, and then there was a final burst of light.

Slowly, everyone in the group managed to open his or her eyes, only to gape in shock at what they saw. The fox had changed into a humanoid form and now stood upright on two legs in Elemental garb, a long sword strapped to her hip. But she stood totally still, her body as rigid as a statue. Even her eyes were shut.

"Oh. My. God," Crash said.

"Is that ... what happened to her?" Hiro asked.

"And why is she dressed like Joe?" Firesprite asked, pointing at the modified brown and gold costume.

"Better question, is she alive?" Kimiko asked as she walked up to the new manimal. The vampire waved her hand in front of the creature, snapped her fingers, and even lightly slapped her furry face. But throughout it all, the manimal stood unmoving.

"I think she's broken," Kimiko said.

But the fox suddenly took in a breath, opened her eyes, looked about, and promptly screamed. Kimiko backed away in shock, and the others tried to do something.

"It's all right, please," Hiro said, speaking as calmly as he could. "I know this isn't the temple, but surely you remember me?"

"What in the hell are you talking about?" the fox suddenly spat out. "Who are you? Jesus Christ what are *they*?!" she yelled, pointing at the knights.

"Oh crap, she can see us," Crash said. "Please, if you just let us explain—"

"Oh no. I've had enough weird shit today, thank you," the fox said, backing away from all of them. "Now you just get away from me until I can get the cops and show them how you fucked this place up."

"We didn't do anything," Firesprite said. "Look, I can prove we aren't a threat."

The lizard reached behind her, drawing her spear and holding it away from her and then started to drop it. But apparently the gesture only panicked the fox, who suddenly reached to her side and drew the long, golden sword, with a hilt made of gold wings that melded into the blade itself. She pointed it at Firesprite, and a beam of light suddenly shot out and struck the lizard, knocking her back.

"Holy *shit*!!" the fox exclaimed, staring at the weapon. "Where did *you* come from?"

But as she stared at the sword, another was staring at her. Stalker, who had not moved since the fox had emerged, was staring ahead with a mix of elation and terror. Because unlike the others, he recognized the red hair that fell from the fox's brow, even with the ends colored white. He recognized the green eyes that still glimmered in her face. And he knew the profanity-laden voice that came from her throat.

"No. No, no, no, no, *no*!" he cried out as he all but ran toward the fox.

She held out the sword against him, but the bat pushed it to the side and grabbed her by the shoulders.

"Get off me, freak!" the fox yelled, struggling under his grasp.

"It's me!" the bat said. "Sara, it's me."

At the sound of that name, the fox stopped struggling and looked at the bat in puzzlement. "Mark?" she asked.

The bat spoke the words of the glamour, and the fox gasped as his disguise washed over him and then faded away.

"Oh my God, what … what are you?"

"I'm … I'm complicated. This is why I left. I couldn't get you involved in—"

"Get me involved in what?" Sara snapped, pushing his arms away. "What the hell did you think you were doing? You'd get involved with me and lie about *this*!"

"She remembers who she is?" Crash said.

"Of course I do!" Sara snapped. "What I don't know is who you are or why I'm in these clothes or what this sword is—"

But that was where Sara stopped. In holding out the blade, she finally saw her fur-covered hands. She dropped the blade in shock and stared at her hands, at the red fur that covered them, the short claws that extended from the fingers, the black pads that extended over her palms. She glanced at the bat before her and then went to her face, feeling the fur there, the sharp teeth in her mouth, the small muzzle where her nose had been, the ears that poked through her long, red hair. She stood there stunned, until Firesprite coughed and gripped her scaly tail. Sara stood stunned, and then her hands slowly reached back, to pull out her own red and white tail.

"Sara, I swear I never meant for any of this to happen," Stalker said. "I don't know why—"

"What did you do?" Sara whispered.

"I-I didn't, I don't know—"

"*You son of a bitch, what did you do to me?!*"

EPILOGUE

"Just a dream," he said aloud as he placed the pen down. "If only I'd known how far it would go."

Then again, there was likely little chance things would've been different anyway. Dealing with Him was never anything but what he expected. And neither had that last step of Joe's journey into who he was now been expected. But that part of the tale would come later. As always, duty called him, as another disruption of balance had occurred on Earth. He would look into it and then return to his work. He had to, after all. Things were about to get very interesting for him and for all the knights.

ACKNOWLEDGMENTS

My parents, for their continued support.

Kristen, for always listening and believing in me.

My editors at iUniverse, for their help in sculpting the story and with writing the romantic elements (monsters I can do, romance …).

Shane McGowan and the Pogues, for writing the songs that helped me see Mark and Sara's romance form.

All my former teachers and personal editors who gave me the skills to do what I love; your help is always appreciated. Special thanks to Carol Lomardo for slogging through another novel of mine to check "then" and "than."

Everyone who bought Volume 1 of *Lightrider* and the friends and family who continue to inspire me to complete this story.

My writing heroes, Stephen King, Terry Brooks, Michael Dante DiMartino, and Bryan Konietzko, for showing me the way.

And to the ones who got to the end of this book with me, thank *you*.

ABOUT THE AUTHOR

Eric Nierstedt's work has been published on *Suite101.com*, the *Westfield Leader*, a local newspaper, and his blog on *wordpress.com*. His writing was featured in the Unlimited Potential Theatre Production's Wordsmith Competition. He has a BA in English from Kean University. Eric lives in Garwood, New Jersey, where he is hard at work on the Lightrider series.